# The Evolution of

*Sean Cam*

**The Evolution of a Serial Killer**

First published in Great Britain by De Minimis 2017.
This edition published by Partners in Crime Publishing 2021.
Cover design by www.nickcastledesign.com[1]



10 9 8 7 6 5 4 3

By Sean Campbell:

*Dead on Demand*
*Cleaver Square*
*Ten Guilty Men*
*The Patient Killer*
*Missing Persons*
*The Evolution of a Serial Killer*
*Christmas Can Be Murder (a novella)*
*My Hands Are Tied*
*The Grifter*

1. http://www.nickcastledesign.com/

# Chapter 1: Stupidity

'Most criminals are stupid. They're easy to catch because they make mistakes. It's the smart criminals you have to watch out for. That's my job. I catch the weird, the wonderful, and the downright dangerous.'

Morton paused to survey the room in front of him. Eight pairs of eyes stared back from the darkness of the small lecture hall, which was illuminated only by the glare of the projector. Ayala was sitting at a desk to the left of Morton's podium, half-heartedly clicking through the PowerPoint presentation between stifling yawns and trying not to look thoroughly bored. The whole team had been assigned to teaching duty, and yet only Ayala had made it to the first lecture of the week. Rafferty had been summoned away for a meeting, and Mayberry was hiding in his office. Morton didn't blame him. Poor Mayberry wouldn't have been much help, anyway. With his stutter, the six-week course would have taken three months.

A hand in the front row shot up. It belonged to a lanky man with caterpillar-like eyebrows adorning eyes that were much too big for his face. He smiled earnestly as his hand trembled in the air. Nobody else had joined him in the front row. The other students had the good sense to hide on the back benches in the shadows. Morton nodded at the overly-eager student.

'Sir, how do you know you're catching the really smart criminals? Aren't the truly smart criminals those you never even investigate because they didn't leave any evidence?' The man spoke quickly, the words running into one another breathlessly. A verbal machine gun firing at full pelt.

'And you are?'

'Crispin Babbage, sir.'

Morton glanced at the clock. Half past ten. It was going to be a long day. 'Well, Mr Babbage, I can't disprove the existence of something for which we have no evidence. What I can say is that for every ten bodies, we get nine convictions. That's higher than virtually anywhere else in the world.'

'But, sir, what if they were so devious that they never left a body for you to find? Who are the one in ten who get away with it?'

Morton waved for Ayala to click over to the next slide.

'They, Mr Babbage, are the dangerous ones. I don't fear the axe-wielding maniac or the wife-beating coward. I don't even fear the spectre of a serial killer. The murderers we have to worry about aren't the mentally ill or the dregs of society. The true evil is the emotionless psychopath, the man or woman who can look at you and make a cold, calculating decision based on whether or not they will benefit from your death.'

Babbage's hand shot up again.

Morton exhaled deeply. 'Go on, Mr Babbage. One more question, and then I'm going to have to ask you to keep your hands to yourself for the rest of this presentation. Otherwise, you're all going to be working right through lunch.'

At this, a collective groan rose through the room. Babbage grinned sheepishly, seemingly oblivious to the other trainee detectives staring daggers at the back of his head.

'Sir, how many psychopaths are there? Didn't Neumann and Hare think it was about 2% of the population?'

Morton felt his eyebrows arch into a frown. Bloody know-it-alls. 'Mr Babbage, did you just ask me a question you already know the answer to? Brown-nosing is unwelcome in my classroom, and it won't do you any good, anyway. I'm not going to decide which of you get to become detectives. If you're looking to curry favour, then feel free to leave a bottle of Scotch on my desk, preferably one older than you are.'

'But, sir, I wanted to know how many you've come across. It can't be that hard to plot a murder, can it? Surely, any intelligent person could get away with it if they put enough time and effort in. You can't be that much smarter than them, can you, sir?'

Morton glared. If Babbage wanted to match wits, Morton would gladly school the arrogant young man. He smiled politely, the kind of smile that doesn't reach the eyes, and watched as Babbage melted back into his seat, slinking down under Morton's glare. He made a decision on the spot. Babbage needed to be taken down a peg or two.

'Let's find out. Homework!' Morton cried. 'I want each of you to spend the rest of the day planning how you'd kill Detective Ayala, here. I want the specifics. You tell me how you'd do it, and I'll tell you how I'd catch you.'

A few students grinned. The rest looked mortified. Morton motioned to Ayala to pass him his overcoat, then slung it over his shoulder. He nodded to the class, then headed for the exit. He paused in the doorway. 'We'll meet back in this room at oh-nine-hundred hours. You have twenty-two hours to plan the perfect murder. Good luck. Class dismissed.'

***

Rafferty exhaled deeply. She could feel the hairs on her arms standing on end. The waiting was the worst part. Rafferty didn't like the endless paperwork, getting shot at, or canvassing witnesses door-to-door until her feet blistered, but she'd take any of those over sitting still.

Whatever the reason for the wait, it couldn't be good. The new chief, Anna Silverman, had summoned Rafferty with the briefest of emails:

*My office, 12:00 sharp.*

Rafferty knew better than to email back and ask for details lest she be accused of wasting the chief's time. It couldn't be a reprimand. Or could it? Rafferty strained, trying to think of anything she'd done wrong that would warrant Silverman's personal attention, but she drew a blank.

Rafferty's gaze wandered around the room as the clock ticked loudly. The antechamber to the chief's office had changed since Roberts had retired. Gone were the personal knick-knacks, the sporting goods and photos collected after a lifetime in high office. Gone, too, were the motivational posters. *Good riddance,* thought Rafferty. Any man who needed such platitudes was too vapid to hold a rank as important as the Commissioner of the Police of the Metropolis.

After an agonising wait, the intercom buzzed. The chief's private secretary, a young man with a neatly trimmed beard and wire-frame glasses that covered half his face, answered the phone, murmured a few words, and placed the receiver back down almost immediately.

He turned his attention to Rafferty with a thin-lipped smile. 'Ms Silverman will see you now.'

Rafferty nodded her thanks, gathered up her handbag, and headed for the door. She knocked loudly to announce herself and proceeded in without waiting for an invitation.

'DI Rafferty, take a seat,' the chief answered without looking up from her laptop.

Rafferty sat down awkwardly, resisting the urge to fidget. 'Not going to offer me a coffee, then?'

'No,' the chief said simply.

'Then, what am I doing here?'

The chief tore her attention away from her laptop and locked eyes with Rafferty. 'I'm giving you your first case. The next murder that comes in is yours. Any problem with that?'

Rafferty's eyes widened. Her first case. Wait. Shouldn't Morton be deciding if she was ready? If the chief was going over his head, it spelled trouble. Any idiot could see that Silverman and Morton weren't exactly friends, but to cut the Met's most senior detective out of the loop was unprecedented.

Rafferty bit her lip. Finally, she said, 'Chief, I'm honoured, but why me? I'm not the most senior DI on the force.' She wasn't even the most senior DI on the team. Even Ayala had seniority by dint of having been with Morton for two years longer than Rafferty.

'No, you're not. I think you've got potential. Am I wrong?'

'N-no...'

'Good. Then, the next body that drops is all yours. Borrow Detectives Ayala and Mayberry to assist you. It's not like they're busy.'

Silverman bared her teeth in a smile that hid the truth. Ayala and Mayberry weren't busy because Morton's entire team had been side-lined after the incident in Canary Wharf. They'd been given the bare minimum workload, the boring easy cases that needed no real detective work: stabbings, strangulations, and road traffic accidents, the sorts of cases new detectives cut their teeth on. It was a far cry from the serial killers they usually hunted. Morton ought to be fuming, but he was being as stoic as usual. If he was angry, he wasn't sharing it with Rafferty.

She felt the chief's eyes boring into her.

'Right. Thank you.' Rafferty looked at the chief, still confused. The chief began busying herself once more with her laptop. *Should I go?* Rafferty wondered.

The chief looked up. 'Don't you have work to be doing? Oh, and one more thing – not a word to Morton. He isn't supervising you. I am.'

# Chapter 2: Ways to Kill

The class ambled in slowly as the clock ticked towards nine. Morton resolved to be strict: any latecomers would be turned away. These weren't undergraduates, and Morton was in no mood to babysit. Ayala had joined him fifteen minutes ago, his arms laden down with two boxes of doughnuts.

'Ayala, what are you doing? You're not seriously going to feed the students, are you?'

'Should I not, boss?'

'Do what you like, but be careful. One kind gesture, and they'll think you're a pushover. Is one of those for me? I'm starving.'

'Yep. Salted caramel, and a black coffee.' Ayala placed Morton's breakfast on a side table and set about connecting his laptop up to the projector system.

Morton sipped at his coffee, surveying the class as they arrived. Babbage was the first to arrive. As usual, the pompous young man made a beeline for the front row, and then proceeded to spread out his notes. He even had a small tablet on a kickstand.

'You can put that away. You won't need it. I want you listening, not tapping away.'

'But, sir, I always make notes this way,' Babbage said.

'Not my problem.' Morton glanced over at Ayala. Morton didn't care about tablets being used during his lectures. He just didn't like Babbage.

Nobody else sat in the front row. They slunk in at the back, avoiding making eye contact. Small cliques had begun to form already. Little clusters of two or three students gathered among the rows, with the occasional lone student interspersed between them.

Morton leaned in to the microphone attached to the lectern. 'Move forward, please. I want your attention, and I don't want to shout.'

Slowly, they shuffled forwards. Morton could only see two women among the group. It wasn't for want of trying. The new chief had been aggressively recruiting for women to join the training program.

'Just three women, eh, boss?' Ayala whispered.

'Three?'

'The two in the third row–'

'I see them,' Morton said tersely. 'Where's number three?'

Ayala nodded towards the back row. Morton followed his line of sight. He hadn't clocked the person at the back: small, slightly built, with a delicate feminine nose and a military-style close-shave haircut.

'What's her name, Ayala?'

'Hang on,' Ayala said. He fetched a clipboard from the side table and scanned down. 'Sam Rudd. Gender NB.'

'What on earth is NB?'

'Non-binary, boss.'

'Right,' Morton said as if he understood. 'Sam, would you move forward, please, and join the rest of the group?'

Sam looked aggrieved, but slowly meandered forward to take a seat a few rows from the front, as far from the others as possible. The clock chimed for nine o'clock.

'Is that everyone? Right. Let's go, then. Yesterday, I asked you all to plan how to murder Detective Inspector Ayala. Who wants to go first?'

Predictably, Babbage's hand shot up straight away. Morton ignored him and looked for other volunteers. A few students averted their eyes as if hoping that, if they couldn't see Morton, Morton couldn't see them.

Morton picked his first victim at random. He was a man in his late twenties wearing a herringbone suit and an obnoxiously bright red tie that matched his hair. 'You, there. Red. What's your name, and how are you going to kill Inspector Ayala?'

'Eric O'Shaughnessy,' the man said without a trace of an accent.

'Okay, O'Shaughnessy, how're you killing Ayala?' Morton asked again.

The young man looked around the room, searching for an ally. It was obvious he hadn't prepared. 'I'm going to shoot him.'

'With what?' Morton asked.

'A gun?' O'Shaughnessy said with a nervous chuckle.

'What kind? Handgun? Shotgun? Sniper rifle?' Morton reeled off the most common firearms at a rapid pace. 'Where are you getting it? Even if you get a gun, there are plenty of forensic markers. Gunshot residue–'

O'Shaughnessy interrupted him. 'I'll wash my hands afterwards.'

'Striae evidence,' Morton continued as if he hadn't interrupted. 'Every gun is unique. We can recover serial numbers with acid etching, and we can match the bullet to the gun. If you shoot Ayala, we'll find you by dinner time. Next.'

'What if I don't use real bullets?' O'Shaughnessy said. 'Can't I use ice bullets so they melt and leave no bullet for you to find?'

Morton sighed. That old chestnut. 'No, Mr O'Shaughnessy, you cannot fire a bullet made of ice. The friction from the inside of the barrel would melt the bullet before you hit your target.'

'What if I shoot him at really close range?'

'It won't work,' Morton said. 'Metal is used for its high mass. It's basic physics. Force equals mass multiplied by acceleration. Bullets travel two and a half thousand feet a second. If I could throw a beanbag at you at that speed, it still wouldn't kill you because there isn't enough weight behind it.'

Ayala tapped away at his laptop as Morton spoke. When Morton was done, Ayala stood up in anticipation. 'And if you want to prove it, ice has a density of 0.9167 grams per cubic centimetre. Copper has a weight of 8.94 grams per cubic centimetre.'

O'Shaughnessy looked impressed. 'What about a bullet made of meat, then?'

'Plausible,' Ayala conceded. 'But you'd leave obvious trace evidence behind. It's a gimmick, and one that gives you no advantages over a generic copper bullet. If anything, it would be easier to link back to you than something store-bought.'

O'Shaughnessy turned to the student next to him with a shrug. He'd survived the opening salvo.

The room fell silent. Who could follow the idea of a meat bullet?

Babbage's hand shot up again. He waved it excitedly, like a small child who wanted permission to go to the bathroom. There were no other volunteers.

'Yes, Mr Babbage?' Morton said.

Babbage puffed up his chest proudly, as if he'd invented the most novel murder ever devised. 'I'm going to use a police radio to listen out for when everyone is distracted, and then I'm going to strike. With no witnesses, you'll never be able to prove it was me.'

'Right. First off, you'll need a radio, so chances are you're one of us, and Professional Standards are pretty quick to spot a dirty cop. Secondly, that won't tell you when Ayala is alone. Why would he be the only one not responding? Third, and finally, you've done nothing to prevent the forensic markers of whatever method you actually use. What you've devised is a way to isolate your victim. It isn't a murder method at all. I'm very disappointed.'

Babbage's lower lip trembled, and he blinked rapidly at the moisture forming droplets in the corners of his eyes. Morton almost felt guilty. Almost.

Morton turned his attention to the others. 'Next. Give me your name and your method.'

'I'm going to throw him out that window,' a gravelly voice answered.

Morton looked around for it and found a hulk of a man with a weatherworn face. The big man nodded in the direction of a large window behind Ayala.

He looked as if he could do it easily enough. He had the build of an East End hard man who lived for the gym, but he was wearing the suit of a banker. He said, 'And the name's Danny Hulme-Whitmore.'

Danny was jammed between two other students, his gargantuan arms folded neatly across his chest. The others, Morton surmised from the register, were the last men on the list: Sulaiman Haadi al-Djani and Kane Villiers.

'And Inspector Ayala is just going to let you, is he? One scratch, and your DNA is under his fingernails.'

'Then, I'll have to be quick, won't I?'

'Okay,' Morton conceded. 'Let's say you get lucky with a blitz attack. It's the same brick wall as the ice bullet. How're you going to overcome basic physics?'

'Physics?' Danny said, his accent making it sound like he was saying 'fizzicks'.

Morton held up three fingers and counted them off. 'Jump, push, fall. Three scenarios, three different distances. If you fall out the window, you'd be right up against the side of the building. You'd probably grab out at window ledges, ivy, anything you could. By the time you hit the bottom, you'd already be scuffed up and bruised. If I push you out the window, you'll be a bit farther away. If I throw you, you'll be a lot farther away.'

'Prove it.'

Ayala stood up. For a moment, Morton thought he might actually be about to jump. Ayala rolled an old blackboard in front of the class and began to scribble the outline of a building.

'The horizontal distance away from the building to the point they hit the ground is determined by the take-off, flight, and landing distance. Imagine the centre of mass in someone's body as the first measuring point, and then think about that window. There's a small ledge just outside it, and if you were to jump, you'd swing your legs over, stand on the ledge and step off. We're on the fifth floor, so we're just over fifty feet up. That's the vertical distance.' Ayala drew a vertical line beside the building, going from the fifth floor to the ground.

'Okay. We're up high. So what?' Danny said.

'If you step off, you're going to go maybe two feet from the building. That's our horizontal travel distance, and it's based on how far the victim can step off the ledge. He's got no velocity, because he's just falling straight down. The only force acting on him is gravity.'

'But he could jump.'

'He could. But with no run-up from the ledge, he isn't going far. Ignoring wind resistance, which ought to be negligible, his flight path will look a bit like this.' Ayala scribbled a soft curve arcing from the building down to the ground and labelled it 'Fall'. He then drew a second arc showing the man's jump such that the curve arced above the ledge and then fell down slightly farther away.

'And now, if we throw the man from the window, he'll be starting a few feet higher than the outside ledge, and he'll have a lot more velocity behind him.' Ayala began scribbling again, an equation this time. 'Distance, which we're calling D, is going to need us to calculate the launch speed multiplied by the sine of the launch angle divided by gravity, or G, which is then multiplied by one plus two g times the height over the square of the launch velocity times the sine of the launch angle, all divided by two.'

Even Morton was impressed. The entire class looked at Ayala with awe as he translated his theory to the graph with a curve that pushed much farther away from the building.

Ayala flashed Danny a smile. 'Sorry, Mr Hulme-Whitmore, but you'll have to kill me another way.'

He looked stunned. Emboldened, a couple more of the students put a hand up. As Ayala rolled the blackboard back out of the way, Morton picked another student to try their method out.

'Sulaiman Haadi al-Djani,' the man said. 'But just call me Sully. Everybody else does.'

'Very well, Sully. How're you killing Ayala?'

'I'm going to have somebody else do it. Detective Inspector Ayala is in the line of fire, and that means he sometimes has to wear body armour. Kevlar fails if it's stressed too much, especially if you put it somewhere really hot. I wear out his body armour, and someone else gets him. No link back to me.'

Morton nodded appreciatively. 'Very good, Mr al-Djani. I like the outside-of-the-box thinking, and you can set up an alibi for the time of death. But there are three flaws here. One, you need access to the body armour in question. Two you're assuming Ayala doesn't replace his Kevlar, and that he only uses one vest. He's lazy, so I'll give you that. Three, you're assuming Ayala will eventually get shot while wearing that Kevlar, and that it will fail in a fatal way. That's a big ask. As murder methods go, it might be hard to track, but it's not likely to succeed, either.'

'Fair enough,' Sully said with a grin. 'For the record, I'd never murder a man who brings me a free doughnut.'

'Who's next?' Morton asked. 'How about one of the ladies? You're awfully quiet in the back, there.'

Two of the women, one blonde with pale skin and the other a raven-haired beauty, were hiding behind Danny, shielded by the big man's bulk.

'Maisie Pincent,' the blonde said. She looked over at Ayala with a mischievous smirk. Ayala was sipping his drink and looking bored.

'And how did you murder Ayala?' Morton asked.

'I poisoned his coffee.'

Ayala spluttered, the hand holding his coffee cup swinging away from his lips. His coffee erupted all over him and his laptop. He yelped as he jumped from his seat, brushing his thighs as the coffee – thankfully lukewarm by now – trickled down his legs.

'I like your sense of timing, Ms Pincent,' Morton said. 'Poison is the most common method by which women commit murder. It is clean, simple, and often effective. You don't have to watch your victim die, and you can be miles away when it happens. The big flaw is that it requires access both to a suitable poison and to the victim. You need to get physically close, and if you can do that, there are better options.'

As Morton spoke, Ayala's laptop turned to a blue screen, casting a blue tinge over the entire lecture theatre.

'We have time for one more before we break for poison-free coffee,' Morton said. He pointed at the woman next to Ms Pincent. 'How about you?'

'Almira el-Mirza. I'm going to blow up the building he's in. Nobody needs to know he was the target, so tracing his murder back to me would be impossible.'

Morton's jaw dropped. The potential for collateral damage was enormous. But she wasn't entirely wrong. It *would* be hard to track.

Similar expressions of horror spread throughout the room, and an awkward silence fell.

'Okay,' Morton said, trying to buy time to think of an appropriate response. 'Can you be more specific about how you'd do it?'

Ms el-Mirza cocked her head to one side, watching Morton's reaction. 'I could fly a drone through the window with an explosive and kill everyone in this room. The evidence would go up in smoke with us.'

'Very... violent. Three problems. Number one, you'd need the right expertise. Not many people know how to make a bomb and how to fly a drone. That would narrow it down. Number two, you'd need access to the right materials to make a bomb. Some household cleaners might give you a small bang, but if you really want to make a mess of all the evidence, you'd have to lay your hands on restricted materials. Number three, you'd need to get around the no-fly zone around this building. Any drone on approach would be shot down long before it got through the window.'

'And,' Ayala added as he continued to mop up coffee, 'you'd have to be willing to go down with us. You're in this room too.'

El-Mirza looked unperturbed.

'Time for a break,' Morton said. 'I think Ms Pincent owes Inspector Ayala a fresh cup of coffee.'

# Chapter 3: Shot

It was nearing nine-thirty, and the Dog House was already rammed. Leon hated Saturday nights behind the bar. The music was too loud, the clients were too drunk, and it was ten to one on that someone was going to puke before midnight.

The crowd was young, dumb, and desperate to spend their parents' money. The Old Brompton Road was an alcoholic's paradise with pubs, bars, and restaurants in every direction. For the rich and the soulless, it was home. At the centre of it all was the Dog House, the oldest bar in the road and the rowdiest.

Leon tapped the other bartender on the arm and yelled over the music blaring through a nearby speaker.

'Missy, can you cover me? I need a smoke.'

She nodded, and Leon headed for the fire exit behind the bar. He briefly acknowledged the photographer circling the dance floor as he passed by, and then ignored the 'Fire Exit Only: Do Not Open' signs warning of a non-existent alarm, propped the door open with an old cinder block, and proceeded out into the alley.

The night air hit him immediately. It was cool, almost refreshing, as a light drizzle found its way between the buildings. Leon pulled out his vape and turned it on. A sweet cherry-flavoured nicotine mist hit him immediately. He inhaled deeply, pulling the mist into his lungs in a way he never could quite do with real cigarettes. Gone were the shallow, rapid breaths of the tar addiction of his youth.

As he smoked, he listened to the sounds of the night. The bar's techno music thumping away inside had been reduced to a dull throb that assailed his temples. Cars buzzed by at the end of the alleyway as Leon smoked.

Then he heard it: a muffled bang. He wasn't quite sure what it was at first. It was much too early in the year for fireworks, and seldom did anyone fire just one of those. Leon scanned the sky above him for a moment in case it was that simple. A less sober man might have dismissed the noise as part of the club music. It sounded almost like a gun, though not quite as loud as Leon had seen it portrayed in the movies. One shot.

He had to find out what it was, so he ran towards the source of the noise. It hadn't sounded very far away, almost as if it were just to the south of the club, where a shortcut ran down to Drayton Gardens. Leon sprinted around the corner onto the road, ran down to the next alleyway over where the sound appeared to be coming from. He never stopped to think of his own safety, and that was when he saw her.

There was a woman slumped on the ground, limbs akimbo, as if she were a rag doll tossed aside by a giant. Her chest was stained crimson as blood spurted in time with her heartbeat. Leon knelt next to her and pressed two fingers against her neck. She was still alive. Barely.

Leon tore his shirt off, wadded up the fabric, and pressed it to the woman's chest with one hand. He had to stop the bleeding, else she wouldn't last long enough for an ambulance to arrive. He could see her heartbeat dropping as the interval between spurts of blood increased. He didn't have long.

With his free hand, Leon dialled 999 and hoped he wasn't too late.

***

Rafferty's phone rumbled to indicate a text message a little after ten o'clock. This was it. Her first case as lead. Her hands trembled as she read the message summoning her to the Brompton Road, and the nerves hadn't quite worn off by the time she reached the Old Dog pub. She doubled-parked on the main road and stepped out into the drizzle.

The familiar blue-and-white crime scene tape signposted where the victim had been shot. It was an alleyway behind the pub that Rafferty knew all too well. The Old Dog had been a favourite of hers ever since she was old enough to drink.

Uniformed officers were guarding the perimeter. The nearest man saluted as she approached.

'Detective Inspector Rafferty,' she said. 'Where's the body?'

'Body?' the man echoed. 'You're getting ahead of yourself. The vic is down at the Royal Brompton Hospital. By all accounts, she's in bad shape, but she ain't dead yet.'

Rafferty's stomach churned. Ten seconds in, and she was already making mistakes. She quickly checked her phone for the initial message. It read: 'Shooting, Old Brompton Road. Victim: Angela King.' It didn't say she was dead.

'Err, right,' Rafferty stammered. 'Then, where *was* our vic?'

'Halfway down the alleyway, equidistant between the lampposts. One of your boys is waiting for you.'

Rafferty squeezed between the officers to find Mayberry loitering awkwardly with a digital SLR in his hands.

'R-Rafferty! W-where's Morton?'

'He's not coming,' Rafferty said.

'He's n-not?' Mayberry said, his tone dubious.

Rafferty looked around the crime scene. Techs were waiting nearby. It took a moment for her to realise that they were waiting for her to direct them. Morton seemed to get everyone working without any real effort.

She motioned for them to come closer. When everyone was in earshot, she raised her voice and called out, 'I'm in charge tonight. Come on – our crime scene is getting wetter by the minute, and we need to get to work. I want fingerprints, DNA, anything and everything we can get. Mayberry, show me what you've found so far.'

Mayberry looked confused but complied nonetheless. There wasn't much to see. The position of the victim had been marked both by the police and by her own blood loss. The rain was still pelting down, and much of the evidence had been washed away.

'W-what are we l-looking for?' Mayberry stammered.

Rafferty stopped in her tracks. What *were* they looking for? The victim was at the hospital, no doubt in surgery by now if she was still alive, so there was no witness to talk to, no body to look at, and the crime scene was being washed clean by the September rain. There was little point in having Mayberry loitering by her side, doing nothing to help out.

'Go find whatever CCTV you can,' Rafferty ordered. There weren't any obvious cameras in sight, but some of the businesses on the adjoining road had to have coverage. At the very least, it would give her time to explore the crime scene without being the centre of attention.

Mayberry nodded his acknowledgment and set off down the alleyway. He had barely gone ten feet when he was out of sight.

Rafferty made a mental map of the surrounding area.

The alleyway wound around the properties to the north and to the west, joining up the Old Brompton Road and Drayton Gardens. Both were major thoroughfares with lots of foot traffic, yet few ventured down the alleyway. Rafferty didn't blame them. The cut-through was dimly lit, with only two lampposts covering a three-hundred-yard stretch, and the high fences on either side backed onto private gardens. It was eerily quiet for somewhere so central.

It seemed like the perfect place to commit a murder. Or to dump a body.

Lighting had been set up around the place where Angela King had been shot. Her blood had pooled on the ground. It wasn't easy to spot because of the weather, but judging from the size of the pool, Angela King had lost several pints of blood before the ambulance arrived on the scene.

Rafferty ran her torch along the ground in either direction to look for blood droplets that might indicate movement. There were none. Either the victim had been shot on this spot while standing still, or the killer had cleaned up.

Rafferty rubbed at her temples. A migraine was beginning to set in. Did Morton feel like this when he was on a scene? He always looked so composed. *Think,* she told herself. There had to be some physical evidence. The victim had been shot. Where was the bullet?

There was no glint of metal in sight. Perhaps the bullet was still in the victim.

Rafferty was still searching when Ayala appeared on scene.

'Evening,' he said. 'Where's the boss man?'

'No boss man. Tonight, it's the boss lady.'

Ayala didn't even bother to hide his disdain. The scowl on his face and the set of his jaw said it all.

'The new chief's orders. I'm in charge of this case. You got a problem with that?' Rafferty asked.

She knew he did. Ayala had been on course for his own murder investigation team when Rafferty had re-joined the force. She'd displaced him as Morton's right hand in no time, and he'd never let her forget it.

He shrugged his shoulders as if he couldn't care less. 'Fine by me.'

'Good. Not a word to Morton, either. That's an order direct from Silverman. I need you to start going door to door. Canvass the flats to the south and east, and then go door to door among the clubs and restaurants.'

'On a Saturday night? That's going to be utterly fruitless,' Ayala complained, then quickly added, 'boss.'

'So be it.'

***

Angela King was in bad shape by the time she arrived at the Accident and Emergency department at the Royal Brompton Hospital. The paramedics in the ambulance had done their best to fill the gunshot cavity with gauze. They'd stemmed the bleeding, given her oxygen, and tried to reassure her so she wouldn't go into shock.

Doctor Hannah Cornell had seen it all before. She'd been a trauma surgeon for over twenty years, but even after all this time, it was still a rush. That wasn't something she'd ever admit to a patient. If you weren't an adrenaline junkie or a sadist, you didn't survive more than a short stint in Accident and Emergency.

She stood in her favourite room in the hospital, the operating theatre, and surveyed her patient. This was her domain. These were her staff. And tonight, Angela King's life was in her hands.

A nurse bristled at her elbow. He was already fiddling with the patient's IV. 'Patient presented with a bullet wound to the chest. Paramedics have filled the cavity with gauze.'

'Mainline six units of blood, stat. Get me a 32G chest drain.' Cornell stared intently at the woman's injury as she considered her options. The patient's heartbeat was weak. Her venous pressure was rising, and her systemic pressure was falling in response. Beck's Triad. Fluid was accumulating around her heart.

But before Cornell could deal with the heart, she had to drain the patient's chest cavity.

Bullet trauma was typically indirect. The bullet followed a narrow trajectory, obliterating everything in its path. That could be fatal, although in most cases, it wasn't. With it, the bullet brought enormous kinetic energy transfer, which damaged all the tissue around the bullet's path.

And then, if the patient lived long enough, they were at high risk of an infection from whatever bacteria the bullet had dragged in with it.

Cornell smiled. She felt most alive when death was in the air.

She jabbed the drain into the patient's chest. The lung and chest walls had collapsed, flooding the area with blood. The fluid began to spurt out of the drain. There was too much. She'd have to go in surgically.

'Nurse, scalpel.'

This was the tricky bit. The tension from the pneumothorax would have pushed the trachea to the other side. Cornell could barely see through the blood. She ran her fingers over the cavity, feeling for the right place to cut, and then, with a jolt of adrenaline, she pressed the scalpel to the patient's chest.

Blood erupted from the incision. It seemed like gallons, though Cornell knew it to be no more than three pints. In less than ten seconds, the operating theatre went from sterile, cold, and clean to a scene out of a horror movie.

'She's going into cardiac arrest!'

Cornell glanced at the monitors. Timing was everything. The few minutes between the patient being admitted and getting her into the operating theatre might have cost Angela King her life.

'Paddles. Now.'

The nurse desperately wiped away at the fluid on the patient's chest. They couldn't use the paddles until she was relatively dry.

'Charge.'

'Are you sure?' the male nurse asked.

'I'm damned sure. Do it,' Cornell barked.

The paddles began to hum as they charged. Moments later, they were ready for a Hail Mary to save Angela King's life.

'Clear!'

Cornell pressed the paddles to the patient's chest the moment the team was clear. The patient convulsed on the table, a violent spasm as she clawed to hold on to life.

'Clear!' Cornell repeated.

The electricity coursed through the patient, her every muscle tensing and twitching. Cornell glanced at the monitors once more. It wasn't helping. Angela King's heart wouldn't start.

One more try. One more.

'Clear!' Cornell thrust the paddles into place and jolted the patient's heart once more. Cornell's own breathing stopped as she craned her neck expectantly towards the monitors.

Nothing. She was going to have to call it.

'Time of death, ten thirty-two p.m.'

# Chapter 4: No Backup

Rafferty left Mayberry to get on with the general canvass, which normally would have suited him just fine if Ayala had bothered to make an appearance. Ayala was supposed to be there, but he seemed to have disappeared.

Mayberry wasn't confident that he'd find a reliable witness. The alleyway was dark and dingy and ran behind the busy thoroughfares of Drayton Gardens and the Old Brompton Road. At this time on a Saturday night, it would be a small miracle to find someone who wasn't drunk, high, or too busy working to notice any goings-on.

And he had to talk to them. His aphasia was better than it had once been, but he still hated talking to anyone except those close enough to know he had to take his time.

He fumbled in his pocket, searching for the reassuring presence of the little moleskin notebook and pen that Morton had given him the previous Christmas. Writing down what he wanted to say helped, but explaining that he needed to write it down – and that he really was a police officer on the job – was never easy. Especially with drunks. His first encounter of the night proved that.

'You're a copper, are ya, lad?' The speaker was a homeless man who was camped outside an ATM machine a couple of hundred feet away from the alley. He had a can of White Lightning in one hand and a cigarette in the other.

Mayberry nodded. 'H-have y-you seen anything un-un-unusual tonight?'

'I met this guy. He can't speak English proper, and he's pretending to be a policeman too. Now, you gonna spare us a quid, or you want to move on? Only you're scaring off me marks.'

Mayberry sighed inwardly. He wished Ayala were here. Ayala had a way of getting witnesses to talk, and it left Mayberry free to do what he was good at: to watch, to listen, and to make extensive notes.

He pulled his phone from his jacket pocket, swiped his thumb against the reader to unlock it, and opened up Messenger.

*Ayala, where are you?*

He hit send. It wasn't like Ayala to be late to a crime scene.

Mayberry turned slowly on the spot. He was on the Old Brompton Road, looking west from the Old Dog past Drayton Gardens. The people there were passing through, heading out for the night or heading home. Most had been in the bars or the restaurants. That left a few homeless people who hadn't seen or heard a thing. It didn't help that there were tourists everywhere. Mayberry could barely speak English, let alone try his hand at Urdu or Chinese.

There had to be something to find. The crime scene had yielded nothing. There were no prints, no trace, no things to find, only the blood, and that was being washed away by the weather. He hadn't even found a bullet. From his brief conversation with Rafferty, it sounded like the victim had been shot at close range, but if it had been a through-and-through, then the bullet should have been in the fence. It wasn't.

The CCTV had largely been a bust. The convenience store around the corner had been happy to hand over their tapes, but there was no guarantee the killer had walked past.

He decided to try inside the Old Dog once more.

He found the bar and flagged down the barman by flashing his police identification.

'Are y-you L-L-Leon?' Mayberry yelled over the music.

The barman nodded and beckoned for Mayberry to follow him. He led the way back to the alleyway in which he'd been taking his smoke break when he'd heard the gunshot. There, he turned on his vape once more and looked expectantly at Mayberry.

'I'm D-D-DI Mayberry. You f-found the victim?'

Leon was polite enough to pretend not to notice Mayberry's stutter. 'That was me. Want me to tell you what happened?'

Mayberry nodded, grateful that he didn't have to speak.

'I came out here to vape. I'm on shift 'til one a.m. tonight, and I get a headache with the music being so loud. That was about half nine. As I was smoking, I heard... well, the shot. Only it didn't sound quite right. I know what guns sound like. You never forget that sound.' Leon shivered. 'I was in the army, see?' He rolled up his sleeve to show off a tattoo depicting a crest with a tank and the words "Fear Naught".

'S-second R-royal Tank Regiment?'

Leon took a drag from his vape. 'Bingo. I did a full tour, and then I came back here. It's probably why I don't like the loud music. The gunshot wasn't *right*. I don't know why. It was definitely a gunshot. She had the hole in her chest to prove that. I don't know, maybe I'm imagining things. I'm sure it was a gun. It had to have been. I'm sorry I can't be more helpful, Detective.'

'D-did you see anyone unusual t-tonight?'

'Not that I remember. It was the usual crowd inside, and I didn't see anyone at all out here. I told the other detective that. Is there anything else? I only get one five-minute break, and if I don't get back to work, I'll be in trouble with my manager.'

'Y-you're f-free to go.'

***

Angela King was in the mortuary by the time Rafferty arrived at the Royal Brompton. The receptionist at the front desk helpfully escorted her downstairs.

'Hold on here one moment, please,' the receptionist said when they were outside the door of the mortuary. She slipped inside, and Rafferty could hear her talking to someone. She returned carrying two plastic bags.

'This,' she said as she handed over the first bag, which was a satin evening bag, 'was brought in with her. We looked inside, but only to find her ID.'

Rafferty took the bag. For a moment, she wished the rest of the team was there with her. It was usually Mayberry who handled the chain of custody paperwork for Morton. Now that she was the senior investigating officer, she'd have to do it herself.

'And the other one?'

The receptionist hesitated. 'The victim's clothes. The surgical team had to cut her top off to operate on her. I hope that's not a problem for you.'

Rafferty took the second bag. The clothes wouldn't be of much evidentiary value. At best, there would be a bullet hole they could measure, and, given the relatively narrow alleyway, there would probably be gunshot residue on there too.

'Not a problem,' Rafferty said. 'Is there anything else?'

'That's everything.'

Rafferty gestured at the door to the mortuary. 'Can I go in?'

'I'm afraid not, ma'am. The pathologist arrived five minutes before you did. He's in there right now, and he said...'

'He said what?'

'He said, "Morton can fuck off until I'm good and ready. The body is mine 'til I choose to release it." Does that mean anything to you?'

*Chiswick*. Rafferty smiled politely. 'I'll wait.'

***

The death was simple to explain from a forensic point of view. She'd been shot.

Doctor Larry Chiswick ruled it murder the moment he saw the body. There was a gaping hole in the victim's chest where the bullet had struck her. The actual cause could be exsanguination, hypoxia, or collapsed lung. Not that it mattered. One bullet, one hole, one dead woman. It was the sort of autopsy that Chiswick did on autopilot.

The gunshot wound had been made worse by the surgeon's mangled attempt to keep her alive. Her ribs had taken a beating, which would normally be suggestive of an assault, but Chiswick knew from the Accident and Emergency records that this damage had occurred when they tried to resuscitate her. The damage made his job a little more complex, but a single gunshot wound was a closed case as far as Chiswick was concerned.

Chiswick set a recorder down on a tray next to the gurney and spoke aloud to record his thoughts.

'The victim is female, late forties, and in good health. Apart from being dead.'

Chiswick hit pause on the recording, chuckled at his own joke, then hit the button again to resume recording.

'She was shot at close range, face-on, as evidenced by the presence of gunshot residue. From the angle of the entry wound, it appears the victim made little or no attempt to flee, which suggests she may have known her attacker. It is impossible to definitively determine the calibre of the bullet due to attempts to save her life. It is probable that a small-calibre weapon was used, due to the lack of perimortem damage sustained. According to the treating surgeon, the cause of death was a cardiac incident caused by acute bullet trauma. The manner of death was undoubtedly homicide.'

The bullet had passed close to the heart, and kinetic energy transfer had done the rest. It was a simple gunshot death.

Except for one thing.

The bullet had penetrated approximately five inches through Angela King's body. When Chiswick rolled her over, there was no exit wound.

'Odd,' he mused. She had been hit at a sufficiently low velocity to avoid a through-and-through, and yet there was no bullet inside her. He x-rayed her chest to be sure, and then updated his audio findings. 'No bullet is present in the chest cavity. I presume this is the result of removal by the Accident and Emergency department, but the senior investigating officer will wish to confirm this.'

He hit the pause button once more. There wasn't much more he could do here. The body would need to be transferred to the police morgue at Scotland Yard, where he could perform a full autopsy, send off blood samples to check for intoxication, and add her DNA to the system. That could wait until business hours on Monday morning.

Chiswick snapped closed his carry bag, slipped his audio recorder into his pocket, and disposed of his gloves in the yellow bin marked for biological waste.

He found Detective Inspector Rafferty waiting for him in the corridor. She was staring off into space, her headphones blaring out some awful pop music at much too loud a volume. He tapped her on the shoulder to get her attention.

'Where's David?' he asked.

'At home, I presume. This is my case.'

Chiswick used a fat forefinger to push his glasses up to the bridge of his nose and smirked.

'Good one. So, where's David, really? I've got news.'

'It really is my case. Tell me what you've got.'

Chiswick's smirk melted. 'Okay, I'll humour you. Your victim was shot at close range with a low-power weapon. There wasn't a bullet inside her chest, so I assume you've been given that by the trauma surgery team.'

'I haven't,' Rafferty said. 'It must be in there. You must have missed it.'

'Detective, I've been doing this since before you could legally drink. I didn't miss anything. There is no bullet in her. It would have shown on the x-ray.'

Rafferty frowned. If it wasn't inside the victim, and the surgery team hadn't taken it out, where had the bullet gone?

'What else can you tell me?'

'I'd guess she knew her killer,' Chiswick said. 'At the very least, she didn't have time to turn and run. She was shot while looking him or her in the eye.'

# Chapter 5: One of Us

By the time Rafferty and Mayberry had finished the initial evidence collection and located the next of kin, it was early on Sunday morning.

The victim lived with her husband in up-and-coming Muswell Hill. Their home was a new-build flat around the corner from the North Finchley allotments, with views of greenery just across from their front door. If not for the presence of the North Circular Road cutting straight past the flat, it would have been picturesque.

Rafferty knocked on the door, and a man in his boxers answered.

'Mr Brian King?' Rafferty said. 'Metropolitan Police. Can we come in?'

Brian loomed above her in the doorway. He looked from Rafferty to Mayberry and back again. From their expressions, he must have realised something was up.

'Okay. Give me a minute,' he said gruffly. He shut the door in their faces, leaving them waiting on the doorstep.

'My God, I thought the name sounded familiar,' Rafferty said when they were alone.

'W-who is he?'

'That's *the* Brian King. He's with the Serious Organised Crime Agency. Don't you recognise him?'

Mayberry shook his head. He looked quizzical. 'S-should I?'

Rafferty planted a hand on her right hip and stared down at Mayberry. 'He was in the newspapers a few weeks back. The misfire in Leicester Square? Some random civvie got shot because we thought they had a gun. SOCA got dragged over the coals by the press because of it.'

Mayberry still looked blank.

Before they could discuss it further, the door opened, and Brian King reappeared fully dressed. He led the way through to a small kitchen, where a pot of coffee was boiling away.

'What is it, then? Am I needed? You could've just called.'

'Mr King, would you care to sit down?' Rafferty began.

King's face turned ashen, and his eyes darted from Rafferty to Mayberry and then back again. 'Oh, no, you don't get to do that to me. What's going on? Is it my Angie?'

Rafferty paused. She hated death notifications just as much as every other police officer. 'Mr King, I'm sorry to have to tell you that Angela King died last night.'

The wail that emanated from the big man ricocheted around the kitchen, echoing off the bare walls and reverberating down the hallway. It was a sound that Rafferty instantly knew would haunt her forever. Then King slammed a ham-hock-sized fist down on the countertop, causing his coffee mug to leap into the air. It fell to the floor with a crash, flooding the linoleum with black coffee.

Mayberry leapt into action. He nabbed the kitchen roll from the counter and began to mop up the mess. Brian King continued to sob, seemingly unaware.

'How did it happen?' King demanded between sobs.

Rafferty watched him intently. 'She was shot.'

His eyes went wide. '*Shot?* By whom?'

If he was acting, the man deserved an Oscar. 'That's what we're going to find out, Mr King. Did Angie, or do you, have any enemies?'

Out of the corner of her eye, Rafferty saw Mayberry produce a notebook and pen and begin scribbling away.

'No,' King spat. 'Who'd want to hurt my Angie? She's a schoolteacher, for fuck's sake.' He slammed his fist down once more.

'I'm sorry,' Rafferty said. 'We can do this another time if you need to contact family.'

'No. Let's do this now. What do you need from me?' King demanded.

'What would Angie be doing in Kensington, just off the Old Brompton Road, on a Saturday night?' Rafferty asked.

'We used to live there. We rented just off Dove Mews. She often goes back for a night out with the girls or to visit her folks. I don't know who it was last night, though. She didn't mention it before I went to work, so I assume it was a last-minute thing.'

'How were things between you and Angie?' Rafferty asked.

'How dare you ask that? My wife is dead, and you want to know about our sex life?' King thundered.

'I have to ask, Mr King. I'm just doing my job,' Rafferty said. *You ought to know that better than most,* she thought.

'It was fine.'

'Then, why didn't you notice she was missing?'

King hesitated. 'Because I slept on the sofa.'

'You weren't sharing the marital bed? Why was that?'

'I get called a lot on weekends. I don't like disturbing her. My gaffer warned that something might be going down last night, so I slept on the sofa, just in case. I didn't want to say because I knew you'd take it out of context.'

'We'll have to check that. Who's your gaffer?'

'Xander Thompson.'

*Brilliant,* Rafferty thought. Xander Thompson was chummy with Morton. He was going to find out about the investigation in no time at this rate, and then Rafferty would be caught between his ire and the chief's direct orders to keep her assignment from him.

Brian King had begun to cry again. He was in no fit state to continue. Rafferty briefly wished she carried a pocket square like Detective Inspector Ayala often did.

'Is there anyone we can call for you?' she asked.

King nodded and pointed towards the wireless phone by the microwave. 'Me mam. Her number was the last I called, so just hit redial.'

# Chapter 6: Evolution

Morton found himself back in the lecture theatre on Monday morning. He had overslept, and arrived just after nine. He walked through the doors expecting to see Ayala had started without him. Instead, the students were milling around, chatting.

'Seats, please,' he called out as he swept past the rows towards the front of the lecture theatre. Ayala was nowhere to be seen, so he asked, 'Anyone seen Detective Inspector Ayala?'

'Nah, he ain't been in,' said the man in the second row. He was the only student to wear a full three-piece suit despite the weather.

Morton ran a gnarled thumb down the class list perched on the lectern. Daniel Hulme-Whitmore. He was a transfer in from SCD9. It was properly called the Serious Crime Directorate for Human Exploitation and Organised Crime Command, but everyone just called it "vice", much to the chagrin of those in charge of department names.

'Danny, right? What made you want to leave vice?'

'The hours, boss,' Danny said in an East London accent. 'The missus don't like it when I'm asleep all day and at work all night. We barely see each other.'

'Some couples like it that way,' Morton said with a wry smile. It was a story as old as time. The job or the family. It was a line that was far too easy to cross.

'Speaking of, did I hear Brian King's missus is dead?' Danny asked.

'You know him?'

'Of course. He's on the force rugby team with O'Shaughnessy and me. Did he do it?'

News travelled fast inside the Met. Morton was unsurprised that the death of a policeman's wife had quickly become force gossip, but now wasn't the time to comment. He ignored Danny's enquiry and turned his attention to the rest of the class.

'Right, that's five minutes,' Morton called out. 'It appears you've just got me today, so eyes front.'

No Ayala meant no PowerPoint. He really was on his own. He waited until all attention was focussed on him. The hum of chatter died down almost immediately.

'We've talked about basic murder methodologies. You know that the common murders – shootings, stabbings, poisonings, and defenestration – are usually easy to solve. The harder crimes to solve are those where the criminal adapts their modus operandi. The evolution of a serial killer is fundamental to catching them, because they're most likely to make mistakes early on.'

He sensed it coming before it happened. The moment Morton stopped talking, Babbage's hand shot into the air. *Oh, come on!* Morton thought. The man never missed a chance to interrupt him.

'No questions, please. I'll deal with those at the end. Unless you'd like to get up and teach this class, Mr Babbage?'

Babbage recoiled. He sat down in his seat in the front row and averted his gaze. Behind him, Danny, Sully, and Eric giggled like schoolgirls. It was only the second week, and cliques had already formed among the students.

'Something funny, Mr Hulme-Whitmore?'

Danny twirled his pen around his fingers absent-mindedly. 'Yeah. That was the first time Babbling Babbage wanted to speak that I thought I might ask a question too. I guess I'll just shut up now, though.'

'What did you want to ask?'

'Do all of 'em do that? Follow a pattern from shitty right up to polished? Can't a smart killer start off strong?'

'The starting point can vary,' Morton conceded. 'Criminal sophistication is on a broad scale. Some start relatively sophisticated and work their way up to almost uncatchable. Some start at the bottom and fumble their way into competence.'

'Almost, eh? Wouldn't a smart killer avoid mistakes?'

'They all make mistakes. They can't watch instructional videos on YouTube and then just give it a crack. You're underestimating how difficult, how bloody, how physically demanding a murder is. You can't just be smart. You have to be willing to get dirty, to lift heavy, and to take risks. Like any activity, it takes practice. Criminals become more sophisticated over time. I caught one man because he used cheap bleach. If you want to get rid of blood, you need oxidising bleach. That's not a lesson he'll forget in a hurry.'

The red-headed Irishman whispered something in Danny's ear, and Danny smirked. 'But what if they practiced somewhere else? Y'know, fuck off to Bumfuck Nowhere and strangle a few hobos to learn the ropes, and then come back to kill their real victim here in London?'

'Lovely imagery, Mr Hulme-Whitmore. No doubt you remember the class of criminals you had to deal with during your time with vice. Did any of them strike you as that smart?'

'Nah, but I wouldn't have met the smart ones, would I?'

He had a point. Cases with itinerant victims and crimes that were geographically removed from the killer would be more complex. Geographic profiling was a massive win for Morton's team. Serial killers felt safest near home, so the murders they perpetrated tended to be geographically concentrated. The idea of a killer who had no such compunction, someone so criminally sophisticated that they started by killing far from home in ways they never intended to use again...

A shiver ran down Morton's spine. The day he came up against such a killer would be the day he seriously considered retirement.

'Like I told you last week, we catch nine killers for every ten bodies. Show me a better way of doing things, and I'll listen. Until then, I fail to see what you expect me to do about the faintest possibility of a Moriarty-like serial killer roaming the streets and practicing on the homeless. Thankfully, if the number of beggars who accosted me for change on my walk from the tube this morning is any indication, he doesn't exist. Now, if you'll let me get back to the topic at hand, we were talking about being as flexible as the killers we hope to catch. Let me give you an example from my own cases. We had a man dumping bodies in the water. He'd picked a pond in north London.'

Babbage tentatively raised a trembling hand. His expression was that of a man who expected to get slapped down.

'What now, Mr Babbage?'

'Why did he dump them in the water? Was it a forensic countermeasure?'

'The man's mother had drowned when he was a young boy,' Morton said. 'Dr Jennings thought it was a compulsion. He wasn't choosing to dump the bodies in water for fun or as a forensic countermeasure. He felt he had to do it. After we discovered his primary dump site, he couldn't do that anymore. We were able to catch him by staking out similar dump sites and waiting for him to show up with his latest victim.'

'But, sir,' Babbage said, 'what if we come across a killer who doesn't have an Achilles' heel like that?'

'Then, God help us all.'

# Chapter 7: The Usual Suspects

As incident boards went, Rafferty's first was pathetic. It was an old cork board that Mayberry had pilfered from God knew where. It was full of holes from old pins and had a slightly musty smell. In the middle of the board, Rafferty had pinned a large picture of the victim, Angela King, and to the right, underneath Suspects, Mayberry had written the name Brian King in a beautiful cursive script.

There were no fancy projectors, no conference table to sit around. It was a far cry from the way Morton ran his cases.

As Rafferty hadn't been formally assigned rooms, she had pilfered a key to one of the disused offices on the third floor. Officially, they were supposed to be for task forces set up for specific, temporary purposes. Rafferty didn't see the harm, and this way they wouldn't accidentally run into Morton. His office was three floors up, and the lecture theatre was in another building. She felt a sense of betrayal running around behind Morton's back, but that knot of fear and irrational guilt could wait until after she'd caught the killer.

Only she and Mayberry were in attendance. Ayala still hadn't surfaced since skipping the crime scene callout on Saturday, and Rafferty could only assume he was off working with Morton.

"And that's it," she said, then turned to Mayberry. 'So, where do we begin? Who benefits from Angela King's death?'

'N-n-nobody,' Mayberry stammered.

'Someone has to. She didn't get murdered for no reason. Look at the modus operandi. She was shot at point blank range in the chest. Her husband is a firearms officer for SOCA. Doesn't he seem like the prime suspect?'

Mayberry looked dubious. 'W-why would h-he need to shoot her at close r-range?'

Rafferty deflated. He wasn't wrong. It didn't take an expert marksman to shoot somebody up close.

It was a weird murder. In some ways, it was thoroughly professional. The hit had occurred in a dark, quiet alleyway at a time when there would be few witnesses. There was little to no forensic evidence. All they had so far was the gunshot residue on the victim's clothing and body.

'Isn't it a b-bit im-p-p-personal, too?'

It was a cold-blooded and thoroughly ruthless kill. Rafferty tried to imagine shooting someone she loved, or had once loved, at the very least. To kill a spouse was one thing. To do it at point blank range in a meticulous, calculating way and to leave her bleeding out on the ground in a dark alleyway... well, that was something else entirely. Was Brian King that kind of psychopath?

Rafferty changed the subject. 'Any luck finding that bullet?'

'N-no. The d-d-docs are adamant there wasn't one.' Mayberry had spent all day Sunday chasing down the missing bullet. He'd been back to the crime scene, and had even had the body x-rayed by one of the dieners in the morgue.

'And we're waiting on the full autopsy,' Rafferty continued. 'Can you handle that?'

Mayberry nodded.

'Good. We've got two theories, then. Our prime suspect has to be the husband. He could have done it himself. We need to run down where he says he was.'

'H-he s-says he won't t-talk without a r-rep present.'

'Typical. He could also have had somebody else do it. I need you to run down his financials. If it's a professional hit, he'll have had to pay for it somehow. See what Angela had by way of life insurance, too. Money makes the world go round.'

***

Brodie's corner of the office was as messy as ever. The big Scot's desk was smothered not with reports or chain-of-custody paperwork, but with Cheetos and empty bottles of Pepsi Max. He hurried to hit alt-F4 as Mayberry's shadow loomed over him. He spun on the spot and grinned.

'Bloody hell, laddie. You gave me a heart attack,' Brodie said.

'S-sorry, B-Brodie.'

Brodie hit shift-alt-T on his keyboard, and the eBay window he'd quickly hidden sprang back to life. It looked like he had been checking out a custom mechanical keyboard. 'Nae problem. I was just having a canny bid or two. What can I do you for?'

'B-B-Brian K-King. I need–'

Before he could even finish speaking, Brodie had set to work. The clack of Cherry keys abounded as Brodie began to sift through the databases at his disposal. By starting with something as simple as Brian King's full name and address, he soon had records from insurers, banks, credit reporting agencies, and the Met's own personnel files.

'Here we go. Brian King, age forty-two. Bloody heck, he's with Trojan?' Brodie said, referring to the Met's Trojan Protective Unit. Brian King was one of just two dozen officers tasked with patrolling high-risk crime hotspots to deter potential criminals.

'Y-yes. H-he's one of us.'

'Should we be calling in the Professional Standards Department? If we're investigating one of our own...?' Brodie trailed off with a shrug and held up his hands. 'OK, it's none of my business. What do you need to know? Job history? Finances?'

'E-everything.'

Brodie's hands danced over the keyboard at lightning speed. 'Bank accounts look about normal. Ten grand and change in a current account, thirty in stocks. Not bad for a man earning maybe fifty grand including overtime.'

'Any d-debts?'

'One mortgage,' Brodie said. 'Plenty of equity in the family home, so nothing unusual. I'm not seeing any late payments on his credit record. He seems to be doing just fine.'

Mayberry leant over Brodie's shoulder to look at the screen. Brian King had two hundred thousand pounds outstanding on a property worth half a million. It was well within his means. 'What about l-life insurance?'

A few more clicks brought up the right documentation. 'He's insured for just under half a mil in the event of an unexpected death. His wife is on the same policy for the same amount. They're each other's beneficiaries.'

Half a million pounds. Half a million reasons to kill. Mayberry had seen people die over much less.

'S-she's d-dead.'

'Then, Brian King is soon to become a very rich man. You think he killed her for it?'

Mayberry hesitated. He didn't want to jump to a conclusion. 'Rafferty t-thinks so,' he said diplomatically.

'What does Morton think?'

'H-he's not involved.'

Brodie turned to face Mayberry with an incredulous stare. 'You're running a case without the big man? Does he know?'

Suddenly, Mayberry found the insurance documents on-screen absolutely fascinating. He could feel the heat of Brodie's eyes boring into him.

'He doesn't, does he?' Brodie tutted. He seemed almost cheerful at being ahead of the office gossip. 'Who's running the case? Bertram? No, not the new girl? How's Ayala taking that?'

Mayberry gestured at the screen. 'W-why f-five hundred thousand?'

'I'd guess they picked an amount just big enough to cover the total amount they had on their mortgage. They borrowed half a mil to buy their place originally, and they've got just over two hundred grand still to go.'

'T-that's a lot,' Mayberry said. He didn't need to add "on a policeman's salary".

'That's London for ya, laddie. I sold my place in Glasgow before I moved down here to take this job. It was only just enough for a bloody deposit.'

Brodie had never mentioned his past before. Mayberry looked at him curiously.

'What? Ya wonderin' why I moved? The missus wanted to live in the big city. The world's yer oyster down here, isn't it? The world's best museums, thousands of pubs, sporting events and gigs every night. There's always something to do. I guess we just needed a change. Not that I don't miss Glasgow, mind you. I can't find a battered Mars Bar and a pint for three quid in the East End now, can I? Anyways, is there anything else you need?'

'W-what's his credit like?'

Mayberry expected Brodie to turn his attention back to the computer once more, but Brodie was ahead of him. 'Eight hundred and change. Need the exact number, laddie?'

'N-no.' It wouldn't make a jot of difference. If Brian King's credit record was clean, his bank accounts were healthy, and his mortgage high but manageable, then he probably didn't have motive to kill his wife for money. 'W-what about social m-media?'

'Sod all, laddie. He tweets about Aston Villa far too much for my liking, but if being a card-carrying member of the Claret and Blue Army is a criminal offence, then we're going to need more resources to tackle that hive of scum and villainy. Those Brummies seem to get everywhere, even this far south.' Brodie gave a hearty laugh and pointed across the room to another desk, where an IT analyst Mayberry didn't know was sitting with headphones on. He hadn't heard a thing. On the desk was an Aston Villa mug.

'T-thanks for everything,' Mayberry stammered. His next stop was the morgue for the autopsy results. He hated talking to Dr Larry Chiswick. He never could get a word in edgeways.

'Don't mention it, laddie. And don't worry, I won't breathe a word to Morton.'

# Chapter 8: Too Perfect

It was too clean, too professional. Whoever had killed Angela King had to have killed before. To leave a body but no witnesses, a gunshot wound but no bullet, to kill without leaving a hair out of place – that took skill, practice, and training.

Rafferty knew just who had those skills. The vic's husband was a police marksman. He had confirmed kills on record. He'd been through the Met's forensics training. He had access to guns. And Rafferty just didn't like him. There was something definitely off about him, but before she could confront him, she needed evidence.

Rafferty looked around the empty Incident Room. It wasn't the same as Morton's, and she regretted having to hide away from him, but Silverman had been explicit: Morton was not to know that Rafferty had been assigned her first case.

In the corner farthest from the door was the tatty old cork board with the victim's name and photo at its centre. Everything they knew had been noted in Mayberry's meticulous handwriting, just as Morton would have ordered done. The beauty of Mayberry's cursive seemed to mock the empty space on the board. Where there ought to be definitive forensic details, evidence samples, fingerprints, and witness statements, there were none. All they had was a preliminary report from Dr Chiswick, not that they had needed a pathologist to tell them that Angela King had been shot. There was also a short statement from Leon, the bartender, outlining how he'd come to find the body.

It just wasn't enough evidence.

The case seemed simple: a woman dead by a method that screamed trained marksman; her husband a trained sniper. Rafferty desperately wanted one and one to equal two. Knocking out her first case in record time would bode well for her future.

It just seemed too perfect. Morton had always taught her to look at the domestic partner first. A husband – and it was almost always a husband, rather than a wife – was the most likely suspect in any murder investigation.

King's background fit the profile, too. He had reprimands on record for using excessive violence, and, not even a month ago, he'd been involved in a misfire incident on Pall Mall where a businessman had been mistaken for a terrorist.

Rafferty was jerked out of her thoughts when her phone buzzed. King's partner was waiting for her downstairs. Rafferty looked around the incident room on her way out, then pocketed the key. She hurried downstairs hoping she wouldn't cross Morton in the hallway. She felt like a fugitive on the lookout.

She made it to reception unscathed and found Abby Fields waiting for her. She was older than Rafferty by perhaps half a decade, with elegantly carved features and piercing green eyes that stared unblinkingly at Rafferty. Fields was part of the blue berets. It was her job to drive the BMW X5 that had been specially modified to carry all of the weapons that Brian King might need. She'd been with him for years, and her disdain at being summoned showed on her face.

'Why am I here, Inspector?' she demanded almost immediately.

'Ms Fields, thank you for taking the time to see me. Would you be so kind as to come up to my office?' Rafferty said.

Fields cut her off with a glare. 'I have nothing to hide. If you have questions, ask them.'

Her voice was just loud enough to draw the attention of passers-by in the lobby. With a nod of her head, Rafferty led Fields to the west side of the lobby, where a cluster of empty chairs awaited them. Once they were sitting down, Rafferty leant forward and spoke quietly. 'I need to ask you about Brian King and his relationship with his wife.'

The older woman sighed, leant back, and regarded Rafferty warily. 'It's not what you think,' she said.

Rafferty raised an eyebrow, keen not to let on that she had no idea what Fields was talking about.

'They've had some trouble, okay? And it's not because of me, before you ask. I know the rumours that go around this place. Every man in here thinks that a single woman must be in want of a suitor,' Fields said.

'So, why was their relationship on the rocks?'

'He took the job home with him. He hasn't stopped talking about that accident–'

'The misfire?'

Fields nodded. 'It hit him hard. He's always been an emotional one, but guilt isn't something Brian is used to. He tried to use her as an outlet, and she got sick of it, resentful, even. He used to be so loving and attentive, and since then, he's been preoccupied, moody, withdrawn. He hasn't been sleeping properly, and she booted him to the sofa so she could get some shut-eye. After a while, she threatened to leave if he wouldn't agree to counselling which he did. He's getting better, but it's not an overnight thing.'

Rafferty locked eyes with Fields. 'So, he's emotionally all over the show, but you don't think he killed her.'

'I know he didn't.'

'How?'

'He was with me.'

Rafferty stared.

'Not like that. We were on a job. Check the logs if you don't believe me. Thompson should have signed off on them by now.'

Rafferty thanked her for her help and rushed off to her makeshift office to check the paperwork. Sure enough, there had been a call-out on the night of the murder, which Abby Fields and Brian King had both attended. His alibi was rock-solid.

And yet, Rafferty mused, the kill had all the hallmarks of a professional. It was clean, quick, and well-planned. It was the sort of kill that took training to accomplish without leaving evidence.

Could Brian King have arranged Angela King's murder without getting his hands dirty? Rafferty wondered. For now, it seemed, that was the best lead she had.

***

The drive to Ayala's was supposed to give Rafferty time to clear her head, but by the time she parked up illegally outside his home just south of the Millwall Docks, Rafferty was downright angry.

He'd texted her claiming to be ill. She knew damned well he wasn't. The odds of Ayala claiming his first sick day in six years the moment he was assigned to work for Rafferty were one in a million.

She walked the path along the dock quickly and found his front door nestled down a short pathway through his front garden. She banged on the door.

'Ayala! I know you're in there!'

When he didn't answer straight away, she banged on the door again. 'Police! Open up!'

The door finally cracked ajar, still latched, and Ayala's mug appeared in the crack between door and frame. 'Very funny. What do you want? I'm sick.'

'Let me in. We need to talk.'

Ayala made to shut the door, forcing Rafferty to jam her foot in the gap. 'We don't need to do anything, boss,' he said. 'I'm allowed to take a sick day.'

'Not when you're not sick.'

'Fine. Move your foot.'

Rafferty complied. For a moment, she half-expected him to slam the door shut again, but he duly undid the latch, opened the door, and stood aside to let her pass into a small house with kitschy memorabilia on every available surface. He beckoned her to follow him through to a small kitchen, where he set a pair of teacups down on a rickety old oak table.

'Tea?'

'Go on, then.'

She watched him in silence as he fumbled to make tea the proper way.

'Milk? Sugar?'

She nodded for the first and declined the second. Ayala seemed to be dragging his heels as if he were desperate to avoid a difficult conversation. He finally sat himself down opposite her and met her gaze.

'What's really up?' she nudged gently.

'It's not fair,' Ayala said through gritted teeth. 'I've been with him for years, I've been a detective inspector for the last three, and you get a shot before I do? Who'd you blow?'

The hairs on Rafferty's neck rose up, and anger coursed through her veins. As quick as a flash, her hand shot out to slap him. It only registered when she saw the outline of her palm upon his cheek. 'How dare you. You know why I'm in charge? It's because I act like I'm in charge. You're a competent detective, Bertram, but you never show any initiative. You wait for Morton to tell you what to do, like a puppy dog. Just lingering on his team for years doesn't earn you the right to lead. If you want to lead, be a leader. Right now, I'm in charge. Are we going to have a problem, or are you going to get in line and help me give Angela King justice?'

She had just slapped a subordinate. In any normal circumstances, that would be grounds for dismissal, but she didn't care. She had earned this. If Ayala wanted to be petulant, he could do it on somebody else's time.

Ayala stared glumly at his tea, veering between shock and indignation. Finally, he looked up, his expression cowed, and bit his lip. 'I can't. I won't work for you. And if you try to force me, I'll tell Morton you've stolen a case we both know should be his. If the new chief hadn't put him on desk duty, he'd have solved Angela King's murder by now. You want justice for Angela King? Morton's the man to get it for her.'

As Ayala spoke, Rafferty's rage grew. Her jaw was set, her arms tense. Through clenched teeth, she growled at Ayala.

'Be in work tomorrow morning, or else. This is the last chance I'm giving you.'

She swept from the room without a backwards glance. How dare he?

# Chapter 9: The Union Rep

Brian King was not alone when he arrived at the interview suite at New Scotland Yard. No doubt his partner had tipped him off that they were looking at his relationship with his wife, so he had brought back-up. The man accompanying him, Kirk Addison, was wiry and grey-haired, with a ruddy complexion that belied an intelligent wit. He was a veteran of the Metropolitan Police group of the Public and Commercial Services Union, and honour-bound to attend any hearing at the request of a union member.

There was no sign of Detective Inspector Ayala. He had not listened to Rafferty's demands. Ayala had to know he was forcing her hand, but dealing with that would have to wait. There was a killer to catch, and Rafferty was still convinced she was staring right at him.

Rafferty shook Addison's hand, careful to match her grip to his. He wasn't one of those men who tried to crush her hand in a primal show of dominance, unlike the man he represented, and Rafferty felt a surge of grudging respect.

The formalities were sorted without ceremony. Once the tape was recording, Rafferty shuffled forward in her chair, made direct eye contact with Brian King, and let an uncomfortable silence begin to build. It was a technique Morton had used many times before. Suspects felt compelled to fill the void with something – anything – to avoid the silence. But not this one. Brian King was too old and too smart to fall for such a basic tactic.

Eventually, Rafferty caved. 'You and Angela were in counselling.'

'Yep,' King said, his face betraying nothing. If Rafferty could imagine the cold, hard, expressionless features of a cold-blooded killer, Brian King would fit that description perfectly. His eyes were steel grey tinged with a hint of blue, and they bored into Rafferty like a drill.

'Why?' she prodded simply.

His eyes narrowed angrily for a moment, then the emotionless mask returned. He could feel, after all.

'That's private,' he said.

'I'm sure it is. Are you declining to answer?'

'Yes.'

'Okay,' Rafferty said, and pretended to shuffle her notes as if searching for something. 'Let's talk about what happened in February.'

King glared and looked over to his union rep.

'That's a matter of public record,' Addison said slowly. He looked searchingly at his client as if wondering why this was an issue.

'It is. I'd like to hear it in his own words, if I may,' Rafferty said with a mirthless smile.

'Fine,' King said. He exhaled deeply, flexed his fingers against his forearm, and began. 'On the third Saturday in February, we were called to an incident at Covent Garden market. It was late at night, the bars were crowded, and there was movement everywhere. The call was that a man was holding up the crowd with a gun in the lower level outside the Punch and Judy. We quickly assumed a position on the level above, and I was the point man.'

'What happened?'

'A man was wearing a hoody. He was tall, dark–'

'Black?' Rafferty prompted.

King glared. 'Yes. As I was saying, he was in a dark corner, and he had his right hand inside his pocket. There was blood on the floor nearby, and members of the public were screaming and running back and forth.'

Rafferty watched King carefully as he spoke. His voice had begun neutral, even, and low. As he told his story, there was a quiver in his voice, a staccato of emotion.

'He wouldn't take his hand out of his pocket–'

'Which hand?'

'Right. He was screaming something, but I couldn't hear what over the din. He had his left hand raised in a pointing gesture and kept jabbing it at a woman nearby as if he were threatening her.'

'Was he?'

'No. But I didn't know that until... after...'

Rafferty folded her arms and looked across the table at him, her manner that of a stern schoolteacher. 'Until after you shot him,' she finished for him.

'Yes,' King said, his tone suddenly matter-of-fact once more. 'I believed there was a danger to life and limb, and I acted accordingly. I'd do it again.'

'For someone with very little regret, it's weird to see a counsellor about the guilt,' Rafferty chided.

King howled, an animal wounded. The sound reverberated around the interview suite as he sobbed. 'He was a child, OK? I didn't mean to kill him. How was I supposed to know he was the victim?'

'He was the victim?' Rafferty echoed.

The police rep interjected. 'I think you know the rest, Inspector Rafferty. The victim was a young man who had been stabbed. His hand was inside his jacket to stem the bleeding, and the screaming was from pain. The blood was his. Mr King had no way of knowing this in the split second he took to make the decision. After Borough Market, the acid attacks in the East End, and everything else that had happened, he couldn't take the chance. It's obvious he regrets it. How and why is this pertinent to your investigation?'

Rafferty was forced onto the back foot. If King was genuinely contrite, and it was some form of post-traumatic stress disorder that had fractured his relationship with his late wife, could he be an innocent man?

'Who does Mr King think killed his wife?'

'How would he know?' Addison said.

'Okay,' Rafferty said thoughtfully. 'I'll rephrase the question. Angela was shot at short range by someone who knew how to handle a gun. Mr King works with firearms professionally. Would he not agree that her murder has an element of professionalism to it?'

'You want him to agree that his wife's murder was professional?' Addison echoed in disbelief. 'What is this, TrustPilot for criminals? Five out of five stars, would be murdered by again? This interview is over, and I will be talking to Ms Silverman about your lack of sensitivity.'

# Chapter 10: Coming Clean

The thirty-third game of solitaire in a row saw Morton's average time dip below a minute for the first time in forever. He sighed as the window tempted him to play game number thirty-four. Desk duty just wasn't for him. He knew others who did it much better. They seemed to revel in lazy morning coffees, plush office chairs, and getting home to see the family every evening.

The truth was, he hated teaching. He enjoyed having taught, knowing he had made a difference to young detectives, but the actual teaching itself was so boring. He'd rather have a prostate exam than teach a bunch of overgrown children how to solve crimes, and that was a task he'd been putting off for as long as was humanly possible.

The pile of cold cases on the corner of his desk was a constant reminder of what he craved. He told everyone he wanted to bring justice, to serve the community, to protect those he loved from those who would harm them. All that was true.

But his real passion, the thing that made him excited to stand in the rain at five in the morning to inspect a crime scene, was the challenge. There was a satisfaction to being the better man that he could find nowhere else. To take the puzzle, to solve it faster than anyone else: this was his raison d'être.

A shadow loomed in the hallway, and his office door swung open a moment later.

'Can I come in?' Rafferty asked. She was carrying a tray of doughnuts that she slid across the desk as she sat down. Morton knew instantly that it was a peace offering.

'Well, I do have some important business to attend to,' he said as he quickly closed his card game. 'But I guess I can spare you a few minutes. What's up?'

'I don't know if you know where I've been this week–'

'Of course I do,' Morton said, his eyes twinkling. 'It doesn't take a genius to realise that if you bench one detective, another is needed to take his place. I assume congratulations are in order.'

Rafferty sat there slack-jawed. 'Err, yeah, thanks.'

'And I see you've poached Detective Inspector Ayala,' he said with a grin. 'Though you may regret that one.'

'Actually, he was what I wanted to talk to you about. He's been assigned to me by Silverman, and he won't play ball. He's pretending to be sick.'

'Hmm,' Morton mused. 'That makes two of us he isn't working for. I've been left to teach without him. I'm afraid I can't force Bertram to do anything. He'll either give up and act like an adult eventually, or he'll get called into Silverman's office. You'll just have to let nature run its course there.'

Rafferty leant forward to help herself to one of the doughnuts.

'Oi! Not the salted caramel, please.'

She withdrew guiltily, clutching at a plain glazed ring doughnut instead. She nibbled it while Morton eyed her cautiously.

'You're not here about Ayala. What's the problem?'

'I can't crack this case. Angela King was shot at short range in the chest in an alleyway. The killer was close enough to leave gunshot residue blowback all over her. Nobody saw a thing, and there's literally no physical evidence.'

Morton's brow furrowed into a frown. 'None? Not even a bullet?'

'Lost it,' Rafferty said, hanging her head. 'The vic was taken off the scene alive and died on the table. I searched the crime scene for hours, the surgical team that tried to save her swears they never removed a bullet, and Chiswick didn't find any sign of one inside her at the autopsy.'

'That's a pretty major balls-up. I'd love to tell you that you can blame it on someone else, but the blame is going to land in your lap on this one. Welcome to being in charge.'

Morton gave her a crooked grin. He'd been there many a time. In any other line of work, the shit rolled downhill. In the Met, the buck stopped with the senior investigating officer. That, Morton suspected, was why Ayala had been passed over in favour of Rafferty. She could handle the guilt, while Bertram would have fallen to pieces and begun yelling that it was everyone else's fault by now.

'I figured,' Rafferty said. 'But if I can solve the case, all will be forgiven, right?'

Morton chucked. 'That's how it's worked for me... up until Silverman took charge, anyway.'

'No word on when she'll let you out of the doghouse?'

'When I retire?' Morton said. 'She's never going to forgive me. There's no earning redemption in her eyes.'

'Then I'm doubly motivated to solve this case before she finds out I'm missing a bullet. I think it's the spouse, but he has a rock-solid alibi.'

Morton stared at her. 'How solid?' he asked. He knew full well how the most convincing alibi could turn out to be less than the complete truth.

'We're his alibi. The police, that is.'

'We're his alibi? Is he a criminal? Or one of us?' Morton asked.

'Yes,' Rafferty said with a grin. 'He's called Brian King. His wife was Angela King, the lady murdered up by the Brompton Road last Saturday.'

'Brian King?' Morton echoed. He turned to his computer and began to click through the Met's personnel records. 'I thought so. He's one of Xander's boys.'

'Yep. And Xander is hiding behind the rule book. He let King bring in a police union rep, Kirk Addison.'

'Nice guy,' Morton said.

'Nice or not, he shut down my interview.'

'So, work off-book. There's nothing stopping you having a quiet beer with Xander later this evening, is there?'

'I wouldn't even know how to get hold of him.'

'Hmm... I can't really help you with that, being on desk duty and all, but I'm going to take a short walk for some fresh air, and whoops, look at that, I've left my phone unlocked on my desk. Catch you later!'

Rafferty beamed. 'See you, boss.'

As Morton left the room, he saw Rafferty's reflection in the window as she leant over his desk to nab his mobile phone. Sometimes, just sometimes, the rules were made to be broken.

# Chapter 11: Down Low

Xander was at his usual table in the back of the Nag's Head when Rafferty found him, looking visibly put out at the intrusion. She had borrowed Morton's work mobile to request the meeting at a couple of hours' notice, and then put the phone back before Morton returned.

The pub was nearly empty, which was typical of a Wednesday evening. It was a policeman's pub that filled up after work and emptied as the officers headed home after a long day. After a quick scout around the bar to make sure that Brian King was not loitering in earshot, Rafferty set her tankard of Guinness beside Xander's and perched herself atop a rickety stool.

'So, you're Morton's protégé,' Xander said flatly over a sip of his Guinness. A thin strip of foam lined his upper lip, and he licked it with a satisfied smack. 'He's never asked me to meet with one of his lot before. Why's he not here himself?'

Damn, he was quick off the mark. She ignored the question and offered a handshake. 'Ashley Rafferty,' she said.

'Alexander Thompson. Everyone calls me Xander. Morton tells me you want to know about one of my guys.'

She nodded. 'Brian King.'

'Arsehole,' Xander offered immediately. 'Arrogant prick who thinks he's God's gift to marksmanship, which, annoyingly, he probably is. Not a cold-blooded killer. You're looking at the wrong man.'

'How can you be so sure?'

'Gut,' Xander said. 'I've known him for years, and I'm an excellent judge of character. Gotta be, in my line of work.'

'Which line?'

'Did Morton not tell you this? I'm Serious Organised Crime. Morton and I knew each other back in our undercover days. Doing what we did, you get a feel for people, and I don't think Brian King has the cojones to off his missus.'

Rafferty looked at Xander curiously. His was a face that had seen far too much. There were deep crow's feet around his eyes, and his brow was furrowed like the Mariana Trench.

'Do you think he wanted her dead?'

'I don't think he's as cracked up about it as he should be. He didn't want to take bereavement leave, believe it or not. He wanted to work, to keep busy. Said he'd rather be distracted than sit in the empty home they bought together. Not that I told you that.' Xander drained his glass and looked at Rafferty expectantly.

'One more?' Rafferty asked.

'At least,' Xander said with a grin that showed off yellow nicotine-stained teeth. He looked how Rafferty imagined Morton might have looked had he stayed undercover and never met Sarah.

She fetched a fresh Guinness from the bar. By the time she returned, Xander was tapping away at his mobile.

'Here,' he said, shoving his screen in her face. 'This is what you want to look at. There are at least six professional killers on the loose in London that we know, and there could be more. If your girl was killed by a pro, chances are it was one of these guys.'

Rafferty quickly scanned the list. She recognised the first name there, the ominously unnamed Frenchman rumoured to be in the employ of the Bakowski Crime Syndicate, but the rest were complete blanks. 'Can you tell me any more about these guys?'

'I'm afraid not, but I know a man who can. Rocko Mulhall. He's one of mine, and he's undercover, so you'll have to go plain clothes for the meet. If you're looking for a contract killer, Rocko's the man to point you in the right direction.'

***

It didn't matter how nice he'd been to Rafferty. Morton was pissed. In the course of a few months, he'd gone from leading the top-rated murder investigation team in London to playing babysitter to a bunch of feckless new detectives who couldn't find their arses from their elbows if given a map.

Silverman was dismantling his team one by one. First, Mayberry had gone AWOL, not that Morton could blame him. Who could teach a class while suffering such severe aphasia that he could barely stammer out a sentence? Then it was Rafferty, his hand-poached detective. And now it was Ayala too.

Ayala was like one of those trees that stood upright for many years and then fell down in a storm so it was all twisted and gnarly. It was ugly, but it was Morton's, and he wanted Ayala back.

He huffed his way up the six flights of stairs to the chief's office, letting his anger carry him up. The more he thought about it, the angrier he became. This was his team, his life's work, his legacy, and, though he'd never say it to Rafferty, she just wasn't ready for her own team. Less than a week into her first investigation, and she had already lost a key piece of evidence. The defence solicitors would have a field day with that one.

'Hey!' a voice called out. 'Do you have an appointment?'

He ignored the protests of Silverman's secretary as he barrelled down the hallway. He slammed a fist against the door, bursting it open, and stared Silverman down.

'Ah, David,' Silverman said with a tight-lipped smirk. 'I thought you might show up. Have a seat.'

*Expecting me?* Morton glared. Silverman had always been able to get under his skin. He remained standing, choosing to lean against the seat instead. Silverman looked entirely unsurprised.

'Here to thank me for giving your protégé a shot at her own case?' Silverman said. 'I was expecting flowers or chocolates, but something tells me you're not feeling like much of a gentleman today.'

'You poached my entire team.'

'Yes. Yes, I did. The incident on the Westferry Road was your fault, not theirs. I refuse to punish your subordinates for your failure. Or would you have me condemn three promising careers so they can go down with your ship?'

Acid rose up in the pit of Morton's stomach. He had been thinking of his own career and hadn't stopped to consider that moving on might be in his team's best interest. Had he betrayed their trust by coming in today?

Silverman was revelling in his confusion. 'What's the matter, David? Cat got your tongue?'

Her mirth sent a shiver down his spine. She was enjoying this.

He stood up straight and said with a steely determination, 'You benched the best murder investigation team in the Met, and you've promoted my juniors too far, too fast. Rafferty may have the potential to be one of the best detectives in the force, but she isn't there yet. Don't pretend you were doing her a favour. This isn't about advancing her career. It's about humiliating me. I demand you take me off desk duty. Let me assist Rafferty with her first case. She can take lead, but she needs a voice of experience behind her. Justice demands that much.'

'Request denied,' Silverman said. 'Now, if you're quite done ranting, I've got an official meeting in the next ten minutes. Besides, don't you have a lesson to prep or something?'

Morton stomped from Silverman's office with all the grace of a raging bull. This was all going to end in tears.

***

The drudge work always fell to Mayberry. Ever since the accident that had left him with aphasia, he hadn't been much good for anything else, but this he was really good at. His IT skills were coming on in leaps and bounds, and, after four years on the force, he knew the ins and outs of every major CCTV network in London. There were hundreds of them, from small private cameras outside local corner shops right up to the eye-in-the-sky cameras run by the biggest London councils.

With Brodie's help, Mayberry had everything at his fingertips. Normally. This time, the CCTV footage he was after belonged to a local silverware store. Brian King had allegedly been called there to respond to an armed robbery on the night his wife was murdered. Unfortunately for him, the Chancery Lane-based company did not want to release their footage. As far as they were concerned, the occasional theft was a cost of doing business, and advertising that fact would invite more harm than it would prevent.

The crime had been an elaborate one. The would-be robber had posed as a customer to get into the vault and had then pulled a prison-style shiv which he had smuggled past the scanner. The remote CCTV service for the silverware store saw everything, put the place in lockdown, and called the police. It was a simple system, and it worked.

Except when they wiped the footage.

Mayberry had managed to secure a warrant for the hard drive platters with little difficulty. No magistrate would turn down a request when there had been such a blatant attempt to destroy evidence. Now, it was time to wait.

He watched as Brodie carefully reassembled the drive. It had been smashed into a thousand tiny fragments, but even in such a broken state, there was data to be had. Even a square millimetre of platter could hold a file, and that was what Brodie was trying to recover.

'See, laddie? Told you I could put her back together again. Humpty Dumpty fell off a wall, and then ole Brodie came to call,' the Scot said with a chuckle.

'C-can you s-see f-files n-now?' Mayberry stuttered.

'Hold your horses, laddie. We've got a way to go, yet. Data storage leaves a physical trace, but the way data is encoded and then stored on a platter is proprietary. Every hard drive manufacturer has their own method, and they don't like to share. This one's a Western Digital, and their tech folks are always cooperative, so I'm hopeful.'

'H-how l-long?'

'Hours, if you're lucky. Months, if you're not. You want me to call you when I'm done?'

Mayberry nodded. 'T-thanks.'

'Don't sweat it, laddie. Just keep the single malt coming, and we'll get along grand.'

# Chapter 12: The Meet

Hawker House was a decidedly hipster venue for a meet-up. On Fridays and Saturdays, it was a bustle of hipsters eating street food, sipping cider, and enjoying what little sunshine Canada Water had to offer.

Fortunately, Rafferty was meeting with Rocko Mulhall on a Thursday. She found him near the entrance, casually staring off into the sky with a cigarette between his fingertips.

'Alright, love,' he said as she approached. 'Looking for a good time?'

Rafferty rolled her eyes. Rocko was every bit the younger version of Morton: brash, insecure, and hyper-masculine. He had a slight Belfast twang to his accent.

'The colour of the day is indigo,' Rafferty said, hoping against hope that Xander Thompson wasn't having a laugh at her expense. It sounded ridiculous, but it did the trick. Rocko's persona changed immediately. He snapped upright as if he'd been bent into position by a benevolent God. His previously unfocussed gaze now locked on to Rafferty with an intensity that surprised her. His eyes were a piercing bright blue with the hint of a smile lingering beneath every look. They were what many would call 'bedroom eyes'. The cigarette dangled between long, tapered fingers.

'What's up? Boss man need me?'

'Xander sent me,' Rafferty said. 'He told me you know the players in the professional hit market here in London. I'm investigating the death of Angela King.'

Rocko's eyes widened. 'Brian's missus? She's dead?'

'She was shot at point blank range in an alleyway last Saturday.'

He exhaled slowly and then gave a sad shake of his head, as if he had lost a dear friend. 'Blimey. Brian do it?'

'Not personally.'

'Ah, that's why you're here,' Rocko said. 'You think he had a pro do her in?'

'Is he capable of that?'

Rocko took a long drag of his cigarette and glanced up and down the path as if he was suspicious they might no longer be alone. 'Nah. No way. Brian's a tight git. He's the kinda guy who turns out the lights to save on the electricity bill. There's no way he'd stump up the money for a kill as clean as the one you're talking about.'

'But these professionals exist.'

'Of course they do,' Rocko said. 'You'd need connections with one of the bigger gangs just to know how to get in touch, and you'd need money, but for the right price, there's someone who'll do pretty much anything.'

'What if you haven't got money?' Rafferty said. From what she knew of Brian King, he had just enough to live on and little more.

'Then you're out of luck, aren't you?' Rocko said in between puffs of his cigarette. 'The cheapest pros will set you back five grand. For someone good enough to leave no evidence, add a zero. It's a high-risk gig, and nobody wants to go to jail for sod-all money.'

***

The light in Brodie's office flickered as he squinted at the grainy CCTV footage of Brian King on the night of his wife's death. Despite his only having been able to assemble video fragments lasting a few seconds apiece, the CCTV was conclusive. King had been four miles away at the time of her death. He had his entire unit as alibi witnesses, and the CCTV backed him up, too. He had not murdered Angela King.

There wasn't anything to suggest he'd hired a hit man, either. His bank accounts were nearly empty, and they had been for years. The expenditure on his credit cards matched the couple's combined income, with little or no money left over to stash away. Brodie would bet his life that King could not have saved up enough to pay for a hit man.

Brodie had even looked for any windfalls that might explain it: bingo wins, inherited money, compensation from a lawsuit. He had found none.

And aside from a few questionably sexist emails sent to the rest of his unit, Brian King's email account was as clean as a whistle. If there were skeletons to be found, they were buried so deep that even Brodie couldn't find them.

# Chapter 13: Brick Wall

Friday morning brought with it a sense of dread. Rafferty had had her first case for less than a week, and it was already dead in the water. Maybe Ayala had been right to say she wasn't cut out for leadership just yet.

Rafferty trod the stairs with a heavy heart, her favourite boots clanging against the floor and reverberating loudly. She slowly ascended towards Silverman's office. It was just gone eight o'clock, and the chief would be in at any minute. It would be easier to get the meeting over and done with while it was quiet.

Sure enough, not two minutes after Rafferty had reached the seating area outside Silverman's office, the chief strolled out of the corridor with a newspaper tucked under her arm.

'Detective Inspector Rafferty. To what do I owe the unexpected pleasure?' she asked as she approached.

'I'm here to offer my resignation, ma'am.'

Silverman surveyed her with the curiosity of a small child visiting the zoo for the first time. 'Dear me. We'd better step inside. After you.'

Rafferty's hands began to shake. She hastily stuffed them inside her jeans pockets as she sat down.

After taking what felt like an age to make herself comfortable and set her coffee down on her desk, Silverman said, 'Case not going well?'

'No,' Rafferty said. 'I have nothing to work with. We have no suspects, no motive, and no evidence. Angela King appears to have had no enemies, no debts, and was involved in no arguments. She wasn't robbed, raped, or subjected to sadism. There was, as far as I can tell, no reason whatsoever for her to have been murdered. She was a model citizen. Her husband, while thoroughly dislikeable, has a rock-solid alibi backed up by CCTV footage we recovered. I would like to tender my resignation.'

'Denied,' Silverman said, thoroughly unperturbed by the bad news. 'You're not getting off that easily. If the case can't be solved, I don't expect you to solve it. Did you follow proper procedure?'

'Of course.'

'Did you document the crime scene?'

'Yes, but–' Rafferty stammered.

'And did you make use of all available leads?'

'Well, yes, but–'

'But, nothing,' Silverman said. 'Morton may have given you the impression that I am an unreasonable woman. Do not let that cloud your judgement of me. All I ask is your best foot forward. Hold a press conference today, see if anyone out there knows anything. If that bears no fruit, then so be it. If you cannot solve this one, I will give you another chance with the next body that comes in.'

Rafferty's jaw slackened. 'Thank you. I won't let you down.'

'Ashley,' Silverman said as Rafferty rose from her chair, 'This is your last chance. If you don't prove yourself with the next one, you're fired.'

***

The idea of a press conference terrified Rafferty. She spent most of the morning with the media liaison team setting it up, and the remaining time before three o'clock shuffling her notes, touching up her makeup, and triple-checking that she was sufficiently presentable to appear on television.

It was a quiet news day, and the conference room filled quickly as the clock ticked towards three.

She took the lectern without ceremony, and silence fell quickly in the room. At the back, a door opened, and Morton sidled into the room. He gave her a crooked half-smile and nodded his reassurance.

It was a good thing there was a lectern between her and the rest of the room. It hid the trembling of her hands. She arranged her notes so they didn't flutter, cleared her throat, and looked around to see if she recognised any of the journalists present. There were a few old hands whom she'd seen Morton chatting with before, but she knew none of them herself. She did recognise Brian King's partner, Fields, lurking in the front row. She nodded acknowledgement, then stared down at her notes.

*Come on, Ashley,* she thought. *You've got this.*

With one deep breath, she began in earnest.

'Today, the Metropolitan Police will provide an update on the investigation into the murder of Angela King. This investigation remains of paramount concern to the department, and all leads are being aggressively pursued. At approximately twenty-two hundred hours last Saturday night, Mrs King was shot at near-point-blank range with a small calibre weapon. She was taken to the Royal Brompton, where she died in the operating room. We are appealing for any witnesses who were in the area around the Old Brompton Road to come forward with any information they might have. It was a busy Saturday night, and we believe it is likely that there are witnesses who may have seen the murderer as they fled the crime scene.'

The room was near-silent. She expected a barrage of questions, but none were immediately forthcoming. She saw Morton give her a thumbs-up from the back of the room, and the knot in her stomach began to loosen.

'Uh, any questions?' she finished lamely.

A hand in the front row shot up. 'Martin Grant, *Galleon's Reach News*. Did the husband kill her?'

'No,' Rafferty said firmly. Fields stared from the front row as she spoke. 'Mr Brian King was on duty at the time of the murder, and this has been confirmed by CCTV footage taken from the night. We have no reason to suspect his involvement.'

'But didn't he kill an unarmed child a few weeks back?' Grant prodded again.

Rafferty saw Morton slide a finger across his throat. It was time to end the press conference before it got out of hand.

'No comment. We're not here today to discuss Brian King. If anyone has any further questions about Angela King's murder, please contact the press office or find me immediately. Thank you for coming.'

She shut her microphone off and made a beeline for the exit. As she passed Morton, he whispered, 'Well done.'

# Chapter 14: Close Protection

The life of a close protection officer sounded glamorous and exciting, but for Warwick Kimmel, the exact opposite was true. His life was hours of standing by, come rain or shine, with only the briefest of moments of excitement when an opposition protestor got close enough to throw an egg or a shoe.

It didn't help that he wouldn't mind punching the man he was assigned to guard. His protectee, Hudson Brown, was a royal douchebag. The man offended virtually everyone he met. Lord knew how he'd managed to get himself elected to Parliament.

Warwick gave a wan smile. Maybe that was exactly where the man belonged. They all seemed to be much of a muchness these days. Big talk, little action, and always more cuts to the police service.

He was supposed to have a partner with him tonight so they could take brief breaks without risking Hudson Brown's life, but nobody was dumb enough to spend their Saturday night parked up outside a townhouse near King's Cross while the whole of London danced the night away. Except for Warwick, that was.

Two more years, he told himself; two more years. Retirement was but a brief stint of boredom away. From his seat in the front of his unmarked car, he could see the dozy old Hudson Brown pottering around in his front room. The git knew Warwick disliked him and took a perverse pleasure in the fact that his guardian would rather dance on his grave than go out for a beer with him. Hudson Brown gave a small wave as he did the ironing, then pulled the curtains shut.

'All units, please respond. Reported torture in progress: civilians report a woman screaming in agony. Polygon Road. Repeat, all units, please respond.'

Warwick was jolted from his boredom by the radio. Polygon Road was right around the corner. This was his chance. His time to finally get to be the hero. He threw open his car door with a spryness belying his age, leapt out, and slammed it shut. With barely a backwards glance towards the man he was supposed to be guarding, Warwick sprinted into the darkness.

***

It worked. I saw the doddery old fool guarding Hudson Brown sprint off into the darkness. By the time he returned, I would be long gone, and Hudson Brown would be dead.

It had been child's play to lure him away. One fake emergency phone call, a few snippets of screams stolen from television crime dramas, and the only barrier between me and my target had disappeared without a second thought.

There was still the house, of course. Reinforced glass, comprehensive CCTV, a ram-resistant front door, and a nervy politician who would no doubt stay safely tucked away in his ground-floor flat. I wasn't just expecting it. I was counting on it.

The plan was beautifully simple. My van was parked a safe distance away from the cameras, well out of range. My clothes were as nondescript as they come: I looked like any other freelance courier running around London. The payload was in the boxes. I just had to get them in position, and physics would do the rest.

***

Warwick found the address in Polygon Road easily. He knew the area like the back of his hand, but when he got there, something didn't feel right. The lights inside were off, as if nobody was home. If he'd stopped for a moment, he might have noticed the settled dust on the door handle, the post piling up just inside, or the boarded-up window upstairs.

Adrenaline coursed through him. His heart thundered in his chest. He felt alive for the first time in years, but his excitement was short-lived when his shoulder failed to break through the front door. He yelped in pain, drawing a giggle from two teenagers who were passing by. Even a courier across the street stopped to smirk. He tried again. There was a loud crack, and searing pain shot along Warwick's shoulder. In a fog, Warwick was unsure if the crack had been the door or his shoulder.

The third try was the charm. The door gave way with a mighty heave, collapsing inwards on top of the post pile. A cloud of dust emanated from the edges of the door.

Warwick stepped inside, his ears prickling for any sign of the screaming woman, but found only silence. He crept forward in the darkness, desperate to flick the light switch but smart enough to know that if he did, he would be silhouetted against the light, an easy target for a would-be assailant.

The ground floor was deathly quiet. Cobwebs ran amok as if the home belonged only to the spiders. There was a thick showering of dust on virtually every surface. Warwick left an impression of his work shoes in the dust with every step.

He sidled towards the stairs, the least dirty part of the house. Was that a creak upstairs? Could the assailant and the girl still be here?

Warwick trod lightly as he ascended. There was a smell of iron in the area, which was no doubt the result of the rusting iron bannister. With a little tender loving care, the house could have remained a beautiful family home, but whoever owned it was decades behind on the maintenance. The ceilings were beginning to sag, the paint was peeling from the walls, and there was a damp, musky vibe that didn't bode well.

He felt his side subconsciously and wished that he was armed. As he approached the landing, his bravery gave way to a nagging doubt that it had been a bad idea for an unarmed, aging, out of shape cop to confront a violent sadist in the dark. Flashbacks of his time in the navy danced in front of his eyes, comforting him. He had been a younger man then, but that core defiance and bravery were still somewhere deep inside him. He dredged up the last of his courage, crouched low, and made a beeline for an ornate door at the end of the corridor. He guessed he was heading for the master bedroom.

The door was ajar, and the room within was encased in darkness. Warwick readied his torch, approached the door, and took a deep breath.

With one smooth motion, he kicked the door open, flicked on the torch, and shone a beam into the room in the hope that he could temporarily blind any would-be assailant.

Empty. The last room was empty.

He picked up his radio, thumbed the on button, and called it in to dispatch. 'False alarm. There's nobody here. It must have been those teenagers outside playing a prank.'

And with that, Warwick's last chance of becoming a hero disappeared into the ether.

Five minutes later, he was back outside Hudson Brown's house. He knocked on the door politely, thinking it best to reassure his charge that he hadn't been gone too long.

Hudson Brown opened the door, glared, and snarled, 'What is it?'

'Just checking up on you, sir,' Warwick said through gritted teeth. 'Is everything okay?'

'I'm fine,' Hudson Brown said tersely. 'Bit of flu, maybe, but nothing you can do anything about.'

'Then I will bid you goodnight, sir.'

Half an hour more until the ghost shift would come switch. Warwick made his way back to his car, watched Hudson Brown turn out all the lights, ready for bed, and then kicked back in his seat to wait for the end of his shift. His shoulder hurt, and his ego had been bruised, but at least nobody would ever find out.

# Chapter 15: Domestic Bliss

There was one silver lining to being side-lined at work: Morton could now knock off exactly at five o'clock, wave merrily to his many colleagues who would be there for at least an hour or two more, then go paint the town red with his beautiful wife. He had done a half-day Saturday purely out of habit, and tonight was all about Sarah. She deserved more. She always had. Somehow, she'd put up with over thirty years of his workaholic ways, with only the briefest respite for holidays. Tonight, he would make it up to her.

The limousine was borrowed. An old friend of his had retired from the force and gone into providing a high-security car service for visiting dignitaries. It made an impressive sight parked on the road outside his home.

'You didn't pay for this, did you?' Sarah asked as Morton held the door open for her.

'God, no,' Morton said. 'Not with money, anyway.'

'Good. Because we need that money for Stephen's wedding.'

He resisted the urge to roll his eyes. Wasn't the bride's father supposed to pick up the tab for the wedding? Morton stepped in behind Sarah and produced a single red rose from behind his back.

'I did spend three quid on this, though.'

He grinned as she took the rose. That coquettish smile was the same as the day they'd met. It had been like being struck by lightning back then, and he felt the same jolt now. Five minutes after he'd first met Sarah, he had turned to Xander and whispered, 'This is the one.' Fast forward three decades, and Morton still couldn't believe his luck.

'You're an old fool, David.' Sarah sidled up to him, snuggled against his shoulder, and Morton felt all of the anger of the week drain away.

'Don't you tell a soul. The boys down at Scotland Yard still think I'm one of the lads.'

'If they genuinely think that, they really shouldn't be detectives.'

Morton laughed. She had a point.

'So, are you going to tell me where we're going?'

'Clos Maggoire,' Morton said. He knew from her expression that he'd made the right call.

Sarah smiled broadly. 'And then it struck, a bolt from the blue. One moment alone, one moment there's you.'

'Even after all these years?' Morton said, gobsmacked that she could still recite the poem he'd written for her on their very first date.

'Always.'

Sometimes, just sometimes, life was grand.

***

The eight o'clock changeover from the ghost shift back to Warwick was when they found the body.

The night shift had watched from the car all night. Nobody had been in or out. The doors were locked from the inside. Somehow, someone had killed a man through two locked doors under the watchful eye of a close protection officer, a dozen CCTV cameras, and some of the best home security money could buy.

And yet, there he was, as dead as a doornail, lying in his bed.

'And that's not the weirdest thing,' Warwick said to the outgoing night-shift guard. 'Look. He's not even moved out of bed. There's not a mark on him'

'Weird.'

Warwick saw an opportunity to be important. This wasn't just a crime scene. This was his crime scene. He puffed up his chest. 'I'm going to call it in. Can you stand guard by the body?'

'Sure. I could use the overtime.'

The ground floor was small. The bedroom and the only bathroom, which was an en suite, were at the back of the flat. In the middle were a galley kitchen, a small panic room installed just for Hudson Brown, and a sitting room in which it would be impossible to swing a cat. Warwick marched through to the front door, called it in, and sat down on the front step. No doubt a pathologist would be on-scene in no time, and Warwick had until then to work out how he could use Hudson Brown's death to make his name.

***

Rafferty's Sunday morning started as it always did: with a blistering hangover.

She rolled over in bed, reached for the bottle of water that she had pre-emptively placed on her nightstand, and took a sip. It was still dark out, and she briefly wondered what had awakened her until she saw her phone flashing on the dresser.

A flick of her thumb unlocked the phone, and she blearily read through the page. Another body. Another case. She bolted upright, the sleepiness vanishing from her eyes as the adrenaline kicked in.

The chief had been as good as her word. Despite her lack of progress with Angela King, Rafferty had her second case.

It took twenty minutes to pull together her clothes, make her mussed-up hair look vaguely professional, and jump in the car. She sped towards King's Cross flat out, pushing her little Alfa Romeo GT up to 85 thanks to the lack of early-morning traffic. No doubt several speed cameras flashed her on the way. Those she'd deal with later.

It was only as she pulled into view of the familiar blue-and-white crime scene tape that she finally clocked the name of the victim. Hudson Brown wasn't just any victim. He was a Member of Parliament and one of the most outspoken voices of the far right. The man had decried human rights, hated the fact women could vote, and believed that all minorities "ought to be shipped back where they came from". It didn't take a genius to realise just how many people might want the man dead. Had Rafferty's luck already run out? It felt like she was coming up against a second impossible case before she had even started.

The street was already filling with officers by the time Rafferty had parked up. An older-looking officer with a slight paunch was standing by the door of the victim's home.

'Detective Inspector Rafferty. What can you tell me?'

The older man nodded. 'Warwick Kimmel, ma'am. I found him. I found the body.'

There was a hint of pride in Warwick's voice, as if this were some sort of achievement. Rafferty gave the older man the once-over. 'How did you find him?'

'I'm his close protection officer, day shift.'

*And yet,* Rafferty thought, *you're almost bragging about the fact that your charge is dead.* 'So, what happened?'

'Don't know, ma'am. All was quiet on the western front last night. I looked in on him before I went off for the night. He said he was feeling a bit tired – maybe a touch of the flu, he said – but knowing him, it could just have been the booze, and then he went to bed. When I came back on-shift this morning, he was dead as a doornail.'

Rafferty perked up. Could it be this one wasn't murder after all? 'So, what's the cause of death?'

'No idea, ma'am. The pathologist is in with him now.'

***

Another Sunday morning, another body. By now, Chiswick had seen it all and was fazed by none of it. There had been the dismembered corpses with their fingertips removed to prevent identification, the many bloaters dredged from the Thames, and a handful of bodies charred beyond the worst of Chiswick's BBQ cooking.

This one sounded routine. An older man in a high-stress position found dead overnight sounded like every other natural death case of Chiswick's career. As much as he would like to pretend otherwise, the human body was remarkably frail. Even if what's-his-name outside thought it was murder. Of course he did. The slightest sign of excitement could send a close protection officer rabid. It was a remarkably dull job, babysitting a politician. Chiswick couldn't have done it, and he literally spent his days talking to stiffs. Somehow, the corpses were still better company.

It was a nice flat, no doubt appointed at the taxpayers' expense. The living room appeared to have been decked out exclusively in Kesterport furniture. What Chiswick wouldn't do to have a taxpayer-funded personal shopper at Harrods. His wife might finally be happy with the house if he could wave a magic wand

and make designer furniture appear in a matter of hours. Rumour had it, they even offered horse-drawn delivery bedecked in the company livery for the most discerning of shoppers.

He found the bedroom easily enough. The door lock was broken. Allegedly, the close protection officer outside had done that. If anything, it was another sign that this was a natural death. Both the front door and bedroom locks were high quality and had been firmly locked when the body was found.

Chiswick nudged the door gently to avoid it falling off its hinges and set his bag down. The bedroom was small – no more than a box room, really – but there was a large en suite at the end of the room. It appeared to be the only bathroom in the property. Chiswick hoped the late Member of Parliament didn't host too often, as guests traipsing through the tiny master bedroom to the loo would have been a real inconvenience.

The man of the hour was in bed, his body covered by a large sheet that had been pulled up over his eyes, a mark of respect that Chiswick wouldn't have afforded the man. The bedding was soft, expensive, and, again, probably taxpayer-funded.

Chiswick pulled the sheet back in one smooth motion and froze on the spot. The body showed all the classic signs of asphyxia, except Chiswick knew that nobody had been in or out of the house, so he couldn't have been smothered. It was only then that Chiswick noticed how much colder than normal the room was. His own laboured breathing echoed in the darkness.

Carbon dioxide poisoning. 'Run!' he yelled.

Leaving his bag on the floor, he sprinted from the crime scene in a gangly fashion. When he reached the hallway, he yelled at the close protection officer again. 'Out! Now!'

He ran thirty feet beyond the front door, carried by adrenaline. He was oblivious to the reporters gathered around the crime scene who immediately turned their cameras on him.

Rafferty jogged over, startled to see Chiswick so panicked.

'What's up?' she asked.

Chiswick panted, pointed back at the house, and said, 'Carbon dioxide. Move the perimeter back. Get the neighbours out!'

He fell to his knees, panting for breath. It was not to be such an ordinary case after all.

***

The hour after Chiswick's dramatic sprint from the building was a flurry of activity. Rafferty felt her pride swell up as she barked orders left and right. The police line was moved well back, the neighbours were evacuated just in case, and the fire brigade was on-scene in minutes.

'Ma'am, that means you too.'

Rafferty turned in the direction of the voice. A handsome fireman was looking directly at her. She pointed at herself as if to be sure he meant her.

'Yes, ma'am,' he said with the hint of a crooked smile. 'I have my orders. Everyone gets checked out today.'

It took a moment for Rafferty to realise what he meant. There was an ambulance set up beside the fire truck to check those who'd been on-scene for carbon dioxide poisoning.

'But I feel fine,' Rafferty protested. 'I was barely in there for a minute.'

'And you look fine too,' the fireman said. 'I'm Dermot, by the way. If you wouldn't mind, it'll take just a minute. For safety's sake. I can hold your hand if you like.'

Smooth, Rafferty thought. She subconsciously ran her fingers through her hair, all too aware that she was dressed for work but looked like death warmed up. 'I think I can manage,' she said.

'Oh, okay.'

He looked crestfallen.

She grinned. It was much too easy. 'But I'll let you know if I'm feeling faint and need you to catch me.'

With a brisk stride, she left him standing staring at her. He didn't want to see her go, but damn if he wasn't enjoying watching her walk away. *Still got it, girl,* Rafferty thought.

A quick once-over by an emergency medical technician revealed she was just fine, despite her time inside the house. By the time she was given the all-clear, the firemen had finished checking out the home. Rain had begun to fall, and the assembled journalists, now pushed back a hundred feet or so, were huddled under umbrellas, snapping pictures with long-range telephoto lenses. There was even a BBC News van filming the scene. There wasn't much to be seen, but that wasn't stopping the journalists.

'It's all clear,' Dermot said to her. 'But stay safe. We don't know where the gas came from.'

'I'll let you know if I'm about to fall over,' Rafferty said.

He gave a cheesy wink and said, 'If you're ready to fall, I'm ready to catch you.'

'Promises, promises.'

Rafferty left Dermot standing in the rain. She'd have to deal with the press sooner or later, but she needed to check out the crime scene. Someone had killed a man through two locked doors while a close protection officer was standing guard outside.

Just as she was about to head in, a familiar face ducked under the police barrier. Ayala was, as usual, overdressed for the occasion. He was wearing his trademark three-piece suit and an immaculately pressed Brioni tie, and had paired them with a sheepish grin.

'Sorry,' he said, as if one word would make up for his betrayal.

'Noted. Get to work. The vic was gassed with carbon dioxide. Nobody has been in the house. I need to know how the killer got to him.'

'On it.'

She watched him disappear into the house. If he was dealing with that, she'd better handle the journalists before things got out of hand.

***

Ayala was flummoxed. There was no obvious source of gas anywhere. The flat was nearly empty. Hudson Brown was a minimalist with a place for everything and everything in its place. Even his socks were neatly ironed and folded and then placed in a drawer, grouped by colour and pattern. Ayala had to wonder what kind of mind was so twisted that it had to control circumstances so precisely.

The most obvious source of gas would have been the kitchen but for the fact that there was an electric induction hob. Hudson Brown didn't have gas central heating, either; the flat was warmed by underfloor electric heating. There were no gas-driven appliances, no power generators, nothing that could explain the carbon dioxide. He had a fire alarm, and a carbon monoxide alarm, but there was scant need to put a carbon dioxide alarm into a domestic property, particularly one which didn't even have a gas supply.

Apart from the overly neat clothing, the flat was virtually empty. It was laid out – and felt like – a show home for a developer. There were no knick-knacks, no photos, no personal belongings outside the bedroom. Hudson Brown might have resided here, but he didn't live here.

The sound of footsteps alerted Ayala that he wasn't alone. He tensed up, not having expected company. 'Who's there?'

'M-m-me,' a voice stammered back.

'Mayberry, don't creep up on me like that,' Ayala said. 'A man got murdered in here, not more than a dozen hours ago and through two locked doors. It's enough to put a man on edge without you looming like a spectre over his shoulder.'

'S-sorry. Any l-luck?'

Ayala shook his head. 'None. I'm out of ideas. You?'

'O-one. H-how old is t-this place?'

'The building? A couple of hundred years old,' Ayala said. He had seen a blue tourist plaque on the outside saying that some notable person had lived at the address in the mid-eighteen hundreds.

Mayberry's eyes lit up. 'V-Victorian p-p-plumbing?'

'I guess. Why?'

'L-look,' Mayberry said, shoving his phone under Ayala's nose. The image, which Brodie had managed to scrounge up for Mayberry after a phone call, showed a map of the Victorian drainage system.

Ayala squinted.

'One of the l-lines runs r-right under the h-house.'

'You can't seriously be suggesting...'

'Y-yes. T-they g-gassed him t-through the sewers.'

***

It fell to Rafferty to interrogate the two close protection officers: Warwick Kimmel, the older day-shift close protection officer, and his night shift equivalent, Michael Ford.

'Walk me through it again, gentlemen.'

'I said goodnight to him last night,' Kimmel said. 'He was definitely alive then, I watched him turn out the lights. And Michael took over just after.'

'That's right,' Ford said firmly. 'I came on-shift, and spent the night watching the front door. It's the only point of entry, and nobody came or went during the night. I've got the dash cam footage to prove it.'

Rafferty jabbed an accusatory finger at Warwick Kimmel. 'And yet this morning you found him murdered. How do you think that happened?'

'Don't look at me!' Kimmel said. 'I did my job. He was alive when I looked after him. Ask Ford, here. He's the one who was on-shift when Hudson Brown died.'

Rafferty looked between them. They were both wearing expressions of confusion, as if they were shocked that Rafferty might assign blame for a man under their charge dying on their watch. Could it all be an act? Could one of the men standing before her be the killer? Occam's Razor said the simplest explanation was usually the right one. The killer couldn't teleport through two locked doors.

'Do you have keys to the house?'

'Well, yeah,' said Ford. 'We've got a complete set of keys. The bedroom is a simple bolt from the inside, mind you.'

A simple bolt, Rafferty thought, that Kimmel presented himself as having broken in order to get in to find the body. She only had his word that it been broken then, and not earlier, when Hudson Brown was murdered.

'Does anyone else have a set?'

Ford shook his head. 'We hand 'em over if we're rotated out. We do four on, three off, so the B shift takes over for half of the week.'

'And you're always in the same pairs? You two working one complete day?'

'Usually,' Kimmel said.

'Did you like Hudson Brown?' Rafferty asked. 'How was he to work for?'

Ford pouted. 'We don't – didn't – work for him. We're assigned to protect him. What we think of him is immaterial.'

'But you didn't like him, did you?' Rafferty needled again. She knew she was on to something when the pair exchanged a grim glance.

'Nobody liked him,' Kimmel replied. 'He was a despicable human being. I still don't wish him dead, not least because if he died on my shift, that's it for my career. You can't let a Member of Parliament die and expect to remain with the Close Protection Unit.'

***

'We always get the shit jobs,' Ayala moaned as they climbed down into the sewers. The entrance was a subtle metal doorway just south of King's Cross station. The system was a series of overflow chambers running down into the River Fleet deep beneath the surface of London.

The entrance had been unlocked. A broken padlock lay on the floor nearby, which Mayberry had bagged for evidence. It was possible the killer had followed the very route they were on.

They tied a rope off at the entrance and tied the other end to Mayberry's waist. The system ran for hundreds of miles, and they didn't want to risk getting lost without a guide to get them home. Mayberry slowly unspooled the rope as they walked, trying to keep it taut so it didn't dip into the water.

There was a small current underfoot. Few homes were still attached to the old system, but there were still a number of storm drains that flowed into the old drainage tunnels. Ayala tried not to pay attention to what he was walking in. He had covered his loafers with evidence booties, but the water squelched up and over his ankles, and no doubt his custom Goodyear-welt leather shoes would be fit for the bin before the day was out.

'How did you learn about this place?' Ayala asked.

'G-g-geocaching.'

It was the latest craze: hide something where nobody in their right mind should be going, and invite other geocachers to try to find it, like hide and seek for adults.

'I had no idea you were a fan.'

'My w-wife is.'

That explained it. Mayberry's missus was related to the recently retired chief. She had always struck Ayala as Mayberry's polar opposite: sporty, outgoing, and silver-tongued, yet she had stayed loyal through his disability. Ayala had to respect that.

They came upon a fork in the tunnel. 'Which way?'

'L-left,' Mayberry said as firmly as he could. 'I t-think.'

They came upon a dead end and were forced to double back. The rope was no longer taut and was quickly coated in a layer of greasy sewer water. Mayberry grimaced as he ran the excess back into a spool.

As they made their way down the other path, they heard the sound of the River Fleet in the distance.

'Is this tidal?' Ayala wondered aloud. When Mayberry shrugged, it was Ayala's turn to grimace. Drowning in an old sewer drain was not how he wanted to die.

Farther along, they saw something looming in the darkness. Ayala pushed forward, keeping Mayberry behind him, and held a torch aloft.

'W-what is that?'

It was a good question. It looked like a tube, a giant, plastic tube hanging from the ceiling, where it appeared to have been drilled into place.

'It's a kid's play tunnel!' Ayala cried. 'I had one just like it as a kid. Didn't you? They're for crawling through or hiding in. What on earth is it doing here?'

Mayberry stared at him and pointed to his GPS receiver. They were directly under Hudson Brown's house.

Ayala lifted the tube and looked up inside it with the torch. Sewage water dripped all down his trousers as he did so. There, up above, was a pipe. 'Do you think that's the exit pipe from Hudson Brown's house?'

'Y-yep.'

'Let's test it. You got the kit?'

Mayberry took the bag from around his neck and fished inside. He was looking for long pipe cleaners. They were stiff enough to push up the pipe and long enough to be seen at the other end.

Ayala checked his phone. One bar of signal. He texted up to Rafferty: *Can you see a pipe cleaner?*

The reply came back quickly: *Yes, sticking out of the toilet.*

'Bloody hell. He was murdered by piping the gas in from below. But with what?'

Mayberry pointed farther down the tunnel. The current had swept along a bunch of insulated boxes. Ayala jogged down, grabbed one, and brought it back to Mayberry before holding the torch on it.

Dry ice. The killer had brought tons of dry ice down and used a child's play tunnel to funnel it up through a Victorian drain and into the victim's home.

'Holy shit.'

***

The media frenzy over the Hudson Brown murder was fierce. Morton was sitting at home with Sarah when it showed up as Breaking News on BBC One. He turned up the volume of the tiny television fixed above the microwave so he could listen.

'Turn it off, David,' his wife begged him. 'Please.'

The allure of freshly made croissants and homemade jam dragged Morton's attention away from the television for a moment. He smiled wanly at her and hit the mute button so he could keep a half-eye on the case without distracting Sarah too much.

'Sorry. Force of habit.'

'It's not your case.'

'I know,' he said. But whose case was it?

The murder of an MP would normally have come directly to him. It was well within his bailiwick. His entire murder investigation team specialised in investigating the weird, the wonderful, and the downright crazy. To know about a locked-room murder with a famous victim but to have to watch it from the sidelines was tantamount to torture.

'Two locked doors,' Morton said, nodding at the text alert scrolling along the bottom of the television. 'Doubly mysterious.'

'Hey, isn't that the crazy MP?' Sarah asked, her interest leapfrogging Morton's. Aside from psychology, which Sarah had recently returned to education to study, politics was her favourite conversation. 'It is him. I knew it. He was on TV not long ago, arguing we should deport everyone who wasn't born here and anyone who doesn't have two English parents. That'd be half the country!'

'No doubt he had plenty of enemies. It won't be an easy investigation.'

Morton wondered who'd be handling it. There was nobody else with the experience to handle such a high-profile case. His mind flashed briefly to Rafferty, but surely, even the chief wouldn't hand such a train wreck of a case over to a junior officer?

Morton tried to lip-read the news anchor. 'Our informant inside the Metropolitan Police...'

'Oh, for God's sake, David. Just watch it. And then maybe you can remember that you've got a wife who made you breakfast.'

He grinned apologetically and hit the mute button to turn the volume back on.

'...that Hudson Brown was found dead from carbon dioxide poisoning. Despite a constant police presence from the Close Protection Unit...'

'Carbon dioxide?' Sarah echoed.

'It's a new one,' Morton said. 'I've seen carbon monoxide victims, but never a carbon dioxide murder. I suppose that explains the unbroken locks. Whoever did it is smart and experienced. This isn't a first kill.'

'You think it's a hit man?'

Morton mused for a moment, pausing to take a bite of his croissant. 'Hmm. No. It doesn't feel like it. It could be, but there's something very determined about murdering someone this way. There aren't many hit men who would bother with such an elaborate kill. Two bullets – one for the close protection officer on duty, and one for the vic – would have been ample. This is someone who wanted to kill just him, but they didn't mind risking poisoning the neighbours either. That's not clean. That's reckless. Kill one man, and you'll get a murder investigation team on you. Kill an entire block, and you're looking at a joint task force of SOCA, SCD2, and the counterterrorism task force.'

''Then, who?'

'Someone who hated him, I suppose. I don't envy whoever has to investigate this one.'

***

The moment Stuart Purcell heard Rafferty yell that they'd found the gas source in the sewers below, he knew he'd be the one heading into the muck. He could have delegated the job. He was the boss. It would have been the easy route.

Instead, he donned full-body personal protective equipment, got his torch, and headed down the path Ayala and Mayberry had illustrated. The old sewers were thick with grime. The current underfoot swept detritus farther and farther along, and, despite the map Mayberry had pulled from the British Library's archives, nobody really knew the extent of the smaller pipes on the old network.

On the way down, he'd dusted the ladder from the street. There were prints there, more than Purcell had expected. Mayberry mentioned something about geocachers using these old tunnels, and if he was right, that would complicate evidence collection immensely.

There were fingerprints all along the tunnel, too, preserved above the water line. It would be difficult to get in and out of the tunnels without ending up covered in some sort of grime. Purcell's elbows were already greasy from rubbing against the walls, and he was ankle-deep in sewage runoff. Every now and then, he heard a plop as waste was dropped in from above. He hoped to high heaven that nothing landed on him as he collected the evidence.

Before long, he came upon the tunnel Ayala and Mayberry had found. It was still in place, still stuck to the ceiling with some sort of epoxy. The glue was clean and stood out against the grime and dust on the old brickwork. It wasn't well-secured, but it was enough to hold the lightweight play tunnel in place. One edge was beginning to drift away, which neither Ayala nor Mayberry had mentioned when they sent him down here. Purcell snapped a quick photo and then pulled loosely at the tunnel. It came away easily.

The play tunnel was a generic one from a high street retailer. He bagged it for evidence knowing it would be fruitless trying to trace the purchaser.

The dry ice, on the other hand, might prove to be a critical lead. There were few dry ice retailers in London, and the murder had required a fairly significant quantity.

Ayala and Mayberry had said something about boxes. Purcell couldn't see them. He trudged down the tunnel farther and farther until he was well beyond the house of Hudson Brown. Ayala hadn't come this far down. It seemed the boxes had drifted on the current.

He found them at a grate half a mile downstream. They were large white polystyrene containers, the kind Purcell had delivered by his online butcher. There was no brand name; they were generic, wholly generic. It looked like another dead end.

Purcell bagged them anyway. There was the off chance that the dry ice had trace imperfections that might identify the manufacturer.

***

Rafferty's day went from bad to worse. The unusual details of the MP's murder had somehow been leaked to the press. There were officers from a number of units buzzing over the crime scene. Forensics were combing through, looking for DNA in the tunnel as well as the house, the fire brigade had been on scene for hours, and ambulances had been around for hours, too.

It was a leaky bucket. Any one of those service personnel could have talked to the press. As a newbie to the leadership gig, Rafferty didn't command the necessary respect to get everyone in line. She wished Morton were here. He'd have calmed things down in no time.

Even the pathologist wasn't happy with her. He clearly thought Morton ought to be in charge, and he was holding a grudge.

Sometimes the old boys' club held strong, even when it was more out of personal loyalty than any hatred of female detectives.

Ayala's new-found work ethic was perplexing. He had gone from hating her guts to trying to solve the crime before anyone else. He was quick to take credit for Mayberry's work in the tunnels. Maybe that was it. Maybe he thought solving this case first would be his ticket to running his own murder investigation team.

The one bright side was Dermot, the cheeky fireman. Part way through the afternoon, he'd sidled up to her, announced that they were off, and pressed a note into her hand as he left. On it was written his number in neat calligraphy.

Even on her worst day, hung over to high heaven and as stressed as she could be, and without any make-up or glad rags, she still had it. It was those Irish eyes she liked. They twinkled as if they were always smiling. His salt-and-pepper hair didn't hurt, either.

Rafferty shook her head, blinked, and forced herself to focus. Now wasn't the time. She had a dozen journalists to face down just to get off site, and she couldn't be distracted by a pretty face.

She steeled herself, set her shoulders back, and stood upright, a fierce woman to be contended with. Cameras flashed as she approached the police barricade.

'Inspector Rafferty, is it true he was murdered by Marxist lunatics?'

Rafferty gave the reporter a withering glare. The conspiracy theorists were already coming out of the woodwork.

'No comment.'

A dozen more questions and a dozen more 'No comment' replies later, Rafferty managed to slip behind the wheel of her car. Just ten more minutes, and she'd be back at home, ready to curl up with a nice cup of tea. It had been a long weekend.

# Chapter 16: The Past, the Present and the Future

Monday morning saw Morton return to the lecture theatre. None of the team joined him to assist. He knew not whether Ayala was still sulking or if he'd finally followed the order he had been given to go and work with Rafferty on the Angela King murder.

The class settled in quickly, and silence fell before the clock struck nine.

'Today, we're going to be covering serial killers. Criminals, like everyone else, get better with practice. They become more criminally sophisticated with each crime they commit, and thus harder to catch. Can anyone see an obvious flaw here?'

Maisie Pincent, the cheeky young woman who had suggested poisoning Ayala's coffee, raised a slender hand as Morton met her gaze.

'Yes, Ms Pincent?'

'Because they've committed a number of crimes, their risk of being caught is amplified by the earlier offences. Each crime in the series shows how they think and how they act, and we can trace their steps back to find out where they started.'

'Exactly,' Morton said. 'And when we find their earlier crimes, we find the evidence they didn't know to hide at the time.'

Pincent was sharp. That much was obvious.

'Can anyone tell me what tools we have at our disposal to match current crimes with historical crimes?' Morton asked, searching out another victim. At the back of the room, the non-binary student was slinking down in their seat as if to hide from his questioning. They were sitting away from the group, a physical outsider. 'Mx Rudd?'

'Err... DNA?'

'Obviously,' Morton said. 'We have the full gamut of forensics to use to match crimes: DNA, mass spectrometry, fingerprints. The hard science can be invaluable. It's usually admissible in court, and if you've got a criminal who hasn't taken sufficient precautions, it can be a slam dunk. But what if we're dealing with someone too smart? Imagine they're aware of how to clean down a crime scene, how not to leave fingerprints or DNA. What do we do then, Mx Rudd?'

'What about geographic profiling?'

'That's one tool, yes. Criminals tend to start out close to home and spiral out away from their home area as they gain confidence. Profiling is the most valuable tool we have at our disposal. Can anyone tell me what Holmes typology is?'

Eric O'Shaughnessy, whom Morton remembered for his herringbone suit and sharp tongue, leant forward and raised a gangly hand.

'Mr O'Shaughnessy?'

'There are two types o' killers. Act-focussed killers and process-focussed killers. For the former, it's about having killed. It's over and done, simply, efficiently. For the process-focussed killers, it's about the process, the ritual.'

'Indeed,' Morton said. 'Act-focussed kills are clean. You've probably seen the news reports of the Angela King murder. Her husband is one of our own. She was shot at close range in a dark alley and left to die. This is an action-focussed killer. By contrast, the process-focussed killers get an emotional kick out of the murder. Some are simple hedonists; they enjoy killing. Some are sexual sadists who get off on the pain of their victim. Some want to "win" money or affection. Others just want to play God.'

'Sir,' said another student whose name Morton couldn't bring to mind. 'Isn't that all dreadfully subjective? Where's the boundary between enjoying a murder for hedonistic purposes and enjoying it for sexual reasons? Is there a difference in how the crime scene looks?'

Morton nodded and pressed the button to turn his slide show to the next slide, entitled 'Criticisms of the Holmes Method'. He didn't know why Ayala had made PowerPoint sound so complicated. All he had to do was click.

'You're right, of course. It's one of the many limitations of profiling. It's a human science, and, by definition, subject to the flaws of both the human being profiled and the human doing the profiling. We can combine the Holmes method with other classifications to help narrow things down. We know some killers fall to the OCD end of the organised/disorganised spectrum, while others are all over the show. It comes down to judgement. After years in the job, you get a gut feeling about suspects. We can follow the numbers and the statistics all day long. We know most serial killers are men, most are white, and most are in their twenties or thirties. But when you come up against that rare killer who isn't so obvious, you have to think outside the box.'

'What about their backgrounds?' Pincent asked. 'Aren't there predictors in childhood and criminal history?'

'Often, yes. Many cold-blooded killers are psychopaths. As Dr Jensen, our in-house expert for the murder investigation teams of SCD2, will no doubt tell you, many killers fit the definition of antisocial behaviour disorder. Many come from broken homes. Some have been subject to abuse, neglect, cruelty. We have two major issues here. First is an information asymmetry. We don't know enough about everyone to be able to make this judgement call early on. It can be useful in winnowing down the most likely suspects on a list, but it isn't an elimination criterion like DNA, which can exculpate a suspect entirely. It is possible to go through hell and come out of it a perfectly functional human. The extent and degree to which any one act affects us is subjective, personal, and complicated.'

'Then, how do we catch these serial killers?' someone asked from the back row.

'We use everything we have. We combine the modus operandi of the crime, the victimology, the profiling, the evidence, and we try on case theories for size. We aggressively chase down leads until we find something. Sometimes, we can't. I have a stack of cold cases on my desk that I revisit every week. It tortures me not to be able to give those victims justice. That comes with the job. And on that note, I think that's all for today. Class dismissed.'

Morton folded down his laptop, sank into the seat behind the lectern that Ayala should have been occupying, and watched as his class began to file from the room.

There was something satisfying about this teaching lark. They genuinely seemed to care what he had to say, and it did make a change not being shot at by violent psychopaths.

***

Mayberry found himself back in his comfort zone on Monday morning. Dealing with the press, members of the public, and generally talking to others was not his bag. Aphasia made it difficult to communicate, even if he knew exactly what he meant to say.

To sit in front of a bank of computers and watch YouTube was a blessed relief. He was in Brodie's office, using Brodie's spare desk. Hudson Brown had been receiving death threats for decades. He had managed to insult and annoy virtually everyone he had come into contact with.

The reason was obvious: Hudson Brown had traded on notoriety for fame and money. Whatever he said had been deliberately crafted to be as provocative as possible. He'd blamed the victims, insulted the survivors, and marginalised minorities, and he'd enjoyed every last minute of it.

YouTube was full of videos of him. Many of them had as many or more Thumbs Down as Thumbs Up, and yet the view count kept climbing. The videos were never reasoned, never logical, but always appealed to a core emotion. Outrage rather than respect drew the viewers to watch his oration.

Mayberry had to admit that Hudson Brown was quite the public speaker. He spoke slowly, calmly, and with gravitas. No matter how bullshit his speech might be, he seemed to earnestly believe every word of it. He was the ultimate charlatan: a con man who had drunk his own Kool-Aid.

It was no surprise, then, when Mayberry received the files documenting the death threats against Hudson Brown. They had been prepared by his parliamentary private secretary, who had carefully logged and cross-referenced over ten thousand pieces of correspondence from this parliamentary term alone.

'Just on the desk, yeah?' the delivery guy asked, placing a fat box down in front of Mayberry. Mayberry's stomach churned as he sliced the top of the box open to see the original copies of the threats. There were far too many to get through, even if he had had a team of hundreds and a year to sort through it all.

It got worse, too. Just as Mayberry thought he was getting a handle on the volume of paperwork, the delivery guy returned with three more boxes.

'Alright to put these on the floor, mate?'

Mayberry nodded meekly. He was going to need some help.

***

Brodie proved invaluable, as always. His tried-and-trusted approach to evidence of digitising it all first and sifting later had proved more than worthwhile on previous cases, and no doubt it would this time too. He and Mayberry fed everything into a commercial scanner fed by a conveyor belt, used optical character recognition to create digital copies, and began to sift through, looking for keywords that could indicate violence.

They still had to prioritise. Hudson Brown's secretary had put those she thought were most likely into the first box, so they had started there.

Many of the criticisms – and there were myriad – were, in Mayberry's opinion, entirely valid. Hudson Brown had been slammed for comparing refugees from Syria to rats, describing old-aged pensioners as hospital bed-blockers on borrowed time, and had angered half the nation by calling stay-at-home mums the feckless unemployed.

'Three thousand, laddie,' Brodie said, pointing at the search through the digital copies for the words "hope" and "die". 'That's just so far. He wasn't a popular man.'

'H-how c-can we n-narrow it down?'

'Let's start with the obvious. He spent all day insulting people, right? Who has Hudson Brown insulted the most? Think now, laddie.'

Mayberry strained his mind to think back to the YouTube videos he had spent hours watching while trying not to become inured to the offensiveness. There was one man, a far-left MP, who was a running joke of sorts.

'D-Douglas Shapiro?'

'Bingo, laddie. Who'd want the man dead more? If Rafferty wants somewhere to start, show her the videos where Hudson Brown digs into Shapiro over and over, and then show her Shapiro's reply videos.'

Mayberry did exactly that. He found Rafferty in the Incident Room, looking more haggard than he had ever seen her.

'Y-you okay?' he asked as he sat opposite her at the conference table.

'Not really. I don't know where to start with this. Nobody liked him. Nobody. He's so thoroughly dislikeable that I'd have happily killed him myself. Please don't repeat that!'

Mayberry smiled. 'I w-won't. W-what a-about t-this guy?' He turned his phone towards her, maxed out the volume, and hit play on the most popular YouTube video of Douglas Shapiro, MP.

'Hudson Brown is a cretin. He's so thoroughly wrong that his "followers" assume the truth must be somewhere in the middle. That's the power of the alt-right, ladies and gents. It isn't in stirring up hatred. Those who hate have always hated; all Hudson Brown does is give them licence to proclaim their hatred and ignorance from the rooftops. Giving Hudson Brown a platform legitimises the illegitimate. Every click, every like, every view on his social media feed is one more pair of eyeballs being exposed to the worst of humanity, and you can't unsee it. It's like when one man says white and another says black: it's much too easy to assume that the answer is some shade of grey. Extremism begets hate and violence. It's time to end it.'

'End it?' Rafferty echoed. 'When was this video posted?'

'Y-yesterday. S-six hours before h-his m-murder.'

# Chapter 17: Left Meets Right

Rafferty found Douglas Shapiro, MP in his office at the House of Commons. She didn't expect trouble, but she had the security staff wait in the hallway outside just in case. She rapped smartly on the door to his office and opened it without waiting.

'Douglas Shapiro?'

'You've found him,' Shapiro said. 'What can I do for the Met's finest?'

Rafferty stopped in her tracks. How did he know who she was?

'Sorry, Detective. I spotted you on BBC News. Please, take a seat. I assume this is about Hudson Brown's murder.'

'It is.'

Shapiro smiled. 'And you're wondering if I killed him. Sadly, no. I'm not sad to see him gone, but he'll be replaced in no time. There's always someone willing to take on the mantle of vile hatred to make a few pounds.'

'Then, explain the video.'

He stroked his chin thoughtfully. 'Saturday's video? It was exactly what it looked like. I disagreed with his views, and I said so.'

'You said you were going to "end it". What did you mean by that?'

This time, Shapiro burst out laughing. 'I was being hyperbolic. That's how these videos work. Nobody wants to hear me spout on about the studies, the numbers, the real nitty-gritty of an argument. Nobody has time for that. They want the broad brushstrokes. We have to end this vitriolic hatred. I'd have supported arresting him for public indecency if it were possible, but kill him? Never.'

Rafferty leant back in her chair. 'And you think I'm going to believe that? Just on your say-so? Where were you Saturday?'

He spun his laptop around so Rafferty could see it. 'Look at this. Here's my YouTube channel. See those view counts on the right? Millions. Look at where I was at a year ago: barely a dozen views a day. Hudson Brown was the best thing to have ever happened to the Marxist cause. He united my grassroots power base in a way that simple argument never could have. He provided a common enemy, and, dare I say it, he probably used me in the same way. Vitriol only works if there is somebody to be outraged. It's a dance we both played voluntarily. He for fame, and I for the cause.'

It made sense, but it didn't answer the question. 'Where were you Saturday?'

'My home, three hundred miles away. My wife, kids, and I had a lovely dinner. Do you want her number so you can confirm my alibi?'

'Yes, please.'

***

Kallum Fielder was out of his depth. Recently promoted from hosting morning talk show *Wake Up Britain!*, he was now moderating the talking heads responsible for speculating just what had happened to Hudson Brown.

Ratings were naturally through the roof. The murder was fast becoming a national scandal in reverse: who killed the villainous MP?

Newspaper headlines from the week flashed on the big screen behind Kal. *The Impartial* had run with the scientifically inaccurate headline 'Tickled Pink: Racist Found Dead', clearly having confused carbon monoxide poisoning and asphyxiation by carbon dioxide, while the more sombre broadsheets had run with some variant of 'Locked Room Murder Mystery'.

'It's obvious, isn't it?' one of the talking heads said. 'The government did him in. They didn't like his message, and the neoliberal elites couldn't let him convince the masses to follow his ideas.'

Kal almost snorted. If the government offed every racist in politics, there'd be scant few politicians left standing. He strained to remember the name of the woman talking. He glanced surreptitiously at his notes: Doctor Jessie Weir. Blimey. They gave doctorates to conspiracy theorists these days?

'Dr Weir,' he said. 'Why him? He's not the only alt-right commentator on the web.'

'No, but he's the biggest, the loudest, and the most accessible. He's been one of the most viewed political commentators in the UK since long before the Brexit vote.'

The other commentator, Douglas Shapiro, MP, leant forward. 'Then, why now? If it's political, he could have been dealt with long ago. Your theory is preposterous. It's akin to shutting the stable door after the horse has bolted.'

'Then, who do you think did it?'

'I think we need to look at his personal life. If he was as ugly a person as his public persona suggested, there's bound to be someone in his past who hated him.'

***

'David, you got a minute?' Rafferty came to Morton's office bearing a peace offering of his favourite coffee.

Morton smirked. 'No. Haven't you heard? I'm exceptionally busy these days.'

'Sorry, boss,' Rafferty said. 'I didn't ask for this.'

'I know. Sit.'

She did. 'I need help.'

'Really? I thought you were bribing me with coffee just for fun. Thanks for this, by the way.'

Rafferty placed her notes down on the table and punted the whole bundle across to Morton. 'Hudson Brown. Where the hell do I start?'

Morton turned through the documents, slowly reading the coroner's report. By the time he was done, the coffee Rafferty had brought was beginning to cool.

'So?' she asked.

'It's not an easy case. You've got an intelligent killer who managed to get in and out without anyone seeing them. The time of death appears to be the previous night, when Warwick Kimmel was on duty. Is that right? Why didn't anyone find him 'til the morning?'

'His close protection detail said goodnight. He was alive then.'

'What time was that?' Morton asked.

'About ten o'clock.'

Morton frowned. 'You've had two cases, and both of them were committed around the same time on a Saturday night? That's some co-incidence.'

Rafferty looked quizzical. 'You think they're related?'

'Nothing suggests they ought to be. It just seems weird. Okay, so this Kimmel was on duty at the time of death. Have you looked at him?'

'He seems... inept. I don't think he liked his charge, but killing him would be – is – career suicide.'

'OK. Let's look up his record. If he's inept, there will be flags somewhere in a career that long.' Morton opened up his laptop, accessed the personnel database, and typed in the name Warwick Kimmel.

Rafferty tapped her foot impatiently. 'Anything?'

'Hmm. You said he said he checked on Hudson Brown at ten, right? At quarter to, he responded to a 999 emergency dispatch around the corner in Polygon Street.'

'Let me see that.' Rafferty edged around the desk and peered at Morton's laptop.

'It looks like a false alarm, according to the report.'

'Could be kids?' Rafferty volunteered.

'Or it could have been a lure.'

'What do you mean?'

Morton looked up at her. 'How better to get rid of the close protection officer than to lure him to a crime in progress right around the corner? If–'

He was interrupted as his office door swung open. Silverman stormed in.

'Morton, what the hell do you think you're doing?' Silverman demanded. 'I've just been told you're accessing confidential files.'

Rafferty raised a hand. 'I asked him–'

'I don't care if you asked him to or not. He is not assigned to this case. Get out. Now.'

She stared across the room until Rafferty swept up her notes and left. Rafferty glanced back at Morton as if to apologise.

'David, you are forbidden from helping in cases to which you are not assigned. She needs to learn to handle an investigation on her own.'

Morton's skin burned with fury. 'She needs help. Nobody takes on the murder of a Member of Parliament for one of their first cases. She's not ready to fly solo.'

'She's ready when I say she is. Stay out of it or face the consequences.' Silverman swept from the room like a tornado, leaving an outraged Morton staring at the closing door.

Stay out of it? Over his dead body.

# Chapter 18: The Call

The pit was quiet when Rafferty arrived. It was a windowless room that housed the emergency dispatchers responsible for taking 999 calls. The staff were in matching uniforms with headsets that made them look more like call centre staff for a bank than the heroes they were.

It was a difficult job. Every call could be life or death.

'This way please, Ms Rafferty,' said her guide. She was an older lady by the name of Anna Glen.

She led Rafferty through to a small private booth in the back which belonged to a manager.

'What does it take to become a dispatcher?' Rafferty asked.

'The ability to stomach the twelve-hour shifts,' Ms Glen said with a wan smile. 'We're four on, three off, four on, seven off. It's a weird work schedule to get used to.'

'How do you do it?' Rafferty asked as she watched Ms Glen boot up a computer terminal.

'You get used to it,' Ms Glen said. 'The money's not great, but going home knowing you've made a difference to hundreds of people, if not thousands, every single week... where else do you get that sort of job satisfaction?'

'I suppose so. Is that thing ready? I need the call that triggered sending Warwick Kimmel to Polygon Street on Saturday night around ten o'clock. And can you get me his acknowledgment, too?'

'I can give you the call. Any radio contact from the officer in question would have been on your own radio system, though.'

She did as she promised, and soon Rafferty was sitting in the manager's chair listening to the 999 call over and over.

It was short. There was screaming, as if someone were being beaten.

'Nobody said a location,' Rafferty said. 'How did you get Polygon Street from this call?'

'GPS. The call came in from a mobile – the details are on the bottom of your screen – and the system determined the location of the call.'

'Is it accurate?'

'To within a few feet.'

'But there was nobody there,' Rafferty said.

'No. We get a lot of prank calls. Kids, usually.'

'Is that what you think this is?'

'You tell me,' Ms Glen said. 'There's something off about the audio. Listen again.'

Ms Glen was right. The screams were ever so slightly muffled.

'I recognise that voice!' Rafferty cried. 'Has that thing got internet access?'

When Ms Glen nodded, Rafferty pulled up YouTube and typed in the name of her favourite TV crime drama. 'I knew it. Listen to this.'

Rafferty played the video to Ms Glen, and then the YouTube clip of the crime show.

'Identical!' Ms Glen cried.

Rafferty's jaw slackened. Holy shit. Someone had used a television crime scene to lure a police close protection officer out of the way and then murdered the MP he was supposed to be protecting.

***

The task of identifying the source of the dry ice fell to Mayberry. Forensics had confirmed that there was nothing unusual about the trace residue in the boxes. In fact, there was no trace evidence left; all of the dry ice had evaporated, leaving nothing behind, which was simple $CO_2$ pressurized and cooled to form a solid.

The containers themselves were more revealing. The insulated foam was much thicker than required and would likely have given the killer a longer window to get the boxes in place before it sublimated. The boys in forensics said 10% per day was a reasonable figure to work off, but the addition of heat would speed it up considerably.

It wasn't – as Mayberry had first thought – carbon dioxide poisoning. It wasn't truly poisoning at all in the chemical sense, but asphyxia brought about by oxygen deprivation. The $CO_2$ displaced oxygen, and that had caused Hudson Brown to suffocate much in the same way he would have if he'd been smothered or strangled. The autopsy report, which Mayberry had on the desk beside him in the incident room, confirmed as much.

What was troubling Mayberry was that Hudson Brown hadn't woken up before he died. Dry ice wasn't named that because it contained ice, but because it was cold, and the quantities he and Ayala had found in the sewage tunnel would have reduced the temperature in Hudson Brown's flat by several degrees.

The autopsy report suggested an answer to that problem. Hudson Brown was an alcoholic. His liver showed clear signs of cirrhosis, and the scene of crime officers had found a number of empty whisky bottles in his recycling. That surprised Mayberry. Someone so vitriolic, so evil, still took the time to recycle. It was an odd contradiction that jarred him.

The use of dry ice implied the killer had worn gloves. If he had not done so, a simple burn would mark out their killer. Mayberry hoped that would be the case, but life was rarely so easy.

More importantly, carbon dioxide was dense. It was heavier than air. To introduce it from below meant the killer had to change the air pressure to force the sublimated gas up the tube. They had yet to find any device – like a fan – that would perform that function. It was possible the killer had taken it with him, and if so, would he have been smart enough to dispose of it afterwards? It wasn't the most incriminating evidence to keep hold of, and dumping it would look weird.

The dry ice itself could be a dead end. Over a hundred stores within fifty miles of London sold the stuff, and the quantity required for the murder, while large, would not seem out of place among sellers who were supplying dry ice for parties.

Despite that, Mayberry had been given his orders, and he'd call every single one of the hundred and twenty-two stores on his list. Three down, one hundred and nineteen to go.

***

The chief had been explicit. Rafferty was not, under any circumstances, to ask for or accept Morton's assistance.

She hadn't, however, banned Rafferty from talking to Morton's wife, Sarah.

They met at the Bow Wine Vaults on Bow Lane, a lovely watering hole that felt a million miles away from the politics of the Met.

'Ashley, this isn't a bad thing,' Sarah said. 'It's nice having him home at a reasonable time every night. I've spent decades wondering if I'd be one of those police wives who got the call.'

She was referring to the call spouses got when there had been a line-of-duty incident. Each year, dozens of men and women were hurt while performing their duty. Most of the time, it was minor. Sometimes, it wasn't. Just last year, one of Morton's team had ended up hospitalised in the middle of a murder investigation.

'He's miserable, Sarah,' Rafferty said. 'He puts a brave face on it, but you and I know he was born to solve crimes. He's the best. My cases – both of them – are the sort of no-evidence, who-the-hell-killed-them murders that David is renowned for solving. I don't have a damned clue where to go. I feel like I've been thrown in the deep end, and I'm chasing down every tiny lead. I need his help. Please. He wants to help. It's just... Silverman.'

Sarah's eyes narrowed, her smile vanishing. She knew of Anna Silverman. 'That old witch? Alright. What do you need?'

'Give him this,' Rafferty said as she slid a USB stick across the table. 'It's got everything we know so far. If he has any ideas – any at all – give me a call, and we'll meet back here for another glass of wine.'

'Okay. Speaking of wine, I think it's your round. I'll have the 2014 Pauillac.'

# Chapter 19: The Leap

It had been Super Saturday at the estate agents where Lauren Shrewsberry worked, with flats going on sale off-plan around the world all at the same time. Over four hundred new homes had sold within hours, and Lauren was looking forward to an early night after such a long day.

She was smart enough to live within walking distance of her office in Canary Wharf. In her opinion, it was the best commute in the world: across the footbridge on the North Dock, down the road to the Millwall Inner Dock, and then cut past the Pepper St Ontiod to get home to Spindrift Avenue.

The weather had turned nasty during the afternoon, and great rolls of thunder bellowed across the sky. It was during one of the lightning flashes that she saw him illuminated against the skyline. He was standing atop a building on the other side of the dock, teetering on the edge.

Lauren squinted up. It was impossible to see much at this distance. She broke out into a jog, crossing over the Glengall Bridge towards the eastern side of Pepper Street. As usual, the Dutch-style Bascule bridge was closed. Come to think of it, Lauren had never actually seen it open.

Another lightning flash. For a moment, she thought she saw two men on the roof.

It happened in slow motion. One moment, the man was silhouetted against the skyline, and then he began to fall. Five storeys later, she heard rather than saw the man hit the ground with a sickening crunch that she knew she'd never be able to forget.

She screamed. The mangled body of a man was visible under the dock lights not more than fifty feet away. His limbs stuck up at jaunty angles as if mocking his final act. Blood had begun to pool underneath him and was now making a beeline for the water.

She retched, tore her gaze away, and promptly threw up on the footpath.

***

The police presence was minimal. The death of Ed Teigan was a non-event, a suicide. One police officer had arrived to guard the scene and keep the body away from prying eyes, and then the scene of crime boys had been summoned to sweep up the body, clean off the blood, and get one of East London's busiest footpaths back in operation.

The death file included only the basics: the position of the body, the time of death, various photographs, and Ed's name. Identification had been easy: he'd been carrying his wallet when he jumped.

His personal effects were bagged for the next of kin, not that Stuart Purcell thought anyone would want them. A bloodied mobile phone, a nearly empty wallet, and a set of smashed-up keys were of little use to man or beast. The body was quickly wrapped and taken away, and Purcell was left with the grim task of power-washing the blood off the pavement. He couldn't do much about the blood leaking into the Millwall Outer Dock.

He looked around the dock. There were dozens of people on the water on kayaks and windboards. The local sailing club was one of the best in London, and a charity to boot. Purcell had no desire to let them know what had gone down. No doubt news would filter through in time; the Isle of Dogs was still very much a community, which was odd for London. Purcell supposed it was because nobody travelled through the Isle of Dogs. It wasn't the way from anywhere to anywhere. The only reason to come here was for work or play. It was a shame that Purcell's first visit was tarnished by a bloody corpse. As the sun began to set, Purcell had to admit it really was quite a pretty part of the world.

***

Ed landed on the autopsy table the next day when pathologist Dr Larry Chiswick made it in to the office that Sunday morning to catch up on some paperwork.

He barely stifled a yawn as he confirmed it was a suicide. They were ten a penny these days. Every recession, every financial crash, and a dozen such schmucks landed in the morgue. It was sad, really, but Larry had no time to be sympathetic to every cadaver that passed under his nose. There'd be an inquest. There had to be.

Chiswick hit his voice recorder. 'The deceased suffered injuries consistent with a fall from considerable height. There do not appear to be any other injuries. The victim's blood has been sent for a full battery of toxicological tests; it has been confirmed not to contain any common narcotics, and the deceased's blood alcohol level was near zero at the time of his death. Witnesses report seeing him jump from a height of approximately five storeys, which is consistent with the state of the cadaver. I am minded to consider this to be suicide.'

The next of kin would be informed of his verdict, and they'd have the opportunity to ask questions in the coroner's court. Few ever did. The perceived shame of suicide was still a barrier to any honest discussion of mental health problems. In the City, you were either a winner or a loser. It was a wholly binary division with no space for those just getting along okay, and it drove men to make irrational decisions.

Chiswick had once briefly considered a career as a trader. The allure of the bright lights, the big money, the women, and the whole lifestyle seemed fantastic, until he met a few traders who were completely out of touch. Selling his soul for the almighty dollar had never appealed after that.

Chiswick set down his voice recorder. No, for him it would always be a life of public service... and a gold-plated final salary pension. Just a few more years to go.

# Chapter 20: The Mother

Morton arrived early on Monday. He had been given the USB stick by Sarah, and he'd read the files. Like Rafferty, he felt there wasn't really enough to go on. The deaths of Angela King and Hudson Brown were both clean. Too clean.

The timing couldn't be a coincidence, either. Ten o'clock on Saturday was, Morton had to admit, pretty close to murder central, but those common late-night deaths were stabbings, drunken fights, and the many domestic incidents that befell the capital.

These deaths weren't like that. Angela King had plainly been killed by someone with significant experience. It was, Morton thought, possibly a fatal flaw that the bullet had gone missing. With it, Rafferty would have been able to determine the calibre of the weapon and pursue that angle. Without it, all she had was someone killed where nobody could see.

Hudson Brown's murder was the more promising investigation. There was no lack of suspects. Even Morton had to admit the world was better off without the man. He hadn't deserved to be murdered, but he hadn't deserved to live, either. It felt like a vigilante murder.

But if the timing wasn't a coincidence and the deaths were linked, then Morton was at a loss to see what connected a firebrand alt-right Member of Parliament and the wife of a policeman. There was no clue they had ever met. She was a registered member of the Liberal Democrats, an active member of the local Women's Institute, and had given off the vibe of being a content 1950s-style housewife. It wasn't an existence that Sarah would ever have tolerated. Morton had once bought her a tea towel while travelling, and he hadn't lived it down for a month. He hadn't been trying to suggest a woman's place was in the kitchen; he'd just liked the design. Convincing Sarah of that had been another matter entirely.

It was no use. He had only a few more minutes until he had to teach, and he had little planned for the lesson. With a yawn, he stretched and forced himself to his feet.

He needed a breath of fresh air before nine o'clock. He headed down the stairs, forgoing the lift for a modicum of exercise, and found himself in the lobby. He was about to head outside when he heard a woman screaming. He spun around, muscles tensed.

The scream was emanating from an older woman, and it was a scream of anguish, not pain.

The temptation was to ignore it. It would have been so easy to just keep on walking and leave someone else to deal with the distraught woman. Instead, he turned, cast the thought of teaching from his mind, and headed over.

'Excuse me? Detective Chief Inspector Morton. Can I be of any help here?'

The woman stammered her name between sobs. Her eyes were bloodshot from crying and bogged down by dark bags. 'Teigan. Amanda Teigan.'

'Okay, Mrs Teigan. What can we do for you today?'

She looked around the lobby. Those who were staring quickly averted their gaze, but the damage had been done. Amanda Teigan quickly realised she had made herself a spectacle.

Morton gently took her by the arm and said kindly, 'Why don't we go on through to the back, and we can talk there.'

He steered her by the arm, waved off security, and made a beeline for one of the ground floor interview suites. He found one empty and motioned for the distraught woman to join him.

'In here, Mrs Teigan. Can I get you a cup of sweet tea?'

'No, thank you.'

They sat in awkward silence for a moment. Mrs Teigan had begun to cry once more. This time there was no stopping her. For once, Morton was thankful his mother had always insisted he carry a handkerchief in his breast pocket, and doubly thankful that it was clean. He handed it over to Mrs Teigan and waited as she let herself cry.

'Thank you,' she said eventually. 'You must think I'm pathetic.'

'Not at all, Mrs Teigan,' Morton said. 'When you're ready, no rush, I'd appreciate if you could tell me what brought you here this morning.'

'It's my son, Ed. They found his... body...' Mrs Teigan began to sob once more. 'On Saturday. Your officers say he killed himself.'

Morton had suspected a bereavement. Few things left a parent so broken as seeing a child, be they adult or not, die. It was a cruelty Morton would not inflict on his worst enemy.

'You don't think he committed suicide,' Morton said.

Amanda Teigan looked him dead in the eye. 'No. I know he didn't. And you lot don't believe me.'

'Why?'

'Because he was happy. He had a good job, a beautiful girlfriend, and he was excited about the future. He's never had depression. He wasn't in financial difficulty. Don't people commit suicide for a reason?'

Morton pondered his response. It was possible that Ed Teigan had simply been an expert at hiding his problems. Maybe he had suffered from depression, but his mother was in the dark. To say so would seem cruel, callous, and unfair. The least he could do was extend the poor woman some sympathy.

'Okay. This might sound... difficult, but is it possible he had a problem of some kind, but was keeping it to himself?'

'Absolutely not. He was making plans for the future. I spoke to him on Saturday afternoon. He was planning to propose to his girlfriend, Aline. He had a reservation at Peninsula for last night that I know for a fact he confirmed on Saturday evening. See!' She pushed her mobile phone across the table to him.

There it was. A text from Ed dated 21:09: *Hi Mum, all set for tomorrow. I've called the restaurant, got the flowers, and I've got my suit. Gran's ring looks beautiful. She'll love it. Wish me luck tomorrow night!*

Morton reread it again. Amanda Teigan had a point. It didn't read like a man about to end his life.

'How long before he... you know, was this?'

'Less than an hour. They tell me he jumped at ten o'clock.'

Morton's eyebrows leaped. Three deaths, three Saturdays, each at around ten o'clock? He tried to shake off the feeling that it was mere coincidence, but the acid churning in the pit of his stomach was having none of it.

'Why else would he be on the roof?'

'He smoked. His office was on the top floor, and he often worked late. I kept trying to get him to quit smoking, but Ed always said his roof time was one of his favourite parts of the day. Could it have been an accident?'

Morton didn't know what to say. He wasn't familiar with the building that Ed had worked in, but virtually all high-rises with roof access had extensive fencing to prevent such an accident. It seemed unlikely.

'Mrs Teigan, I'll look into this for you. I can't promise anything, but I'd like to make a few enquiries, talk to the coroner, and, if I may, speak to Aline. Would you be able to write down her contact details for me?'

Amanda Teigan began to tear up once more. 'Thank you, Mr Morton. Thank you.'

# Chapter 21: Fall, Jump, Push

It was much the same as Ayala had told his students. When jumpers committed suicide, they tended to fall not far from the building. As Ayala had less than tactfully put it, the greatest act of cowardice took ten seconds of immense courage. Overriding the human survival instinct took immense effort.

Few suicidal men had the determination to take a running jump to their death.

Morton wondered what they thought on the way down. Did they regret their choice in the few seconds they were falling? What went through a man's head right before he met destiny in the form of a solid concrete pavement?

Ayala had not answered Morton's summons, so he relied on the forensics department to run him through the calculations.

There was a margin of error. With a relatively low building, the overlap between stepping off and being pushed off was large. According to the scene of crime officer in attendance, Stuart Purcell, Ed Teigan's body was right in this overlap zone.

Morton headed out to the office building where Ed Teigan had worked as an advertising executive so he could look himself. He was not a fan of the Isle of Dogs. When he'd been an undercover officer, many moons ago, he had spent a great deal of time investigating drug running in the East End, and he had no fond memories of anywhere beyond Limehouse.

As he drove over, Morton was struck by how much had changed. Gone were the slums, the cheap cafes, and the industrial sites. Everything seemed so shiny and new. There was little parking to be had, so Morton left the car in the local Asda's car park. He was careful to park directly in front of a CCTV camera, just in case.

The dock was a five-minute walk underneath Crossharbour Docklands Light Railway Station. The DLR was the spine of East London, running right up to Bank, where commuters could switch over to London Underground. While not as convenient as a true tube line, it ran above ground, which gave commuters the chance to see the bright lights of Canary Wharf from another angle.

He found the spot where Ed Teigan had bled out in no time. There were no indications that a man had died there less than forty-eight hours earlier, except for a sole bunch of flowers tied to the railing around the Millwall Outer Dock.

It was a pretty spot, and Morton could well imagine the view from the top of the buildings would be exceptional. From where he was standing, Morton looked west across the Millwall Outer Dock towards the Isle of Dogs Sailing Club. When he turned to his right, he could see Canary Wharf to the north of the island. At night, the lights would be impressive.

As Morton admired the view, he saw someone swipe a card to gain access to Ed Teigan's building. As he was not officially assigned to the case, Morton had to tailgate his way into the building like a common thief. He strode briskly for the stairs in front of him as if he belonged and slowly climbed towards the roof.

There was a fire exit at the very top of the stairs. It was the kind of the door that would automatically lock shut behind him. When he swung it open, he spotted a couple of cinder blocks that had been left just outside. He propped the door open and proceeded up onto the roof.

The view was as breath-taking as Morton had imagined it would be. This high up, the noises of the dock below faded, and the whole of London seemed to be at his fingertips. He walked to the edge of the roof that ran alongside the dock. The building was old, and it appeared to be mostly concrete construction. A ledge approximately four feet high ran around the perimeter.

There was no way Teigan's fall had been an accident. Getting up onto the ledge would require a determined effort.

Morton looked around the roof. There was nothing that could be used as a step. Then he swung a leg up onto the ledge. It would be possible to pull himself up onto the ledge as long as it was dry enough to get a grip on the wall. His quick scan of the roof revealed a number of cigarette butts littering the rooftop. Amanda Teigan had mentioned her son had smoked.

As Morton prowled the roof, a woman emerged from the fire exit.

'Oh, hello,' she said, obviously surprised to see someone in her spot. 'New hire out for a ciggie, are you? I'm Dolly.'

Morton regarded her as she pulled out a cigarette, deftly held it between delicate fingers, and lit up.

'Hi, Dolly. Detective Chief Inspector Morton. I'm investigating the death of Edward Teigan. Did you know him?'

'Know him? I've known him since preschool. He was the year above me, same as my brother. It was so sad what happened to him.'

'How did he strike you last time you saw him?' Morton asked. 'Was there anything to suggest he was suicidal?'

'No way!' Dolly said. 'Poor lamb must have been overcompensating or something. He seemed ever so cheerful, cracking jokes and talking about his plans to propose. He seemed a bit nervous about that, mind, but nothing to suggest he was hurting inside.'

'When was this?'

'Saturday evening. I saw him go up for his cigarette late Saturday night. It must have been right before he jumped. I assumed I hadn't noticed when he came back down. It's a big office, and I was working late on a project – the same one as Ed, actually – so I wasn't exactly concentrating on who was where.'

'Was the project causing Ed stress?'

'Nah,' Dolly said. 'This one was almost in the bag. He was in line for a big bonus for completing it, too.'

Morton made a mental note: could someone else have wanted to stop him getting the bonus? 'When did you realise that he was dead?'

'When I saw the commotion outside. I headed out for the last DLR from Crossharbour at a bit gone eleven o'clock, and there was blue police tape up just outside. One of your officers was escorting our staff out one at a time past the cordon.'

'Did you notice anything when he went up for his cigarette?' Morton asked.

'No. Nothing. Should I have?' Dolly looked suddenly worried.

'Not at all. It's not your fault. Thank you for your time.'

***

Aline was at Ed's mother's when Morton called. It sounded from the stress in her voice that the whole family was holding vigil. Morton swapped his tie for a sombre black affair that had seen far too much use before he headed over.

It was a large family home on the outskirts of Greenwich. Once upon a time, it would have been a cheap property, relative to the rest of London, but up-and-coming Greenwich had long since gentrified beyond the means of most Londoners. Morton was pleased to see an old Victorian terrace that had remained a family home rather than having been carved up into shoebox-sized flats for rent.

Ed had still lived with his mother. While he waited for Aline to finish a phone call with the funeral directors, Morton was permitted to visit Ed's bedroom in the converted attic. It was a handsome space filled with handmade furniture, a neatly concealed television, and an en suite complete with stand-alone bath. Ed Teigan had had a high standard of living paired with minimal costs. It was the sort of low-stress environment that seemed at odds with suicide.

His PC was unlocked. Morton scrolled through his social media pages, combing for any hint at dissatisfaction. He found none. There were dozens of photos of Ed smiling, laughing, and posing. His emails were full of upbeat messages, and he had social plans for many months ahead. His to-do list, which was in a special app on his desktop, included plans for upcoming birthday and Christmas presents. Beyond a handful of 'bored at work' statuses, Ed seemed to have had a remarkable joie de vivre.

Everything Morton saw suggested that Ed had been a happy, well-adjusted Londoner who had it all: the big house, the loving family, the well-paying job, and the beautiful girlfriend. Why would such a man kill himself?

The ring was there too, sitting on the desk. Morton was no expert, but he'd been around Sarah long enough to know an expensive ring when he saw one. There was a diamond report sitting next to it marked Gemmological Institute of America. Morton Googled for a diamond value calculator and typed in the details so he could estimate its value. He gave a whistle: the diamond alone was worth twelve grand. That ruled out financial problems.

Aline found him while he was inspecting a number of personal photos hanging on the wall.

'Mr Morton?' she said. She was a very pretty girl, much like in the photos. She was wearing black, had minimal make-up on, and appeared not to have slept since Ed's death.

'Chief Inspector, actually. Aline, I presume.'

'Yes,' Aline said. 'Do you believe us?'

She looked at him in earnest, hanging on for a response. There was fury mixed with grief twined with the faintest look of hope in her expression.

'Yes,' Morton said firmly. 'I don't believe Ed killed himself, but I need to find something that proves it.'

'What do you need?'

'I need to know if anyone wanted him dead.'

'Ed?' Aline said. 'Gracious, no. Everyone loved him.'

'Nobody disliked him at all?'

'His co-workers loved him. His family loves him. He's never hurt anybody.'

'So, do you think his death was random?' Morton asked. It seemed incredible that a man could be pushed off a roof for absolutely no reason.

She shrugged. 'All I know is that the man I loved was a good, honest, hardworking man. He never set out to hurt anyone. I can't believe someone would be angry enough to throw him from a roof, and I can't believe he jumped. I don't know what happened.'

Morton found himself at a loss for words. She seemed totally earnest in her defence of her would-be fiancé's character, and all the evidence backed her up. Ed Teigan had never been arrested, sued, or fired. He'd never had so much as a parking ticket, although that was probably because he didn't drive.

'Did you know he was going to propose tomorrow?'

'Not until his mum told me and showed me the ring. We'd talked about it many times. I guess it was always a question of when rather than if, as both he and I always wanted to get married. We were hoping to have the whole fairy-tale white wedding one day.'

'I'm sorry to ask, but had you had any sign at all that Ed might have been unhappy? I have to convince the coroner to rule this a homicide.'

Like Amanda Teigan, she volunteered her phone. 'Look at my texts, listen to my voicemails, look through my photos. Nothing anywhere in there shows a man at the end of his rope. Take it into evidence if you have to. Ed was not suicidal.'

One glance through her phone, and Morton was convinced. The smile on Ed's face, the look in his eye, the flirty tone of his texts, showed a man wildly in love, deliriously happy, and looking forward to the future. There was no longer any doubt in his mind. Ed Teigan had been murdered.

# Chapter 22: Scopolamine

'What about scopolamine?'

Chiswick turned to look at Morton as if he were an idiot. 'Overrated. I tried it once and woke up three days later in a bush, buck naked, with no recollection of where I'd been.'

'Very funny, Doc,' Morton said. 'But I'm being serious. Doesn't it cause disinhibition?'

'Disinhibition, yes. Mind control? No. Nobody dosed Ed Teigan with scopolamine. Even if they had done so, the killer would have had to lift him over a four-foot ledge and roll him off the top of the building. There are much easier, much less physical, ways to kill. And he'd have been bruised from that sort of lift.'

Morton just looked at him. 'Did you see any bruises?'

Chiswick stared back. 'I didn't notice any, no.'

'The absence of noticing isn't the same as the absence of bruises,' Morton said, smiling sweetly.

'You're not going anywhere until I get Ed Teigan out of cold storage, are you?' Chiswick asked. He'd seen Morton play this game before, and Morton was always a pain in the bum.

'Nope.' Morton perched himself against the wall as if to emphasise the point.

'Fine.'

Five minutes later, Chiswick's assistant, or diener, wheeled Ed Teigan into Autopsy Room One. Chiswick lit the body up with ultraviolet light.

'Look, no bruises,' Chiswick said. 'He wasn't shoved, pushed, punched, kicked, or otherwise physically forced over the ledge.'

'So, he did kill himself.'

'All signs point to yes,' Chiswick said.

'Except for the fact that he called to confirm a restaurant booking twenty minutes before he died. Doesn't that strike you as a weird thing to do right before killing yourself?'

'I suppose,' Chiswick said grudgingly as he covered Ed Teigan back up. 'There's nothing to suggest he was murdered, though.'

'Don't you find it weird that we've had three victims all die at ten o'clock on a Saturday night, and two of them are Rafferty's first cases? Saturday is never a quiet night, but the odds of that must be astronomical.'

Chiswick turned to face him. 'That is odd. I'd write off two in a row as weird, but if you're right, three is more than a coincidence. The problem is that getting to three means taking a simple suicide and turning it into a murder. There's no way to prove that.'

'Can you at least push for an open verdict?'

'I can try.'

***

The chief wasn't in until the next morning. After her Tuesday morning Pilates, she rolled into the office just before lunch and looked very surprised to see Morton waiting for her.

'David, I don't believe we have an appointment,' she said with false sweetness. She stopped dead in the corridor and didn't invite him into her office.

'We don't,' Morton said. 'I'm here about a miscarriage of justice. Ed Teigan died on Saturday night. It has been preliminarily ruled a suicide. I think it's a murder.'

'You're not being assigned a case,' Silverman said bluntly. 'And this is not a case.'

She walked into her office, leaving a gobsmacked Morton standing in the hallway. For a moment, he stood there slack-jawed, and then he felt the anger begin to build. He roughly shoved open the door to Silverman's office and barged in.

'How dare you!' he yelled. 'I tell you a man has been murdered, and your first thought is to make it about you and me? Have you no sense of justice? Ed Teigan was a happy man making plans for a bright future with his beautiful girlfriend. He had absolutely no reason to kill himself.'

'And you have absolutely no evidence he didn't. Now, get out. If you ever barge into my office uninvited again, you'll be fired. Do I make myself clear? This is for the coroner's office. Until and unless they rule it homicide, nobody in this building is to do a damned thing, and that includes you.'

Morton stormed out, apoplectic with rage. Screw Silverman. He'd get justice for Ed Teigan even if it cost him his job.

# Chapter 23: Coincidences

Technically, Rafferty wasn't supposed to talk to Morton about her cases – but Ed Teigan wasn't a case at all. They met over lunchtime on Wednesday in the Red Lion, a Fuller's that was usually more popular with politicians than policemen.

'Are you sure he wasn't hiding something?' Rafferty asked dubiously.

'Great,' Morton said, his voice dripping with sarcasm. 'Now you're doubting my judgement too?'

'You've got to admit that it's weird, boss. He definitely jumped. There's no way he could have been pushed without bruising somewhere, shy of someone literally lifting him over their head and launching him clean over a four-foot obstacle.'

'He didn't kill himself,' Morton said adamantly. 'And three murders in a row on three consecutive Saturdays, at the same time? That's unheard of.'

'Approximately the same time,' Rafferty said reasonably. She picked at her halloumi salad as she spoke. 'We don't know for sure they all died at exactly ten o'clock. That would be weird, but we don't have that information. And, like Silverman said, you're including a possible suicide in the series. Ed Teigan is not an open case.'

'I'm not wrong, Rafferty. I wish I was. But I'd bet you dollars to doughnuts that there'll be a fourth victim come Saturday night at ten. We've got a pattern.'

Rafferty set her fork down and sighed. 'What pattern?'

'The timings!'

'But nothing else. One woman shot in an alleyway, one Member of Parliament gassed to death under the noses of his protective detail, and a suicide. There's no pattern there.'

'You're just not seeing it. The odds–'

'Of three murders on successive Saturdays are astronomical,' Rafferty finished for him. 'Silverman is never going to believe you.'

'And neither do you,' Morton said, his disappointment evident in his voice. 'I thought I'd earned a bit of trust. I guess not.'

***

Morton made an appointment this time, albeit at short notice. Silverman could hardly refuse to see him when he was warning of an impending murder.

'What is it now, David?' she'd demanded as soon as he walked in.

'Rafferty's three cases–'

'Are none of your business,' Silverman said firmly.

'Look,' Morton said through gritted teeth. 'I know you don't like me. That's obvious. But if I'm right, and this is a serial killer, they're going to strike again, and we know exactly when. The last three murders all happened on Saturday night at ten. Are you going to just sit there and let the next one happen?'

'Yes,' Silverman said flatly, folding her hands on her lap. 'That's a risk I'm willing to take. It's clearly a concoction you've dreamt up to try to get back to active duty. It won't work. Don't let the door hit you on the way out.'

'But, Chief!'

'Goodbye, David.'

'I'm not going unless you tell me you're responsible for the next death.'

'I won't be responsible for the next death because there won't be one. Get out, David. You're spent, past it, done. You're never getting back control of a murder investigation team.'

Morton stood firm. 'Oh, I will.'

'Over my dead body.'

Morton smiled sweetly. That, he thought, could be arranged.

# Chapter 24: The Good Samaritan

I lurked in the alleyway for a good twenty minutes, an unlit cigarette perched between my lips. A few of those who passed me by looked curious for a moment, but moved on when I asked to borrow a light.

Timing was key. There were gardens backing onto the alleyway, all fenced in and several of them dark. I watched until I was sure which one would give me the seclusion I needed.

The brick lay at my feet, concealed by my bag.

It was almost exactly ten when I saw my victim. He was older, unsteady on his feet, and he shuffled along like a broken man. I wasn't really taking that much from him – only the last few years of misery.

As he passed, I asked again for a light. He stopped, apologised, and shuffled on. A quick look up and down the alleyway revealed nobody else in sight. I stooped as if to tie my shoes, picked up the concealed brick, stepped forward, and whacked him hard about the head.

He fell, landing unconscious with a thud. Another glance in both directions showed me the coast was still clear. I dragged him, hands under armpits, into one of the abandoned gardens. I needed to be quick. The bag came out again. Inside was a bag of iron ball bearings. This was the part I had been looking forward to least. I pulled the man's trousers down as he faced the dirt. I pulled a face, swallowed hard, and donned the gloves. Less than a minute later, the ball bearings were inside him. I quickly took his wallet, pocketed the money, and threw the empty wallet on the ground.

With another motion I turned the soiled gloves inside out and placed them into a Ziploc bag in my pocket to get rid of later.

I propped my victim up, pulled him to his feet, shoved him back into the alleyway, and then half-carried him in the direction of the Royal London. A passer-by soon came upon us.

'Help! I found him like this. Someone must have hit him over the head. He needs a doctor!'

The man looked nervous. 'Shall I call an ambulance?' he said in an accent I didn't recognise.

'No, just help me carry him. It's only just over there!' I pointed towards the sign denoting the entrance to the Accident and Emergency department.

No sooner had we crossed Stepney Way than paramedics emerged from a parked ambulance. They jogged over towards us quickly.

'What happened to him?' one asked.

'He was hit over the head,' said the thickly accented man. 'That's all we know.'

'We'll take it from here,' said the other paramedic.

Before I knew it, my job as the apparently good Samaritan was done. The man was taken inside, and they knew he had a head injury. All I had to do now was wait. Assuming they followed protocol, I had just committed the world's most original murder.

***

Nicole Wheelan had spent her life working for the NHS. She was one of a handful of MRI technicians at the Royal London, and today she was the unlucky soul who was in charge of the MRI machine when an old man was stretchered in to be looked at. It seemed routine because it was: the patient presented with a minor head injury, seemed woozy but competent, so she had to check for evidence of resting state changes that would suggest post-concussion syndrome.

She did the usual checks for metal before they began: belt, watch, pockets, glasses and the like. He seemed semi-conscious when she pressed the microphone button and told him to relax.

The job was a simple one for Nicky. She pressed a few buttons, pulled up the images, and sent them where they needed to go. Her training wasn't about pressing buttons at manic speed, but rather knowing which button to press.

She fired up the machine and ran the boot-up sequence that primed the electromagnetic field within, then slid the tray on which the man was lying into the machine. It was a head injury this time, so the MRI was a small, tightly focussed search for any signs of concussion. The man groaned, presumably from his head pain.

'It'll be okay, sir,' Nicky said comfortingly. 'You may feel a little claustrophobia, which is perfectly normal. If anything feels uncomfortable, I can pull you right out of there. Are you ready?'

When he didn't object, Nicky pressed the button to engage the MRI machine. The machine whirred to life, and that was when she heard the most atrocious noise. It was bone-splitting, followed by the sound of metal clanging against metal at ultra-high velocity. The poor old man barely had time to scream.

Blood exploded everywhere, like a Jackson Pollock painting.

And then silence.

Nicky slammed her fist against the emergency stop button. The machine spun back down to zero in less than thirty seconds, and the helium gas contained within, over £25,000 worth, hissed out.

The door to the operator booth banged against the wall as Nicky darted out to see what had happened.

She screamed.

Where moments earlier an old man had been in the MRI machine, all that was now left resembled tiny pieces of offal. Ball bearings were stuck against the magnets, and they began to clatter down as the machine finished turning off, a rain of bloody iron filings falling among the smashed-up corpse of an elderly man.

One final scream escaped Nicky as she bolted from the room. She didn't know where she was running. She just had to get out.

***

None of the staff really wanted to look, but they all seemed compelled to. Everyone knew the risks of using a giant electromagnet. There had been incidents over the years: workmen had lost tools, earrings had been ripped from earlobes, and the occasional coin had ripped through clothing. Never before had a man been eviscerated from the inside by what appeared to be ball bearings.

Speculation was running rife. Where had the ball bearings come from? Why had he had them? The higher-ups were already checking the insurance policies. Losing the helium was bad, but if the machine had been damaged beyond repair, they'd be looking at a loss running to seven figures.

Human Resources, and their in-house legal team, were on top of it in no time. By the time the police arrived on the scene, they had compiled everything they had. The patient's file, the triage nurse's observations, even the CCTV of him being helped inside by paramedics.

One thing bothered them more than anything. There was no record of the paramedics picking him up. No doubt that was just missing paperwork.

Staff were eventually pushed away from the MRI machine by the police, and a cordon was established. God help any other patients in need of an MRI, because the one at the Royal London was out of action for the foreseeable future.

# Chapter 25: He's Back

Silverman called at quarter to eleven that Saturday night.

'You were right,' she said through gritted teeth.

It took a moment for Morton to register exactly what she was saying. There had been another murder, just as he'd predicted.

With a start, Morton bolted upright in bed. Somehow, he managed not to rouse Sarah from her slumber. He tiptoed from the bedroom out into the hallway, closed the door softly behind him, and turned his attention to Silverman.

'What happened?'

'Somebody used an MRI machine to tear a man apart from the inside. A nurse turned the machine on, and the victim exploded. It's the talk of the hospital.'

*Shit!* Morton thought. It was brutal, violent, and yet, somehow, it was a clean kill. The murderer, whoever they were, had been hands-off. They had somehow tricked those responsible for saving a life into ending one instead.

'When?'

'He was brought to the Royal London at ten. He died twenty minutes later. I need you to get over there now, and you're going to need to do some damage limitation with the press.'

Silverman rang off.

Morton exhaled deeply. It wasn't the redemption he had been hoping for, but God damn, it was exciting to be back on a case. He grabbed a notepad from beside the hallway telephone, scribbled an explanation to Sarah, and placed it on the pillow where he should have been. He watched her chest rise and fall as she slept while he got dressed. She always looked so peaceful sleeping. He grabbed a body pillow from the wardrobe, placed it in his spot in case she rolled over in her sleep, and gently kissed Sarah on the forehead before heading out.

***

It was as Morton had expected. The short time between the man's death and Morton's arrival on the scene had been enough to give the press free rein. He dodged a barrage of questions as he headed from his car to the crime scene.

His team had yet to arrive. He hoped Rafferty wouldn't be too upset that she was no longer Silverman's protégée. There were uniformed officers around, and the corridor leading to the MRI machine had two men stationed at either end.

Even in his short walk through the hospital, Morton heard the whispering. The evening's events had become common knowledge among the staff, though none knew the exact details. Evidence booties donned, Morton made his way into the MRI room.

The old man's name was Donald Bickerstaff. He had managed to tell that to the triage nurse when he was brought in, but it didn't seem to matter now. There was precious little left of Donald. His entire body had been smeared up the walls by the force of the electromagnet.

All of the hospital staff had been barred from the room as soon as uniformed officers made it to the scene, but it was probably too late to have prevented gawkers glancing in. No doubt grainy video footage would surface on the news channels in due course.

The MRI operator who had turned the machine on was being treated for shock, so Morton would have to wait until he had her doctor's permission to question her.

There was little to see in the crime scene. Morton found the steel pellets easily enough. There were perhaps thirty of them. It seemed incredible that such tiny ball bearings could have done so much damage.

It didn't look like the MRI machine itself had been damaged, though Morton was no expert. Small chunks of Bickerstaff remained where the ball bearings had missed him. There would be no identification stage for his next of kin.

His staff trundled in, one by one, in varying states of sobriety.

'Evening, boss,' Ayala said as he and Mayberry traipsed in. Ayala looked distinctly unsteady on his feet, not fit for any difficult work. 'Rafferty's gone to find the MRI operator. Where do you want us to start?'

'Crowd control first,' Morton said. 'Find out what the staff here are saying. If anyone came in here, get a written statement. Confiscate any phones that have photos or footage of the crime scene.'

He turned to Mayberry. 'While Ayala is off doing that, I want you to find Bickerstaff's next of kin. I don't want his family being ambushed by the press before we can tell them what happened.'

They nodded, spun about heel, and headed off into the bowels of the hospital.

It was good to have his team back. Ayala looked more relaxed than he had been in weeks, though whether that was down to the reformation of the murder investigation team or the booze, Morton didn't know.

He snapped a few photos for his own records, then left when the scene of crime officers made it in. Chiswick was waiting for him in the hallway.

'Larry, what did they call you out for? Surely, they don't need a pathologist to know he's dead.'

Chiswick's mane shook as he chuckled. 'Had to see for myself, and I want to make sure they get all of him when they bring the body to the morgue. The last thing I need is a missing toe. This is a weird case, even by your standards.'

It *was* a weird one. Four murders, each on a Saturday night. Morton was too tired to think straight, but he knew in his gut that there was something more than the time of death that linked the cases. He just couldn't see what.

Morton found Nicole Wheelan in the staffroom down the corridor. Rafferty was with her. There was a large mug on the table and the faint smell of brandy in the air. Wheelan was crying, her mascara streaked across her face. She was staring off into the distance as if unaware that Morton had entered the room.

'Ms Wheelan?' Morton said gently as he sat down.

She turned slowly towards him. 'Huh?'

'My name is David Morton. I'm with the police. How are you doing?'

She shook her head sadly and held her hand up. It was visibly shaking.

'She's had a brandy or two,' Rafferty said. 'And a lovely young man from the emergency room has given her the once-over. I don't think she's up to talking tonight, though.'

Morton had to agree with Rafferty's assessment. 'Stay with her, okay? When she's ready, get a witness statement.'

# Chapter 26: Connections

Rafferty wasn't there when the team assembled at nine thirty the next morning. Morton had commandeered their usual Incident Room, and Mayberry had spent the past half an hour bringing everything from the room Rafferty had been using on the third floor.

'No, no, no,' Morton said as things were brought in. Things had to go in the right place. 'One board, four victims, not separate boards. We're looking for a serial killer, not four murderers.'

Ayala looked dubious. 'You sure, boss? One, two, and four, sure. But three still looks like a suicide to me.'

He referred to the crimes in the order they had been committed. Angela King, victim one, was placed on the left of the board. To her right, in second place, was Hudson Brown. Ed Teigan took centre-right, and finally Donald Bickerstaff's name and photograph were on the right. Mayberry had found the next of kin, a great-nephew up in Fife, and the local police had been dispatched to perform the next of kin notification.

'Deadly sure,' Morton said, and Ayala shrugged as if to acquiesce. It was Morton's show, and Ayala didn't have any better ideas to suggest. 'Run me through them, Bertram. Name of the vic, modus operandi. There's something connecting them. I just can't see it.'

Ayala produced a laser pointer from his jacket and pointed at each victim in turn.

'Victim one, Angela King. She was shot at point blank range as determined by gunshot residue which was found on her. No bullet was recovered.'

'Why was that?' Morton asked.

'Rafferty said it wasn't at the scene.'

'So, is her working theory that the killer retrieved the bullet from Angela King after shooting her?' Morton asked. 'Because that increases the time the kill would have taken. An alleyway in an area that busy wouldn't be particularly quiet on a Saturday night. Anyone could have seen them. What was Angela King doing out there on her own, anyway?'

Ayala looked blank. 'Sorry, boss man. No idea.'

'Forget it. Second vic?'

'Hudson Brown, Member of Parliament, poisoned–'

'Nope,' Morton interjected.

'Nope? He was definitely–'

'Nope,' Morton repeated firmly. 'Poison requires administration of a noxious substance. Carbon dioxide isn't a poison. Hudson Brown died of asphyxiation.'

'Right...'

'So, why didn't he wake up, go outside, open a window?'

'That, I can answer,' Ayala said. 'He was drunk.'

Morton thumbed back through the autopsy report. There was no mention of any alcohol in his system. 'Where's that in here?'

'It's not,' Ayala said. 'Silverman redacted it. She said we needed to avoid any negative press.'

That titbit stopped Morton dead. 'She *redacted* the pathologist's report?' he fumed. 'And you all went along with this?'

Mayberry, who had been hiding at the far end of the conference table, hung his head. Ayala turned away.

An awkward silence fell over the room. If Hudson Brown was a drunk, it explained how the killer could fill his tiny apartment with carbon dioxide without him noticing. He was either passed out drunk or too far gone to notice the temperature steadily dropping as the dry ice was pumped in.

'What about the pipework underneath his home? How complicated is it?'

'Dead simple, boss,' Ayala said. 'Not even a U-bend other than in the bathroom proper. The old Victorian system used S-bends. All the killer had to do was ensure the pressure in the tunnel full of gas was low enough – which we think he did using a fan and a valve – and voila, dead Member of Parliament.'

'Did you find a fan?'

'Well... no. But the killer could have taken it with him.'

Morton gave Ayala his best withering gaze. 'Did you look?'

'The tunnels go on for miles, boss!' Ayala held up his hands in a gesture of mock surrender, causing the red dot from the laser pointer in his hand to dance on the ceiling.

'Go back anyway,' Morton ordered. 'Map the whole sewer system if you must. Both of you go – after this meeting. What about victim three?'

Ayala turned his laser pointer back to the board. 'Victim number three,' he said, his tone doubtful, 'is Ed Teigan, an apparent suicide that occurred eight days ago. He jumped from the roof of a secure office building to which only employees had access.'

It wasn't, Morton thought, all that secure. He had tailgated in with little effort, and there didn't appear to be any CCTV or other security in the common areas. It would have been child's play for a killer to gain access to the rooftop.

'Ed wasn't suicidal. He was planning to propose the next day.'

'Whatever, boss. That brings us to victim four, the old man Bickerstaff, who was mutilated by an MRI machine. This is where things get interesting. He lived in the area. My best guess is, he was out for a walk. Someone hit him around the back of the head. The coroner has him on the slab now, so he ought to be able to tell us what he was struck with, although he'll be able to give us precious little else, given the damage done to the cadaver by the ball bearings. Before he died, Bickerstaff was taken to the Royal London, where two paramedics helped him inside.'

'How did they find him?'

'I don't know,' Ayala said. 'The hospital admins have closed shop. They seem to be thinking about their liability here. All they said was that the paramedics reported two good Samaritans bringing him across Stepney Way. I had them pull the CCTV, and I can see the paramedics carrying him, but I can't see the good Samaritans.'

Morton stared off for a moment. Four deaths, four victims. What the hell did they have in common?

'There's nothing here, boss,' Ayala said. 'What have they got in common? Shooting, poison, suicide, sabotage.'

'Not poison,' Morton said without thinking. 'Asphyxiation. What about the victims? Have they got any overlap at all? A common social thread? Somewhere they all go?'

'N-no,' Mayberry said. 'I c-checked their F-Facebook accounts. T-they didn't have anything in c-common.'

Ayala pointed at the board once more. 'A policeman's wife, an MP, an exec at an advertising agency, and an old man. We've got a mix of men and women, a mix of ethnicities, and a wide age range from late twenties through to seventies. They couldn't be more diverse than that.'

Morton stroked his chin, deep in thought. There was something that connected all four victims. There had to be. 'What about geography?'

Mayberry tapped away at his laptop, and the projector flickered to life. He brought up a map with the location of each murder marked upon it.

Ayala pointed them out in sequence. 'Brompton, King's Cross, Millwall, Whitechapel. They're all vaguely central, but we can't get a geographic profile from that, can we, boss man?'

Morton looked at the map. There was nothing there jumping out at him.

'Draw me a spiral and overlay it over the map, please, Mayberry.'

Mayberry placed a spiral over the map, but no matter how much he rotated and stretched it, the spiral wouldn't fit neatly over the four points. The theory was that killers started close to their comfort zone and then slowly moved out.

'Okay,' Morton said. 'What about transport links? Any of them connected by a common bus route, tube route, or combination thereof?'

'H-hang on.' Mayberry pecked away at his laptop for a few minutes while Morton looked on impatiently. The clock was ticking towards ten. If Morton's "every Saturday night at ten o'clock" theory held for another week, they had six and a half days to prevent another murder.

'N-no,' Mayberry concluded after a while. 'N-no c-common link.'

Morton swore. There was precious little time. What could the next murder be? He ran through the first four again: Shooting, asphyxiation, apparent suicide, sabotage.

The last word echoed in his mind.

'Ayala, didn't we discuss a sabotage murder in class?' Morton mused.

'Err... let me check.' Ayala dashed from the room. Morton could hear his footsteps fade as he headed out. He came back a few moments later clutching at a pile of notes.

'Had to get these from my office. Okay. Yes, we did. When we discussed plotting the perfect murder with your students.'

*The perfect murder.* All four did seem oddly proficient. A gunshot without a bullet. Asphyxiation without contact. Faked suicide without a clue as to how. And an old man murdered by a hospital that should have helped him.

Ayala continued to shuffle his papers.

'Here we go,' he said when he found the right page. 'The students suggested shooting me, distracting witnesses while they killed me, throwing me out of a window, having someone else do it, poisoning my coffee, and blowing up the building with me in it. Lovely bunch, that lot, especially the little wench who made me spit my coffee out.'

It dawned on Morton. He leapt to his feet.

Mayberry and Ayala looked startled.

'Can't you see it? Our killer is one of the students.' Morton said incredulously. He held up four fingers and ticked them off as he spoke. 'The first victim was shot just as O'Shaugnessy suggested. The second victim had his close protection officer lured away, just like Babbage suggested. The third, instead of being thrown out a window – who suggested that again?'

'Danny Hulme-Whitmore, boss.'

Morton ticked off a third finger. 'Right, Danny. The third vic was thrown off a roof, just as Danny suggested.'

'And four? Nobody mentioned an MRI machine!' Ayala said.

Morton ticked off the fourth and final finger. 'The fourth was killed by a third party, which is what Sully suggested. Our killer was in the classroom.'

Silence fell. Ayala stared back at Morton, wide-eyed. It seemed to fit. Every murder methodology was one that the students had suggested. It had been taken, tweaked, and improved upon.

'They used your feedback,' Ayala said slowly.

'*What?*' Morton said.

Ayala held his hands up in a "don't shoot the messenger" gesture. 'Think about it. You shot down O'Shaugnessy by telling him about striae evidence. There was no bullet at the crime scene, not because Rafferty missed it or the hospital missed it, but because the killer took it with him.'

Morton fell back into his seat. Was Ayala right? Had Morton essentially trained a serial killer to get away with the perfect murder?

'The second vic,' Ayala continued, 'was like Babbage's suggestion of listening to a police radio, but instead of listening passively, the killer lured the cops away with the recordings of a television crime drama before they acted. The killer combined this with Maisie Pincent's idea to poison me, except, as you said, it was technically asphyxiation rather than true poisoning. And the third–'

'I get it, Ayala. The third was better than the window. They used your calculations to obscure the murder. I don't know how they did it without leaving bruises, though.'

This time, it was Ayala's turn to look shell-shocked.

Morton finished the set for him. 'The fourth was Sully's idea: have someone else kill the victim, and the killer did exactly that. They took them to the Accident and Emergency department under the guise of a good Samaritan, and left them there to be brutally shredded by a magnetic resonance imaging machine.'

'So, what do we do?'

'We have to work out what murder they're going to commit next, and stop it before it happens,' Morton said. 'Ayala, what were the other murder methods the students suggested?'

Ayala ruffled his papers once more and turned a pallid shade as he read.

'There was just one, boss. They planned to blow up the building I was standing in.'

# Chapter 27: Loose Ends

Babysitting duty, again. Rafferty had sat with Nicole Wheelan right through the night. She had been kept in at the Royal London, suffering from all the typical signs of shock: greyish skin that the doctors called cyanotic, rapid breathing, low blood pressure, and a clamminess that seemed at odds with the coldness of the night. The staff treating her had extended her the courtesy of a private room at Rafferty's request, which made everything easier when colleagues and well-wishers tried to stop by. Rafferty had seen them off at the door lest they pry sensitive details from Nicole to sell to the press.

By morning, Nicole was looking tired, but she seemed responsive.

'How are you doing?' Rafferty asked as she brought her in a cup of black coffee.

Nicole gave a small shrug. 'I could be better.'

'I'm sure,' Rafferty said. 'It can't have been easy to see that.'

'See it? I did it!'

'No,' Rafferty said. 'You didn't. Whoever was behind the ball bearings did it. You were just doing your job.'

'So, you're not... here to arrest me?'

'Arrest you?' Rafferty echoed. 'Heavens, no. I just need to ask you for a written witness statement for the record, if you're up to it.'

Nicole pulled herself up to a seated position. 'Now?'

'Please.'

Rafferty fetched her a pen and the form that Mayberry had dropped off. Thirty minutes later, she held a completed, signed witness statement in her hands. She scanned through it.

Witness Statement

(CJ Act 1967, s.9, MC Act 1980, ss.5A(3)(a) and 5B, MC Rules 1981, r.70)

*Statement of... Nicole Wheelan*

*Age if under 18... Over 18*

*Occupation... MRI Technician*

*This statement (consisting of one page and signed by me) is true to the best of my knowledge and belief and I make it knowing that, if it is tendered in evidence, I shall be liable to prosecution if I have wilfully stated anything which I know to be false or do not believe to be true.*

*Signed, Nicole Wheelan*

*I was on shift at the Royal London on Saturday evening when a patient presented with a head injury. He appeared to be woozy, but conscious, and was wheeled to the MRI machine by two orderlies. They lifted him onto the tray, and I began the standard procedure. I inspected him for any sign of metal, removed his wallet and his watch, and then headed into the control booth to turn on the MRI machine. At first it seemed normal. The tray retracted, and the machine hummed to life. I spoke to the man, who I later learned to be called Donald Bickerstaff, to reassure him everything was going to be fine.*

*When I turned the electromagnet on, there was an almighty noise as metal was ripped towards the magnets at a high velocity. The man seemed to scream for a moment. I hit the emergency stop button releasing all the helium gas, and the MRI machine whirred down. By then it was too late. The patient was dead, and his blood was everywhere. I screamed, and the orderlies came running. I was escorted from the room, but as I left I looked back and saw him. There were small pieces of metal stuck to the machine.*

'Is that everything you need?' Wheelan asked when Rafferty had finished reading.

'That'll do,' Rafferty said, folding the statement neatly and placing it into her handbag. 'We may be in touch if we need anything else.'

***

There had to be some evidence. Morton headed for the morgue, where he found Chiswick eating breakfast in one of the autopsy rooms.

'Isn't that a bit unhygienic?'

Chiswick smiled. 'I won't tell if you won't. This room is set to be cleaned this morning, so I'm not contaminating any evidence. What're you doing down here?'

'I need to see the body of Angela King.'

'Okay. What are we looking for?'

O'Shaughnessy's idea rang in his mind. 'Evidence of a meat bullet.'

An almighty guffaw escaped Chiswick. He stopped when Morton glared. 'Oh, you're serious?'

'Yep.'

They found Angela King's corpse in the chiller, lucky that the husband hadn't had it removed to a funeral home just yet. She was loaded onto a trolley by the diener.

'Wheel her through to autopsy room two,' Chiswick barked.

'What, not had breakfast in there?' Morton asked.

'Not today.'

They trailed the diener, waited for him to leave, and set about examining the corpse once more.

'You ever seen a meat bullet?' Morton asked.

'Only on YouTube. It should be obvious if you're right. There'd be foreign particulates at the bullet entry site.'

Chiswick swung a large light over the body and pulled it close to the bullet hole.

'I can't see any trace of meat,' Chiswick said as he peered through a magnifying glass the size of a dinner plate. 'Hmm...'

'Hmm?' Morton said.

'Look there.'

'What am I looking at?'

'Right there,' Chiswick said, jabbing his finger at the cadaver. 'Oh, sod it.'

He pulled a camera down from its ceiling mount, flipped on the television screen, and magnified the area he was pointing at.

Morton stared at the screen. 'Is that... glitter?'

There were miniscule flecks that looked golden and metallic.

'Sintered copper,' Chiswick said knowingly.

'You mean...'

'I'll have to pull a sample to be one hundred per cent sure,' the pathologist cautioned, 'but it looks like she was shot with a bullet designed to disintegrate upon impact.'

Rafferty had been right all along. She hadn't missed a bullet. There was never a bullet to be found.

***

On Sunday afternoon, the whole team assembled around the large conference table in the Incident Room. Chiswick and Silverman joined them, both keen to be seen to do everything in their power to prevent a serial killer rampaging through London. Stuart Purcell, the scene of crime officer, lurked in the corner, observing but not contributing; he never seemed to feel that he was a part of the team.

Even Brodie was involved, though only joining them via a video link to Mayberry's laptop.

Morton was convinced they were dealing with a true psychopath. He or she appeared to have no personal connection to the victims. Whoever it was simply didn't care who they killed.

'Then, what are they trying to gain?' Silverman asked.

'Good question,' Morton said, trying to be polite.

'That would be why I asked it.'

Morton debated giving her a non-committal shrug, but the rest of his team deserved an answer too. 'I think they're trying to prove they're smarter than me.'

'Well, that would be a pretty trivial task,' Silverman said nastily. 'But, why?'

'Because of the first class Ayala and I taught. We set the students the task of plotting their idea of the perfect murder–'

'You did *what*?' Silverman thundered, jumping to her feet. 'I never told you to teach someone how to get away with murder!'

'If you want to catch a killer, you have to be able to think like one.'

She stared at him, seemingly unable to formulate a response.

Rafferty breached the awkwardness by leaning past her to talk to Morton. 'What are we going to do? You're supposed to be teaching tomorrow. If you don't go, the killer will know something is up, and they might change their modus operandi.'

'And if I do go and pretend everything is normal, we have until Saturday to work out which student is our killer, lest they blow up a building full of people on Saturday night,' Morton finished for her.

'Or worse,' Ayala volunteered a little too cheerfully. 'All the kills so far have been improved versions of the murders discussed in class. We could be looking at any kind of mass murder incident.'

The thought had crossed Morton's mind. He had explicitly warned his students of how such a killer might get caught. His own words from the lecture floated back to him:

*Three problems. Number one, you'd need the right expertise. Not many people know how to make a bomb and how to fly a drone... number two, you'd need access to the right materials to make a bomb... number three, you'd need to get around the no-fly zone around this building. Any drone on approach would be shot down long before it got through the window.*

What if they didn't use a drone? What if they didn't use an explosive? What if, as Ayala had suggested, they looked for a way to cause a mass casualty event without being seen or heard?

'We need to call in Counter Terrorism Command,' Morton said. 'Silverman, I assume you'll make the call.'

She was still looking slack-jawed from Morton's earlier comments, but she nodded meekly without even protesting that her subordinate had just given her an order. The prospect of presiding over a mass murder that she knew about before it happened was enough to quash her ego.

'And while you're doing that, we need a profile. What sort of person commits these murders? What's their background like?' Morton said.

'David,' Rafferty said quietly. 'We need more manpower.'

'True, but every new body is a red flag for our serial killer,' Morton said. 'If they guess that we know, they could accelerate their plans, escalate their plans, or pause them long enough for us to hope it's over. We have to find justice for our victims, but our main priority must be to keep London safe.'

'I have an idea,' Ayala said. 'Let's change the lesson plan. We can make the students profile each other.'

'That just might work.'

***

They worked through lunch and then dinner. Even Silverman stayed in the room, apparently beset by a sudden rush of guilt that she had not believed Morton's warnings. The boys from Counter Terrorism sent a representative who sat quietly in the corner taking notes but saying little. Morton had ascertained that his name was Mikhail Antonoff, but beyond that knew little about the man. He rarely had cause to interact with the Counter Terrorism Command. When Antonoff wasn't looking, Morton pinged a message over to Xander Thompson at the Serious Organised Crime Agency to see if he had heard of him. The reply came back quickly: *He's sharp, honest, but he's not you. Don't rely on him to bust this case wide open.*

As if Morton would ever delegate his responsibilities to four murder victims and their families. Morton resolved to keep Antonoff in the loop, but to explore every option available to him for preventing another murder. The Met could not afford to let a mass casualty incident happen right under the nose of the new chief. The possibility that Silverman might be fired was scant consolation, given that it would take the deaths of many innocent civilians to get her removed.

At some point in the evening, Ayala disappeared to the Chinese restaurant around the corner and returned laden down with enough food for twenty. Boxes of noodles and plastic cutlery piled up among the files on the conference cable, and the team wolfed down their food as they worked.

The names of the students had been written up on a trio of brand new whiteboards that Silverman had ordered to be brought up from Procurement.

On the left-hand board were the women: Almira el-Mirza and Maisie Pincent. The centre board had three of the men: Danny Hulme-Whitmore, Eric O'Shaughnessy, and Sulaiman Haadi al-Djani. The third and final board had the remaining suspects: the Goody Two-Shoes Crispin Babbage, Kane Villiers and the gender non-binary detective Sam Rudd.

'Who do you like, boss?' Ayala had asked.

'Nobody,' Morton said flatly. 'We have precious little to go on, and I'm not going to impugn an innocent student without good reason.'

'Okay, but who's the most likely?' Ayala said again.

'Statistically, we're looking for a man in his late twenties, early thirties.'

Ayala put a big red X under the names of Danny, Eric, Sully, and Crispin.

'And we're looking for someone who is egotistical, charming, and has an affinity for power,' Rafferty chipped in. 'But isn't that all of them?'

Morton gave her a wan smile. It was true that anyone seeking a position of authority, such as by training to become a police detective, could possess many of the same character traits as a serial killer.

Mayberry tentatively raised a hand up above his laptop screen. He seemed nervous to speak in front of Silverman. 'D-did anyone f-fail the b-background check?'

'Nope,' Ayala said quickly. 'They're all clean on that front.'

'I think,' Morton said, 'we're unlikely to find our killer hiding in the personnel files. We need something tangible, something definitive. We need to work out what they're going to do next and stop it before it happens.'

'What if we just arrest them all?' Silverman said. 'We can hold them for a month if we use the terrorism laws to keep them in custody?'

'And then what? We tail them all indefinitely?' Morton said dubiously. 'Sooner or later, we'll have to give up the surveillance, and all we'll have done is scare the killer into hiding. We'll never catch them. Letting this play out according to the killer's schedule – and winning at their silly game – is the only way to save lives here. The same logic means that any surveillance efforts, if noticed, could force the killer's hand.'

Silverman shot Morton a scathing look. 'Isn't that enough? If we can buy enough time, we don't have to worry about people dying.'

'Unless,' Morton objected, 'the killer has already put their plans for next weekend into motion. For all we know, there could be a bomb out there somewhere, just ticking down towards zero.'

# Chapter 28: Learning by Doing

Morton had the entire lecture hall wired before the morning's lecture. Directional microphones were hidden in every nook and crevice, and a number of cameras had been installed to record video too. Whatever the students said, they'd be watching.

Brodie hadn't been too pleased with the plan. No doubt his office was now crammed with the rest of the team peering at his monitor array to try to see exactly what was going down.

For his own part, Morton had taken twenty minutes before class to sit and breathe deeply. He couldn't let anything slip. If the killer saw his nerves, they could run, they could change their timing, or they could abort. Today's lecture could be the last chance to observe a serial killer ignorant of the fact that they were now being hunted by an entire task force with Morton at the helm.

They began to file in at ten to nine. As was his custom, Ayala brought with him a dozen doughnuts and a tray full of coffees. It seemed almost perverse to knowingly treat a killer to breakfast, but it was necessary to keep up the illusion.

Ayala's performance was impressive. He could easily have been an actor if he had not chosen to dedicate his life to the police.

When everyone was seated, Morton assumed the lectern.

'Today, we're going to put what we learned about profiling suspects into practice. Each of you will be assigned another student. Over the next three hours, I want you to identify everything about each other, note anything you might think significant given the risk factors we identified before, and then write a suspect report categorising your partner's risk level. Any questions?'

Danny Hulme-Whitmore raised a fist. 'Uh, yeah. Why?'

Morton shot him his best "don't be an idiot" glare. 'Because it's a learning exercise. Each of you represents a demographic. Some of the things in your past will be considered risk factors. I want to see if you can identify those factors in each other. Are you not up to the challenge, Mr Hulme-Whitmore?'

'I'm up to it,' Danny said. 'Who am I profiling?'

'Ayala, the pairings, please?' Morton said.

He stood aside from the lectern and sat down at his desk at the front. He paused to scan the faces of his students as Ayala assumed his place behind the lectern. Not one of them looked worried. El-Mirza was sitting at the back with Pincent, smiling over an inside joke. Sully was staring intently forward, eagerly awaiting his pairing. Even Babbage looked relaxed: he had his pen poised to scribble notes and kept looking around the room as if wondering who he was about to be paired up with.

'Right, then,' Ayala called. 'Sully, you're with Maisie. Babbage, you're with Sam Rudd. Kane Villiers, Hulme-Whitmore, and that leaves el-Mirza and O'Shaughnessy. You have three hours. You may begin.'

***

Mayberry and Rafferty settled back in their seats in Brodie's office. Silverman had disappeared, either because her job was done or because she had to deal with coordinating with the Counter Terrorism Command. The rep from counter terrorism was in the Incident Room upstairs, and he had been joined by half a dozen of his colleagues. The students didn't know it yet, but they were about to be subjected to the most intrusive background checks known to man.

'We're live,' Brodie said. 'Sound should be coming through to your earpieces now.'

The audio quality was crystal clear. They could hear everything Morton said.

'Are we recording?' Rafferty asked Brodie.

'Aye. I'll get everything saved, backed up, and then backed up offsite when we're done. If you like, I can isolate each voice digitally, and then perhaps your laddie can transcribe each student's voice as we go?' Brodie looked over to Mayberry expectantly.

'S-sure,' he said.

'Right then, laddie. Take my spare desk and that pair of noise-cancelling headphones. You type, and I'll get the transcriptions sent to the team as they come in.'

# Chapter 29: El-Mirza

Eric O'Shaughnessy tugged nervously at the sleeve of his herringbone jacket and smiled. He had been paired up with the sultry Almira el-Mirza and was at a loss where to begin.

'So,' he said casually. 'Where do you want to begin?'

Almira shot him a withering glare. 'You're the interviewer. You tell me.'

'Where were you born?'

'Riyadh,' she said flatly. 'But I don't remember it. I've lived in Peckham since I was a baby.'

'Peckham? Small world. My brother lives in Peckham, down by...' Eric trailed off as her glare intensified. 'Err, right. Risk factors, risk factors... have you ever hurt someone for pleasure?'

'All the time, but only if they asked.'

'Ohhkay... how about control?'

'I'm always in control,' she said with the hint of a smile. 'Even when I'm not.'

'What do you mean?' Eric asked.

'The submissive has all the power,' Almira said. 'It's all about consent. I'm only talking to you right now because I want to; ergo, I'm the one in control, even though you're asking the questions. And right now, you're not even thinking about how to profile me. My eyes are up here.'

'Sorry,' Eric said sheepishly. 'Doesn't that dynamic change if you're under arrest?'

'Am I under arrest... officer?'

She was clearly enjoying teasing him. He felt his cheeks flush red. 'Can we be serious for a minute?'

'Okay,' she said, pouting her lips. 'Ask away, Detective.'

'Have you ever abused alcohol?'

'Every Friday and Saturday night since I turned eighteen.'

'Not very observant, then?' Eric asked.

Her wan smile said it all. 'Not unless my parents are asking. If they do, I spend my Saturday nights curled up reading the Hadiths.'

'How does that work?' Eric said. 'Isn't it hard having one persona to show your family, and another for the rest of the world?'

Almira seemed to soften, as if she was surprised that Eric could be so sensitive. 'It can be exhausting. Family is family, and I'd hate to disappoint them.'

Eric scratched his head. He was running out of questions. 'On a scale of one to ten, how likely are you to kill someone?'

'Ten, if you don't take this seriously. Ask me if I have any childhood trauma.'

'Did you have a traumatic childhood?'

'No, but I wouldn't tell you if I did, would I?' Almira teased. 'You're being too direct. You can't just outright ask if someone is a murderer. You've got to approach it obliquely. You think of yourself as a player, don't you?'

'Well...'

Almira ignored his half-protest. 'Right. So, would you ever go up to a woman and just flat-out ask for sex? Buy me dinner first. Ask me the groundwork questions. You've got to make me trust you before you move in for the kill.'

'How?'

'Let me show you. Let's swap. I'll interview you.'

***

Rafferty pulled off her earpiece and turned to Brodie. 'Wow. That was downright brutal. Talk about using your feminine wiles to avoid answering any questions. I don't know if it makes her a great detective, but she'd be a hell of a criminal.'

'But what was that "the submissive has all the power" bollocks all about, eh?' Brodie asked. 'That girl is hiding something there. She's clearly got a bit of kink in her.'

'You think?' Rafferty said. 'She could just be rebelling against her strict upbringing. It's the quiet ones you have to worry about.'

'No, it isn't, lassie,' Brodie said. 'Really the quiet ones are quiet because they're too thick to string a sentence together.'

'Ooh, sounds like someone's been burned.'

'Nay, I've just been around a few times,' Brodie said.

'Seriously, though, you reckon either of 'em did it?'

'Can't see why they would have. Being a bit kinky doesn't mean you want to kill four strangers. I'm not getting a serial killer vibe from any of them.'

'Oh, yeah?' Rafferty said. 'Who else do you think it could be, then?'

Brodie shrugged. 'How am I supposed to know? You're the detective.'

'Think about it, dummy. If it's not one of the students, there were only two other people in that lecture theatre. If it isn't them, you've just made Bertram Ayala and David Morton suspects number one and two.'

# Chapter 30: Danny

'This is a waste of time,' Danny Hulme-Whitmore said. 'Shall we just talk about the Chelsea game on Saturday?'

Villiers shook his head with a smile. 'I knew you were a blue. You're so fucking obvious.'

'Let me guess. Gooner?'

'Got it,' Villiers said. 'Highbury born and raised. I grew up on the legends of Dennis Bergkamp, Marc Overmars, and Thierry Henry, and I wouldn't change it for the world.'

'Ever had a box at the Emirates?'

Villiers leant back in his chair. 'Nah, you?'

'Yeah, once.'

'Worth it?'

'Nah,' Danny said. 'It's soulless, isn't it? I want to be where the real fans are. The Shed End.'

'How old are you, anyway?' Villiers asked.

'Twenty-nine.'

'Same. You been a Londoner all your life?'

Danny nodded. 'Born and raised in the East End, mate. I'm as London as they come.'

'So, what's with the posh surname?' Villiers prodded.

'Dad was a banker, innit. He knocked up me mam and sodded off. I haven't seen him since.'

'Sounds traumatic,' Villiers said. He scribbled on the notepad on his lap.

'Nah, it wasn't all that... Hey! Are you profiling me?'

'Obviously. That's the whole point of this.'

'I thought we hadn't started!' Danny protested.

'Too bad.'

'What've you got so far?'

'Male, late twenties, broken home, Chelsea supporter. If that doesn't scream criminal, I don't know what does,' Villiers said with a laugh.

Danny's eyes flashed darkly. 'You watch your mouth.'

'Come on, mate, I'm just taking the piss. You know we have to do this, so let's get it over with, and then we can crack on to the pub for a few pints. How's that sound?'

'Fine. But you're buying.'

'We'll see,' Villiers said, promising nothing. 'So, did you ever fall in with the wrong crowd?'

'Naw, me mam raised me right, she did,' Danny said.

'How'd you avoid that? Poor kid from the East End, and he didn't get in trouble? At all?'

'Well... maybe we did get into a bit of trouble every now and again. Nuffin' serious-like. Just the occasional bowl, bit of shoplifting.'

'You are well gangster, mate,' Villiers said, leaning in conspiratorially. 'You still enjoy the weed every now and again?'

'Why? You looking for a hook-up?'

'Could you sort me out if I were?'

Danny's eyes shot over to the front of the lecture theatre, where Morton and Ayala were watching. He gave a sly wink. 'Naw. Definitely not. I ain't into that sort of fing.'

***

Morton discreetly eavesdropped Danny's conversation with Kane Villiers. He had assigned each pair a primary observer. Ayala was to watch Maisie and Sully, Rafferty was to watch Almira and Eric, and the Counter Terrorism Command were to watch Rudd and Babbage. That way, all suspects should be equally observed.

It was no surprise to see Danny and Kane chatting freely. They had been sitting together with Sully ever since the first lecture, and the trio had clearly begun to develop a friendship. There was rivalry there, too. None of them knew how many detectives would be taken on from the class, nor, for that matter, did Morton. He liked not knowing. If he had been responsible for picking the new detectives, it would have been much harder to be an impartial teacher and observer.

He had to keep reminding himself that, although there was one bad apple in the group, seven of these young people could go on to glittering careers at the Met.

Kane and Danny's conversation had started out slow. Kane was obviously playing a clever game, moving a casual conversation on to sensitive topics without Danny noticing until it was too late. It was a pro move, or would have been if it had worked.

What Morton hadn't expected was for them to discuss marijuana. He knew Danny had been involved in the prosecution of drug-running gangs while he was with Vice, but the wink Danny gave to Kane at the end suggested this was not all in the past.

# Chapter 31: Babbage

Crispin Babbage was paired with the gender non-binary student, Sam, and he had no clue where to start. Sam seemed content to simply sit and wait for him to begin, even though they were supposed to be leading the interview.

'I'm Crispin. I don't believe we've had the chance to chat before now, have we?'

'No, we haven't.'

'Right. So, you're supposed to be profiling me.'

'I am.' They stared at their mobile phone. The Reddit app was open, and they appeared to be looking at pictures of small animals.

He looked at Sam blankly. 'Don't you want to ask me anything?'

'Nope.'

'Should I just talk, then?'

'Nope.'

Frustration began to bubble up inside Crispin. 'Can I ask why not?'

'Nope,' Sam said again.

'Look here, Sam, I want to pass this class. We can't just skip an assignment like this. It's important!'

Sam looked up from their phone briefly. 'Not being graded, is it?'

'Well, no, but–'

'But, I don't give a fuck. I'm here to prove a point. It doesn't matter how good I am – and I *am* better than all of you, and my test scores prove it – I won't make it through this selection process.'

'Because you're gender non-binary?'

Sam finally made eye contact with him. 'Got there in the end, didn't we, Mr Teacher's Pet?'

'You can't know that,' Babbage protested. 'You got into the training program, didn't you? One of eight successful applications from among hundreds. That has to say something.'

Crispin withered under the glare Sam gave him.

'You wouldn't understand, Babbage.'

'Try me,' he said earnestly.

'You're a white guy from a wealthy family. You went to Oxford. Everything you've ever had, while no doubt hard work, has come to you more easily because of it. You're living life on easy mode. I don't blame you for that. Life is a race, and we all have to run it, but you're running it from halfway to the finish line while the rest of us have to trudge the whole distance.'

Babbage felt himself tear up. He hadn't asked for any of that. 'I'm sorry.'

'You... you what?'

'I said I'm sorry. No, I haven't had to deal with what you have. But my life wasn't easy, either. I bounced around the foster system for years before I became a Babbage. I got handed back so many times, I lost count. Nobody wanted to adopt an older boy.'

'What happened to your parents?'

'House fire,' Crispin said. 'I was staying with my grandparents that weekend. They died not long after, and then I had nobody. I spent most of my childhood escaping in books, reading and learning, and pretending I was living any other life than my own. I'm not complaining. I just don't want you to assume I lived some charmed life.'

Sam put down the mobile phone. 'Well, damn. Now, it's my turn to apologise. Can we start over?'

'Absolutely.'
'Hi, I'm Sam.'
'Crispin.'

# Chapter 32: Pincent

Sully and Maisie grabbed a row in the back of the lecture theatre. He was due to interview her, and he was raring to go. He had come prepared with a fill-in-the-blanks profile sheet, a list of talking points, and all the necessary stationery to make notes.

'This is going be fun,' he said.

Maisie tilted her head to one side and looked at him curiously. 'I suppose it is.'

'Okay,' Sully said. 'You ready?'

She grinned wickedly. 'I'd like to exercise my right to have a lawyer present.'

'Uh... what?'

'Lawyer,' she repeated. 'Now.'

Sully's gaze darted from Maisie to the front of the classroom and back again. Surely... she couldn't? He stood, walked past Maisie, who by now looked like the cat that had got the cream, and stomped down to Detective Inspector Ayala.

'Sir?' Sully said. 'Maisie's cheating.'

Ayala looked up from his newspaper. 'What do you mean, she's cheating?'

'She said she won't answer questions without a lawyer present.'

Ayala smirked, impressed by the tactic. 'How is that cheating?'

He'd seen Pincent's file. She'd barely passed the psych evaluation. One of her best friends had been shot, and by a police officer, no less. There were questions about her suitability, given the anger that incident ought to have engendered, but in the end her passion for justice had won out and she'd been permitted to join the training program. Ayala thought, and Rafferty had agreed, that it was not their place to second-guess the psych eval team. This sort of lateral thinking was exactly why they needed her in the program: she had what it would take to become a great detective.

'I'm supposed to be profiling her!'

'And?'

'How can I do that while she's messing about asking for a lawyer?'

Ayala stood up. 'Isn't she entitled to a fictional lawyer, if, in this scenario, she's a fictional suspect?'

'I suppose.'

'Then, Bertram Ayala, fictional defence solicitor, at your service.' Ayala motioned for Sully to lead on.

They walked to the back of the room, where Maisie was waiting. Her eyes narrowed as they approached, as if she somehow knew her gambit was beginning to backfire.

Ayala pretended he had no idea who she was. 'Good morning. I'm Bertram Ayala, the duty solicitor.'

'Funny,' Maisie said.

It was, and Ayala was beginning to enjoy himself, despite the circumstances of the exercise. 'You started this, now you're going to finish it. Do you require a solicitor be present or not?'

'Err, yeah. Have a seat.'

Ayala sat next to his new client and motioned for Sully to begin.

# Chapter 33: Rudd

'Now that we're friends,' Crispin said, 'can I ask a personal question?' He looked at Sam expectantly.

They looked... strange. They had short hair, wore nondescript clothing, and spoke in a voice that was pitched somewhere between feminine and masculine. It confused Crispin greatly, because he'd never met anyone like them before.

Sam looked at him blankly, as if they knew what was coming. 'You're going to anyway.'

'How does the gender non-binary thing work?'

'I consider myself agender,' Sam said. 'I don't feel masculine or feminine. I think they're social constructs designed to limit both genders to a given role.'

'But, biologically...'

'Biology doesn't come into it. It isn't a question of equipment. Nobody really cares if you pee standing up or sitting down, and, outside of a sexual partner, there is no good reason for it to impact upon how I interact with the world.'

'But, are you a man or a woman?'

'Yes,' Sam said simply, ducking the question.

'Okay... why the pronouns?'

'"They" is neutral. It doesn't have undertones of privilege, ownership, dominance, or submission. It's a much simpler, fairer way to refer to someone without labelling them.'

Crispin nodded as if he understood.

'It's not complicated, Crispin,' Sam said, exasperated. 'What I can and cannot do should be judged by merit. I want a fair shot, and the system isn't set up for that. By refusing to conform, I force people to judge me on what I can do, not what they think my biology dictates.'

'Then, why the police force? Isn't it the biggest old boys' club in London?' Crispin asked.

'Now, you're getting it,' Sam said. 'I want to break that cycle. Every time we see men like Morton promoted above and beyond the women who work with him, we continue to perpetuate the system.'

'It sounds like you're arguing for a transfer of privilege. Morton's the head honcho because he's got the best closure rate of any detective chief inspector, anywhere, period. If that isn't a merit-based appointment, what is? And besides, the commissioner of the police is a woman!'

Sam groaned. 'Token appointments don't change a thing. She isn't even actively investigating anything. She's a bureaucrat, a middle-management type with a swanky office. The real work happens much further down the chain. I want to be a part of that.'

# Chapter 34: Villiers

'So, Kane, what's your story?' Danny asked. 'I shared mine with you. Fair's fair, mate.'

Kane Villiers rolled his eyes. 'You're not very good at this, are you?'

'Hey, I'm trying to be direct and honest with you. You're too smart to fall for some sort of trick, so I'll ask you straight up. If you were me, and you had to interview you, what details would you be asking about? I'm just trying to learn.'

'I'd ask about my Uncle Greg,' Kane said.

'Alright, what happened to your Uncle Greg?'

'He died. I was sixteen at the time. He was involved in a protest, and some of those he was with turned violent. The police didn't know who was violent and who wasn't. They kettled all the protesters, engaged them with riot gear, and Greg was beaten pretty badly. His photo made the front page of *The Impartial* the next day.'

'Fuck,' Danny said. 'That's harsh. Sorry, mate.'

Tears were rolling down Kane's cheeks. 'It gets worse. They arrested him, chucked him into a holding cell, and neglected to give him food or water. Three days later, the custody sergeant found him dead.'

Danny reflexively reached out to hug him. To his surprise, the younger man hugged him back.

'Err... sorry. Not sure what came over me, there,' Danny said. 'Wanna forget we did that?'

'Fuck, no,' Kane said. 'I like knowing someone gives a shit. I haven't told anyone outside our family that story before. It feels good.'

'Not tempted to go on a revenge murder streak?'

Kane looked at him sombrely. 'I don't think killing someone else can ever bring back the dead.'

# Chapter 35: O'Shaughnessy

Almira el-Mirza pursed her lips and surveyed her mark. He was sitting on the edge of his seat, leaning forward as if to close the space between them. He was obviously attracted to her. Just as she had planned, Eric O'Shaughnessy was putty in her hands.

He wasn't unattractive, either. He had that Irish vibe going, with a mane of red hair enveloping a chiselled jawline, eyes that seemed to dance in the light, and a smile that showed off some impressive dental work. It was a shame he didn't have that charming Irish accent to go with it. His voice was so indistinctive that he could be from anywhere south of Birmingham.

'Why the herringbone suits?' she asked by way of an opening foray. He had worn three suits so far during the classes, each a different shade of charcoal with the trademark chevron pattern. The only other man she had seen who came close to having such a distinctive style was Detective Inspector Ayala, whose choice of three-piece suit and pocket square had not gone unnoticed.

'I like them,' he said simply. 'They suit me.'

'I'll say,' Almira said, humouring him. 'What else are you hiding? You've got that strong and silent vibe going on. How about you let little old me inside that beautiful mind? What drives you?'

'My job is a small part of who I am. I work to live. I don't live to work.'

'So, if you didn't have to work, what would you do?'

'I'd travel,' Eric said enthusiastically. 'I love seeing the wonders of the ancient world. Where we've come from can tell us a lot about where we're going.'

'Anywhere in particular?'

'I'd love to go exploring in South America. You ever fancied taking a boat down the Pantanal, see a bit of Brazil, a bit of Paraguay, and a bit of Bolivia? Imagine seeing nature at its wildest, enjoying sights no other living human has ever seen. I could make room for two.'

'Slow down, big man,' Almira said. 'Let's start small before we go running away into the jungle.'

***

'More flirtation,' Rafferty said. 'These two need to get a room.'

'She's leading him on,' Brodie said. 'But she's not interested. Look at her body language.'

Brodie pointed at the covert surveillance footage. 'He leans in, she leans back. It's not a mutual thing. She's using her looks to get him talking.'

'Fat lot of good,' Rafferty said ruefully. 'He's not exactly saying anything interesting, is he? He sounds like he's read a book on gap years and has a bit of wanderlust. How on earth do we use that for profiling?'

# Chapter 36: Sully

Morton watched from afar as the final interview took place. His assigned students had long since finished, and so Morton's gaze wandered. Maisie and Sully were taking much longer, probably because of her "I want a lawyer" gambit. While Maisie had played hardball during Sully's interview, he seemed much more relaxed about being grilled. It seemed, however, that she was getting little out of him that they didn't already know. After a further twenty minutes, Morton decided to call time on the experiment.

'Alright, ladies and gents,' Morton said. 'Good work. I hope you've all learned how to start profiling a suspect, or, more likely, learned how not to profile one. Getting someone to volunteer sensitive information is always a challenge. Doing so without them knowing is even better. I wandered around for part of today's session. I heard flirting, I heard rapport building, and I even heard some of you sneakily pretending you hadn't started. Good work, there. Your mark will be at his or her weakest when they don't know they're a mark just yet.'

Ayala stood. 'There will be homework. Not only do we want you to write up your thoughts, but we would also like you to write an essay, no more than 1500 words, describing any risk factors you have identified in your partner. While you're doing this, we'd like you to use any and all lawful resources to inform your report. You can use any information you've learned outside the classroom. You can use social media. You can even talk to mutual contacts. Send those to me by email by tomorrow, and the best report will win a round of drinks in St Stephen's Tavern.'

***

I watched as Ayala summed up the class. He and Morton were right: the unsuspecting fool was a much softer target than the prepared criminal. But as soon as Morton changed the lesson plan, I knew something was up. Somehow, the silver-haired old fool was on to me. He must have recognised that the crimes of the last four weeks were the crimes we'd plotted in class.

That meant he knew what I was planning to do next, but it was too easy. A terrorist incident. There was no way any man could ever work out which target I would hit or how. There were thousands of soft targets, hundreds of ways to kill.

It was time to give the washed-up old detective one tiny sliver of hope. And then crush it mercilessly.

# Chapter 37: Analysis

That Monday afternoon, the extended team convened in the Incident Room.

'That was an enlightening exercise. We now have eight transcribed interviews to assist with our profiles, and, thanks to Ayala's quick thinking at the end of the session, we'll have the students' own written reports that might contain additional information. Let's start with a quick risk assessment on each of our eight suspects.'

He looked around the room, expecting someone to volunteer their thoughts. 'Okay. Who had el-Mirza?'

'We did, Well, Rafferty did, but I listened to the recording afterwards, and I agree entirely with what she concluded.' Ayala said, pointing at himself and then Rafferty. 'I couldn't not listen in to that recording. She's a massive flirt, and she's got some weird BDSM vibes going down, but there are no red flags for "serial killer" in that transcript. She doesn't fit the demographic for a serial killer, either. She's mid-thirties, a woman, not white, and has, as best we can tell from her Facebook posts, a loving, if devout, family. We'd rate her a 2/10 risk factor.'

'Okay, write it on the board.' Morton watched as Ayala put a number two underneath the picture of Almira el-Mirza. 'Who else did you have?'

'Eric O'Shaughnessy,' said Rafferty

'What did you think of him?'

'He fancies the pants off el-Mirza,' Rafferty said with a smile. 'He's a dreamer. He loves travelling, is obsessed with his herringbone suits, and he's a bit of a mummy's boy. I pulled his force-issued mobile phone logs, and he's been calling home every night. He's in the right age bracket, and obviously he's a white male, but I'd say he's a 4 or 5 at best.'

'Which is it?'

'Can we have a 4.5?'

Morton sighed. There always had to be one. 'Fine.'

Rafferty wrote four and a half under Eric O'Shaughnessy's name.

'Next: Danny and Kane,' Morton said. 'I had them. Danny is 29, so he ticks the demographic boxes. He's worked undercover with Vice, so we know he's been exposed to a level of violence some would never tolerate, and it's possible he became inured to it. I know I did when I was undercover. Danny even appeared to offer to sell Kane weed at the end there. If he's still in the life, that's theoretically a risk factor, but I don't think Danny is our man.'

'Why not?' Ayala said. 'If he's engaged in criminality, fits the demographics, grew up poor and without a father figure, then surely he's a seven or eight?'

'I'd agree, except someone dumb enough to deal marijuana in a room full of detectives isn't smart enough to pull off the four murders we've seen. The contrast is too great. I'm going to rate him a six. Ayala, as you're closest, would you do the honours?'

He did, and a third number went up on the board.

'Aren't we going to arrest Danny if he's dealing?' Ayala asked.

'Not now,' Morton said. 'We can't spook the killer by throwing out arrest warrants. We have to ignore the fly to catch the tiger. You can investigate, and if the evidence is there, you can bring him in the moment we've got our killer in custody.'

That satisfied Ayala. He nodded his thanks and returned to his seat.

Morton pointed to the next man up for discussion, Kane Villiers. 'Now, Villiers is much harder to read. Has everyone read the transcript Mayberry prepared? He seems to play Danny like a fiddle. He's manipulative, he's very smart – his test scores are off the chart – and he fits the demographic. What did we think of the Uncle Greg story he told?'

Mayberry raised a tentative hand. He looked nervous at being asked to speak in front of a larger than usual group. 'It's b-b-b-bullshit.'

The urge to laugh hit Morton immediately. He hadn't heard Mayberry swear before. He suppressed it with great difficulty. 'Why?'

'He d-d-doesn't h-have an Uncle G-Greg.'

*Interesting,* Morton thought. 'Could he have changed the name to protect his privacy?'

'D-don't t-think so,' Mayberry said. 'T-there's n-no record of it.'

'Keep digging, just in case,' Morton ordered. 'I think Kane has earned himself a risk factor of eight or nine. What do you think? Hands up for eight? And for nine? Fine, eight-point-five it is. Ayala, if you please.'

Half of the board now had numbers beneath the names:

*El-Mirza – 2*

*O'Shaughnessy – 4.5*

*Hulme-Whitmore – 6*

*Villiers – 8.5*

'Who's that leave?' Ayala asked.

'Crispin Babbage, Sam Rudd, Sulaiman Haadi al-Djani, and Maisie Pincent,' Rafferty reeled off.

'Exactly,' Morton said. 'Who had them?'

Ayala raised a hand. 'I had Maisie and Sully. Counter Terrorism Command had Rudd and Babbage.'

'Thoughts?'

'Sully is the risky one,' Ayala said firmly.

'Why?'

'He's got a PhD in psychology from Cambridge, and his research topic of choice was risk factors in serial killers.'

'Okay, that's got to be a red flag. How old is he?'

'Thirty-three,' Ayala said. 'He's just outside the expected range, but this could be a continuation of an older series. Don't you think these four kills feel a bit too proficient for a first-time offender?'

'Any other risk factors?'

Ayala ticked them off as he went. 'He's superficially charming, an only child, and he's been single forever. I heard him complaining about that before class. At his age, it strikes me as odd that he's never had a serious relationship. It's not as if he isn't handsome.'

'What's your number?'

'Nine.'

'Write it up. Then, tell us about Maisie.'

Ayala did so. 'She's a woman, she's very young, but she's definitely bright. I don't know if she has the physicality to overpower someone or force them to jump. She strikes me as childlike, naïve, and bland. She was very cheeky during the exercise when she asked for a lawyer. I'm surprised nobody else thought of that. I'd rate her a four on that basis. We do know she had a friend die in a police misfire incident a few years back, which is what she says drove her to join the police. Kieran was involved in prosecuting that one, so he might be able to give us some context there. My gut says five.'

'I'll trust your instinct, then. Write it up. Now, where's our Counter Terrorism Command rep gone?'

'He's d-downstairs with B-Brodie,' Mayberry chimed in.

'Could you fetch him for me, please?'

Mayberry scarpered at top speed. Five minutes later, he dragged a reluctant Mikhail Antonoff into the Incident Room.

'Mr Antonoff, so kind of you to join us,' Morton said. 'Your thoughts on your assigned observees, please?'

'Babbage is a risk,' Antonoff replied. 'He's egotistical. He's an only child. And I know he's masochistic.'

'Excuse me?'

'Brodie and I borrowed his laptop. All legal. We searched his history. He has a fetish for fire.'

The entire room went wide-eyed at this pronouncement, and Morton's mind flashed back to the interview transcript. Crispin's biological parents had died in a fire. The possibility of a late-twenties, single male from a broken home, with a fetish for fire... he seemed like the obvious candidate. *Too obvious?* Morton wondered.

'I make him a ten,' Antonov said.

'So be it. What of Rudd?'

Antonov looked directly at Morton. 'Three. Rudd appears to be thoughtful, empathetic, and doesn't fit the demographic.'

'Then, we have our starting scores. Mayberry, can we put them up high to low on that blank whiteboard behind you, please?'

Morton watched as Mayberry wrote out each name in order of the score given.

*Babbage – 10*

*Sully – 9*

*Villiers – 8.5*

*Hulme-Whitmore – 6*
*Maisie – 5*
*O'Shaughnessy – 4.5*
*Rudd – 3*
*El-Mirza – 2*

Morton looked around the room to make sure he had everyone's attention. 'I want each of you to investigate your assigned students. Run anything risky by me. Work hard, work fast. Everybody is on overtime until we crack this. If you have to be here around the clock until Saturday night, so be it. We cannot allow a terrorist atrocity to strike our fair city.'

# Chapter 38: Doorstepped

When Rafferty stepped out of New Scotland Yard that evening, she needed nothing more than a soak in the bath with a large glass of bourbon, some scented candles, and a smattering of eighties classics to chill out to.

Instead, she got ambushed. The moment she was on the public pavement, a pack of journalists descended like ravenous wolves. They crowded around her, including one sneaky so-and-so who slipped behind her to prevent a retreat.

'Detective Inspector Rafferty!' the nearest shouted, shoving a microphone in her face. 'Is it true Angela King was a lesbian?'

'Is that why Brian King was sleeping on the sofa?' another chimed in.

'What was she doing at the Cunning Linguist on the night of her death?'

'No comment,' Rafferty said, pushing past the microphone. She spotted a cab thirty feet out, flagged it down, and jumped in. The questions continued to be shouted at her until the taxi had pulled away.

Lesbian bar? This was the first she'd heard of it. Rafferty Googled the name and found it. It was less than a quarter of a mile from where Angela King had been shot.

Had Brian King been lying? Was there more to the breakdown of his relationship than his post-traumatic stress disorder?

Rafferty knew she had to find out. Tomorrow. Tonight it was time for her to grab a takeaway, veg out on the sofa with *Britain's Next Top Model*, and hit the hay early.

***

The Cunning Linguist was closed when Rafferty arrived. She could see someone cleaning inside, so she banged on the door.

The woman inside yelled back immediately, her voice hoarse and angry. 'No journalists! Get lost!'

'Police!' Rafferty yelled back. 'I'd like to ask a few questions.'

The woman went silent, and then the door was unlatched.

'Sorry. Thought you were another one of them paparazzi. This about Angie?'

*Angie?* Rafferty thought. It seemed an awfully familiar way to refer to Angela King. She nodded anyway.

'Come on in,' the woman said, gesturing towards the lit fireplace. 'It's much too cold and windy to be out.'

The interior of the Cunning Linguist was beautiful. Rafferty had never been in a lesbian bar before, and hadn't known what to expect, but there was one word that seemed to encapsulate it: classy.

Chesterfield sofas were set around low tables. Mirrors and paintings hung from every wall. There was even a crystal chandelier hanging from the ceiling.

'Can I get you a drink, love?'

'I'm on duty.'

'Cup of tea, then?' the woman asked.

Rafferty checked her watch. She had plenty of time. 'Go on, then.'

The combined coffee and hot water machine behind the bar whirred to life as Rafferty set herself down in front of the fire.

'Earl Grey okay?'

'Please.'

It was loose leaf tea served in a china teapot with tiny matching cups. The woman set it down on the table with a gentle chink, poured two cups, then sat opposite Rafferty.

'I'm Grace,' she said. 'This is my bar.'

'You do your own cleaning? I'm impressed,' Rafferty said honestly, then took a moment to study the older woman. Rafferty had originally pegged her as being in her forties, but tiny crow's feet around her eyes, thin skin around her neck, and the skin stretching across her knuckles furrowed with wrinkles all suggested she was much older.

'Trying to guess how old I am?' Grace said. 'Don't worry, love. I'm used to it. I'll be fifty-nine next month.'

Blimey. She looked good for it. 'Wow' was all Rafferty could say.

'They all say that, you know. I've been here nearly forty years. My husband and I bought this place. It wasn't a lesbian bar back then. People weren't so accepting, you see.'

'Your husband?'

'Dead,' Grace said. 'Long gone. Shame. He used to mop the floors, and now I get to do it. But you ain't here to talk about an old lesbian and the beard she married. What do you need to know about our Angie?'

Rafferty took a sip of her tea. 'This is fantastic.'

Grace beamed. 'Fortnum and Mason. It costs a few pence more per cup, but customers'll pay twice as much. Easy money, innit?'

'Was Angie a regular?'

'Yep, she's been coming for years. She always has the same order: tequila sunrise with a vanilla chipotle twist.'

Rafferty was intrigued. Vanilla and chipotle? 'Sorry, how do you make that?'

'Make syrup with the vanilla and chipotle, mix as usual with tequila and top it off with some champers and a dash of bitters. Want to try it?' Grace asked. 'On the house... for research, right?'

Rafferty laughed. 'I wish.'

'Another time, then.'

'I could do that,' Rafferty said. 'Was Angie popular?'

'She did alright, yeah. She had that "sexy older woman" vibe going on – and she was always willing to buy a round for anyone at the bar. She was a bubbly one.'

'Did you know she was married?'

'I did, yeah. She always took the ring off when she walked in, and slipped it back on as she left. It wasn't too subtle.'

Rafferty drained her teacup and poured another. 'Was she really here last Saturday?'

'For a while. I don't know when, though. I heard she was shot about ten, is that right?'

'How'd you hear that?'

'Newspaper.' Grace stood, walked behind the bar, and came back with a stack of the week's newspapers. She flicked through the pile as Rafferty drank her second cup of tea. 'I saved 'em all, just in case. Angie's one of us, and we all want to see her killer bang to rights.'

Grace handed over a newspaper, and Rafferty scanned the text. It said little beyond mentioning that Angie had been shot at ten o'clock and had died less than an hour later at the Royal Brompton. Of course it was *The Impartial.* The byline was credited to Martin Grant, the guy who'd got in her face at the press conference.

'Thanks,' Rafferty said. 'Did you see her talking with anyone in here that night?'

'I don't think so, but you're welcome to come back this evening when we're open and talk to some of the regulars.'

'I just might do that.'

# Chapter 39: Divide and Conquer

Rafferty had texted to explain her absence. The news had broken that morning, and Morton was not best pleased. It was the sort of basic information that Rafferty ought to have turned up during her initial investigation. The cheating spouse angle was as obvious a motive as any, and yet, Morton reflected, it would not have made a jot of difference. Why did it matter to whom Angela King was attracted?

The students had been divided up among the team at random, and Morton himself had drawn Kane Villiers and Danny Hulme-Whitmore. The latter was a non-starter as far as Morton was concerned. He seemed to be dealing, but no minor criminal could have committed the series of murders that Morton was tasked with investigating.

Kane, on the other hand, seemed smart, competent, and dangerous. The fact that he would so brazenly lie to Danny about a dead uncle seemed capricious, but it was the only major flag. There was one man who, though Morton was no fan of his, would surely be able to tell.

He knocked on Doctor Jensen's office door a little after nine thirty. The doc usually set aside Tuesdays to catch up on his paperwork, so Morton knew he would be in the office.

'Hello, Doc,' he said.

'Morton! This is a surprise. What're you after?'

'I need that human lie-detector brain of yours,' Morton said as he lingered in the doorway. 'I want to know if the man I'm dealing with, Kane Villiers, is capable of murder. I think he could be a psychopath.'

That was the magic word: psychopath.

'A real live psychopath, eh? Come on in. Shut the door behind you.'

Morton clicked the door closed behind him, took the sole chair that wasn't piled high with folders, and waited for the doc's full attention.

'I'm investigating a serial killer. My recent class of eight students were set the task of committing the perfect murder. The exercise was intended to teach them how to think like those we have to catch.'

'An admirable goal,' Jensen said.

'That's what I thought!' Morton said. 'But it turns out someone slipped up and let a psychopath get into the course. One of the students has been committing each murder in turn using the feedback I gave them to make their murder more difficult to solve.'

'Fascinating,' Jensen said. 'Absolutely fascinating. What were the murders?'

'A woman was shot with a frangible copper bullet at close range, a man was asphyxiated by carbon dioxide piped into his home from the sewers, another man was somehow forced to jump off the top of his office block, and the last victim was torn to pieces by an MRI machine.'

'I saw those in the news!' Jensen said, suddenly animated. 'I would never have fathomed that they were all killed by the same person. What diversity!'

'Cool it with the admiration, Doc,' Morton cautioned him. 'I need to work out who it is, and I need to do it fast. Each murder has been committed on Saturday night at ten o'clock–'

'Why?' Jensen interrupted him. 'Why ten o'clock? What's so special about that time on that day? It seems ritualistic. Whoever your killer is, that time is significant to their life somehow. Choosing the same time and day is a compulsion, not an active choice. They feel they need to kill then for whatever reason.'

'Good spot,' Morton conceded. 'I assumed they were just taunting me.'

'Oh, they most certainly are.'

'So, this is about me?'

Jensen nodded. 'I think whoever it is thinks they're smarter than you – and they may be right.'

'Then how do I find out which of them it is?'

'Play to their pride,' Jensen said. 'Make them think they're winning. Remember playing Monopoly as a kid? The fun bit wasn't your opponent giving up. It was crushing them slowly. It was that bit where you had a set and they didn't, and every round, they slowly descended towards bankruptcy, and then finally crash-landed at rock bottom.'

'Speak for yourself, Doc,' Morton said. 'I'd have given up the moment it was impossible to win.'

'That's exactly what you need to do. Make them think they're winning. They must know you're investigating a serial killer, but they may or may not know that you know that it's one of them.'

Morton paused, unsure for a moment exactly what the doc had actually said with so many conditional negatives. 'You think I should let them know I'm looking, but make them think I'm looking for someone else.'

'Exactly,' Jensen said. 'If you can't work it out from the evidence you've got, then let the taunts go unanswered. Make them think you're way off track, and lure them into taunting you more.'

'What if they change their plans, accelerate, kill someone else, and swap their modus operandi to something totally wacky that I'll never see coming?'

'They won't. It's not part of the game. They're giving you every chance, here. They didn't have to use the murder methodologies you worked out in class. If they just wanted to kill people, they'd have done it by now, and they'd get away with it, too. These murders are brilliant. They're the work of a superior mind. Does this Kane Villiers fit that mould?'

Morton shrugged. 'He's sharp, but is he smart enough for this? I don't know. The big red flag for me is how easily he lies. During yesterday's profiling exercise, he made up a story in which his uncle died during a botched protest, almost as if he wanted us to investigate him. Could that be him taunting me?'

Jensen looked unsure. 'It's cheeky, but is an obvious lie really a taunt? He had to know that you'd disprove it in minutes. He could be testing to see if you're investigating him, but that doesn't mean he's the killer. Your students might have put two and two together themselves. They know what murders you discussed in class. I'm sure many of them made notes. Wouldn't they have noticed all these murders in the news? It doesn't take a genius to connect them if you've got that inside information.'

***

Morton decided on the direct approach. He would confront Villiers about his fake uncle story and see what he had to say for himself. It was a good thing that he'd left the students the Tuesday free to write up the profiles he'd assigned as their homework. Morton checked with Human Resources to get his address and then had Brodie ping his mobile to make sure he was at home before heading out.

The address was in Wembley Park, not far from the stadium. Victoria Avenue was rammed when Morton arrived. There were cars double-parked all along the road. There must be an event on at the stadium, he decided. He eventually found a space and parked with inches to spare on either end.

The Villiers house looked like most of the others in the row. It was a simple home: two up, two down, semi-detached, with a driveway out front.

Morton walked up to the front door and knocked.

'Coming!' shouted a voice from within. A moment later, the door opened to reveal a plump woman in her mid-fifties.

'Hi, I'm looking for Kane Villiers,' Morton said.

'Villiers… Villiers… I know that name! That was the couple who lived here before us.'

Morton flashed his identification. 'I'm confused, ma'am. I was led to believe this was his address.'

What was even more confusing was that Brodie had confirmed that Villiers' mobile had pinged off a local tower recently. He was definitely in the vicinity of the house.

The woman smiled, humouring him. 'I'm afraid not, officer. It's just me and Jack. We've been here a good two years now.'

'I don't suppose you have any identification that I can see?' Morton asked, and then added apologetically, 'Formalities and all that.'

She looked less than enthused, but she said without protest, 'Come on in, officer, and I'll see what I can find.'

'Thank you,' Morton said as he stepped into the parlour.

The house felt like it belonged to an old couple. The décor was dated. There were few hints of technology to be seen beyond an old radio, and the photos on the wall were of the woman and a husband her own age.

'Wait here.'

The woman disappeared into a back room, and Morton could hear her shuffling boxes around. She came back huffing and puffing, a thin film of sweat upon her brow.

'Will this do?' she asked, handing Morton a thick envelope.

He decanted the contents into his right hand. It was a solicitor's letter confirming that Mr and Mrs Jack Bartley had purchased the home he was standing in from Kane and Alexa Villiers almost two years ago.

Villiers had been married? Morton hadn't seen that coming. There was no ring on his finger, or the tan lines that would have hinted at a recent divorce. It went against the profile, too. Any man who could sustain a long-term relationship such that he got married was markedly less likely to be a serial killer.

'Yeah,' Morton said, his brows furrowed in confusion. 'That will do fine. Thank you for your time, Mrs Bartley. May I make a copy of this for our records?'

She nodded, let him use his phone to scan the documents, then escorted him to the door, obviously pleased to see the back of her unexpected visitor.

The moment the door closed, Morton phoned Brodie back.

'Brodie.'

'Brodie, where's Kane Villiers' phone?'

'I told you, it's at his house,' Brodie said.

'It's not. I'm here. He doesn't even live here.'

'Hang on. I'll ping your phone and tell you how far you are from him. You're twenty feet from him, boss, at most. Are you sure you're not missing something?'

'I'm sure I am, but he definitely doesn't live here.'

Odder and odder. Where on earth was Kane Villiers?

Morton made a beeline for his car and paused before he fired up the engine. He dialled Kane's number and waited.

'Kane speaking.'

'Hi, Kane, it's DCI Morton. Where are you?'

'I'm at home.'

'Right,' Morton said. 'Could you come outside, please?'

'Err... no.'

'Why not?' Morton demanded. There was a pause, and he could almost hear the cogs turning in Villiers' brain.

'I just got out of the shower.'

'Give it up, Kane. I'm not an idiot. What's going on?'

'Honestly?'

'Please,' Morton said.

'I... oh, hell. You're outside it now, aren't you? I'll be there in five.'

True to his word, Kane emerged onto the kerb within five minutes. He appeared not from the front door, but from the bushes alongside the house.

'What the hell was that?'

'I'm a squatter, okay? My divorce ruined me. This house,' Kane said, gesturing at the Bartley couple's home, 'is the house I grew up in. I inherited it. When I got divorced, I had to sell it to pay my now ex-wife and my lawyers.'

Morton looked from Kane to the house. 'How're you squatting in a house two people live in?'

'They don't know there's a basement. I didn't convert it legally, so it's not on the plans. I used to use it as a man cave. Now I live in it, and sneak out of my family home like a thief in the night. Please don't tell anyone.'

It could have been a lie. It sounded utterly preposterous.

'Show me,' Morton ordered.

Kane did. They snuck back the way he had emerged, and came to a fire escape underneath the bushes. An earth-coloured mat lay atop of it. Kane pulled it aside, flipped the hatch open, and gestured for Morton to descend.

'Don't worry,' Kane said. 'I'm right behind you.'

That, Morton thought, was exactly what he was worried about. Had the genius serial killer just pretended to be a moron in order to lure him to a random basement? His biceps flexed as he desperately wished he were carrying a gun right now.

He emerged into what Kane had called a man cave. There was a small bathroom in the corner, a sofa bed extended and covered in cushions, and a large television.

Kane shut the hatch behind him and pressed a finger to his lips in a "shush" gesture.

'I have to whisper, else they might hear me. I wait until they go out before I do anything loud, like take a shower.'

'That's disgusting. You've lived like this for two years?'

'Yes, ever since I sold the house.'

Morton gave the man an astonished look.

'But don't worry. I'm not your serial killer,' Villiers whispered.

'What?' Morton said, a little too loud.

'Shhh. Look, we all know. It's obvious. Someone is committing all the crimes we discussed in class, only better. Everyone's talking about it.'

*Shit,* Morton thought. They did know. Jensen was right.

'I won't tell,' Villiers said. 'As long as you don't.'

'Then, why did you make up a fake uncle who died?'

'Fun,' he said. 'I like messing with Danny. Do we have a deal? My silence for yours?'

It wasn't as if Morton had much of a choice, and what harm was he doing, anyway? It was creepy as hell, but Morton could sympathise with a man losing his home.

'Deal.'

# Chapter 40: Money, Money, Money

The lesbian angle to Angela King's death got Rafferty thinking. Almira el-Mirza had been assigned to her to investigate. Could there be a connection there?

She'd started with the basics: a background check, financial report, and a social media search. One thing had struck Rafferty immediately: el-Mirza was loaded. She wasn't just rich, either. She was filthy rich, or "minted", as Rafferty's brother Paddy liked to say.

Her home in Notting Hill was, according to Land Registry records, owned outright. No mortgage. To own a home at twenty-eight was a miracle. To own a home in Notting Hill was outlandish. To have it without debt was unthinkable. And yet there it was, in black and white: she'd bought it for cash, for just over two million plus stamp duty and legal fees.

Where on earth was the money coming from?

It wasn't, it seemed, from her parents. Her accounts showed a nominal few hundred being transferred internationally. The rest was coming from an online payment processing company. Almira had been making withdrawals of varying amounts. None were huge alone, but the aggregate income was substantial.

'Where's it all coming from?' she wondered aloud as she trawled through the mountains of paperwork Brodie had sent over. It couldn't be criminal in nature, unless the team responsible for background checks had failed miserably. Rafferty couldn't rule that out.

It was no use. The paper trail started and ended with the payment processor.

Rafferty dialled Kieran O'Connor's number. He answered in a hushed tone.

'What is it?' he said. 'I'm due in court in ten, so make it quick.'

'I need to track some unexpected funds. There's no way the payment processor is going to cooperate if I just ask. Do you think I can get a warrant?"

'What's your evidence like?'

'The suspect earns sod all but has loads of dough.'

Kieran tutted. 'Private money?'

'Not as far as I can tell. Her parents are rich, but their support payments are small and regular. This is a pattern of varying amounts over and over.'

'Can't you just ask your suspect?' Kieran said after a pause. 'If she hides it, we can use that to compel records. I have to dash.'

He hung up on her. 'Bastard,' Rafferty muttered. Kieran was always doing that. Mr Important Lawyer never bothered to actually say goodbye at the end of a call.

It was time to talk to Almira.

***

The team were overworked, and the stress was beginning to show. Morton was fielding calls from the press, fending off the demands of the victims' families without offending them, and drowning in leads that went nowhere. Even Sarah's home cooking couldn't lift his mood.

He hadn't managed to rule any suspects out, and yet nobody had left any evidence that they were the killer.

Kane's excuse – that he had been at home on each of the Saturday nights – couldn't be verified, as he lived alone. Morton's gut said he hadn't done it, but gut instinct alone was a poor basis on which to gamble the lives of thousands of Londoners. He picked at his dinner listlessly.

'Penny for your thoughts?' Sarah said. 'You look troubled.'

'I have between now and Saturday to prevent a terrorist atrocity. Four days to save tens of thousands of lives. Of course I'm troubled!'

'Hey,' Sarah said sharply. 'Don't take this out on me because I cared enough to ask. Do you want to talk through it?'

Morton shook his head. 'Whoever it is, they're taunting me. This isn't about the victims. They're almost incidental.'

'Are they? Really? Totally random?'

'You think they're not?' Morton said dubiously. He paused to twirl spaghetti carbonara around his fork as Sarah watched him thoughtfully.

'Nothing is ever truly random,' Sarah said. 'Who are the victims?'

'The wife of a policeman–'

'Brian King?' Sarah said. 'The news said he shot a man in cold blood.'

'He did,' Morton said. 'He had to.'

'And that doesn't seem significant to you?'

'Everything seems significant. His wife was a closet lesbian, he shot a man and now suffers PTSD, but he didn't do it. We know it has to be someone who was in my classroom that first week. Nobody else could be following this pattern. Even the students have worked that much out.'

'What about the other victims?'

'Hudson Brown, the MP. Everyone hated him.'

'But who, specifically, would hate him most?' Sarah asked. 'His whole attitude was offensive, but he loved to extol the virtues of white men. Any ethnic minorities or women on your suspect list?'

It was an angle Morton hadn't considered. Could there be a real victim among the four so far? Could three of them be camouflage?

'What if it's a double bluff?' Morton pondered. 'If the killer is as smart as I think they are – and everything I've seen says we're looking for a high-functioning sociopath – then they could be using the victimology to mislead me.'

'So, that's what's bothering you,' Sarah said.

'The endless wheels-within-wheels logic?'

'No,' Sarah said patiently. 'The idea that the killer might just be smarter than you.'

# Chapter 41: Sex Sells

Late on Tuesday evening, Almira was at her home in Notting Hill. Rafferty knocked on the door a little after seven. The first knocks went unanswered, and Rafferty was forced to keep knocking until Almira answered. What she saw when the door opened shocked her.

Almira stood there wrapped up in a bathrobe. For a moment, it seemed oddly normal, as if Rafferty had caught Almira at a bad time.

Except for the black leather gloves and thigh-high boots.

'What the hell?'

Almira bit her lip. 'Come on in. I'll explain everything.'

In the living room, there was a high-end web camera mounted above a television screen. Leads trailed down from the TV to a computer on the floor. To the right of the TV, there was a microphone on a boom arm. It seemed like the sort of setup Rafferty imagined Twitch gamers might use.

'You're a cam girl,' Rafferty said as everything clicked. That was where the money was coming from.

'I'm a dominatrix,' Almira said. She sounded proud, rather than ashamed, of her side gig. 'I let men feel like the pathetic worms they are, and they show me their appreciation financially.'

'And this didn't get flagged when you applied to the force?'

'Why would it?' Almira asked. 'I passed the physical and the assessment, and the financial status check only makes sure you're not broke enough to be bribed. Having more money than you need isn't a problem there.'

'Why do you do it?'

'It's fun. I enjoy the power. In real life, men dismiss me as weak, stupid, vain. I know better.'

Rafferty could relate. There were still plenty of men who looked down upon her as "not a real detective", and yet would take Morton or Ayala seriously just because they were men.

'When do you... stream?'

'Most nights. I assume you want to know if I was working Saturday,' Almira said astutely. 'I was. I have the video logs to prove it. Do you want to see them?'

Rafferty groaned. She didn't want to see that, but there was no other way to verify if Almira was telling the truth. She hated the job sometimes. 'I suppose so.'

# Chapter 42: One Down, Seven to Go

With Rafferty having confirmed Almira's alibi, they still had seven suspects remaining. Morton called everyone in early on Wednesday morning. With just three days to go, the risk of a major atrocity escalated with every passing hour.

The board with the estimated risk factor had been updated to strike through Almira's name, and Morton had downgraded Villiers two points on the basis of his visit, though he knew he couldn't rule him out entirely.

*Babbage – 10*
*Sully – 9*
*Villiers – 6.5*
*Hulme-Whitmore – 6*
*Maisie – 5*
*O'Shaughnessy – 4.5*
*Rudd – 3*
~~*El-Mirza – 2*~~

'Anyone got anything to add?' he asked, expectantly looking around the room.

Rafferty raised a hand. 'Is it time to bring them all in for questioning? If they've worked out we're looking at them, we've got nothing to lose.'

Morton considered her proposal. He could bring them in, show his hand.

'Or,' Ayala said, tentatively raising his hand, 'we could play them at their own game.'

'What do you mean?' Morton asked.

'You said this is about you, right? Jensen thinks they're playing a game. Make them think the game is over. Force their hand.'

'Okay, but how?'

Ayala looked around the room, paused for dramatic effect, then spoke in a barely audible whisper, forcing everyone to lean in towards him.

'Arrest me.'

*'What?'* Morton said.

'I'm the best way to provoke a reaction,' Ayala reasoned. 'If the killer thinks you're not playing because I did it, they'll be forced to do something to prove it's not me. I was in the lecture theatre when you asked them to concoct the perfect murder. Rafferty and Brodie realised it last week: if I weren't me, and you didn't know me so well, my name would be up there with the others, and so would yours, but we can't very well arrest you, can we?'

'You know what this would mean,' Morton said. 'We'd have to drag your name through the mud. The press would be all over it.'

'And we'll clear my name when the killer comes forward.'

'But what if they don't?' Morton asked.

The question lingered in the air. If Ayala was arrested and the killer chose to take the easy win rather than challenge Morton once more, then he could be vilified, or worse, subjected to vigilante justice.

'Right now, that's a risk I'm willing to take,' Ayala said. 'As long as we explain to the victims' families what we're doing first. I don't mind the press, but I don't want to hurt those people.'

It was an option. At this rate, it could be the only option.

'Not yet,' Morton said, making an on-the-spot decision. 'I'm not ruling it out, but we still have time to investigate further. If we can break the case without going down that route, we should. Antonov, what've you learned about Babbage?'

'His penchant for fire goes back a long way,' Antonov said. 'He is what's known as a pyrophiliac, and he frequents a number of fetish websites looking at that sort of content on an almost-daily basis.'

'That's a result of his parents burning to death, isn't it?' Morton said.

'Our psychologists would agree with that assessment.'

A thought struck Morton. Ten o'clock on a Saturday. It had to be significant. 'When his parents died, was it on a Saturday night?'

Antonov opened up his laptop, fetched the file relating to Babbage, then plugged his laptop into the projector, using the hub in the centre of the conference table. Then he copy-pasted the date into Google. The first result was for a site called "takemeback.to", which revealed it had been a Saturday. Babbage's parents had died on a Saturday.

Morton felt adrenaline pump through him. Sometimes, just sometimes, the hunches paid off. 'And it was the evening? Was it around ten?'

He waited impatiently as Antonov searched the documentation, looking for a time. He eventually found an insurance document with the right details.

'Sorry, midnight,' Antonov said.

'Damn.' It probably wasn't Crispin, then. 'Let's knock a couple of points off Crispin.'

Mayberry adjusted the board as directed, reducing Babbage from a ten to an eight. It left Sully at the top of the list as a nine, way ahead of anyone else.

‘Do we think it could be Sulaiman Haadi al-Djani?’ Morton asked. ‘Mayberry, what did Brodie dig up?’

‘H-hang on.’ Mayberry unplugged Antonov’s laptop from the projector so he could plug in his own, and brought up the bio he had compiled on Sully.

Morton watched as Mayberry became visibly stressed. He wasn’t up to speaking in front of a larger group again. As soon as the bio was on-screen, Morton read it aloud to save Mayberry’s feelings.

‘Sulaiman Haadi al-Djani, born in Libya. He was sent to a boarding school here, where he remained until age sixteen. At that point, the Home Office sent him back to his parents. His family fled Tripoli to avoid the fallout of the Arab Spring, and he was granted indefinite leave to remain. That sounds like a traumatic experience. He’s not a loner, though, and we haven’t seen any of the classic signs of a serial killer beyond the general horrors of living under the Gaddafi regime.

‘He’s our highest risk suspect, now you’ve downgraded Babbage,’ Ayala said. ‘We should bring him in and get an alibi if he’s got one. If he doesn’t, we investigate.’

It was hard to disagree. New evidence wasn’t likely to turn up in the next three days.

‘Let’s do it.’

# Chapter 43: Race

Sully was quickly invited to Morton's office on Wednesday afternoon. The team had debated creating a ruse for the invite, but Morton felt that, if he was the killer, Sully would see right through it.

He arrived earlier than Morton had expected.

'Punctual. I like it.'

'I was nearby,' Sully said as he shrugged off his coat and slung it over the back of the chair facing Morton. He took a seat, then placed his bag on his lap and began to rummage around. 'Mind if I eat? I'm starving.'

'By all means,' Morton said.

A Tupperware box was produced and placed upon the desk.

'Palm dates,' Sully said by way of explanation. 'Want one?'

'No, thanks,' Morton said quickly. He didn't want to end up bloated and gassy.

'Why am I here? You didn't invite anyone else.'

'How do you know that?'

'We have a WhatsApp group.'

*Shit,* Morton thought. Anything one of them knew, all of them knew. His investigation immediately became immensely more complicated. Now, he'd have to arrest others from the group at random to avoid looking like he was singling Sully out.

'Then, you know I have to ask where you were last Saturday.'

Sully popped a date in his mouth, chewed it over, and looked at him searchingly. 'Before I answer, why me?'

It was a fair question. The things that had flagged him were beyond his control. He was the right age, the right gender, and the wrong ethnicity. It was nothing he had done so much as the circumstances of his birth. The pregnant pause was just long enough for Sully to reach the same conclusion: Morton had nothing.

'I thought as much. I refuse to be racially profiled. I am declining to answer.'

'Don't do this,' Morton said pleadingly. 'If you make me do this the hard way and interview you under caution, then guilt can be inferred from silence. If you're not guilty, give me your alibi.'

'No,' Sully said flatly. 'I can't – I won't – be party to the institutional racism within the Met. Go ahead and arrest me. It'll be all over the papers by breakfast.'

He wasn't wrong. Morton wanted to bang his head against the table. If he wasn't the killer, why wouldn't he just give up his whereabouts? It seemed astonishing that any innocent student could be alibi-free for four consecutive Saturdays, and yet nobody wanted to cooperate. Everybody had secrets. Everybody lied.

And why was Sully so unconcerned about being arrested? If he was the killer, surely an arrest would put paid to any plans. Sully had to know he could be held beyond Saturday under the counter terrorism laws... unless he had an accomplice. Or the plans for Saturday had already been put into place. Could the killer already have automated the final murder?

Morton tried again. 'Please. There are lives at stake. You know the last murder method we discussed was a bombing. If there's a killer out there, I have to catch him. We have less than three days to stop a terrorist atrocity.'

Sully's expression softened, and, for a moment, Morton thought he had won Sully over.

'No.'

Morton stood. Damn Sully. Damn his stubborn streak. 'Then you leave me no choice. Sulaiman Haadi al-Djani, you're under arrest on suspicion of the murders of Angela King, Hudson Brown, Edward Teigan, and Donald Bickerstaff. You do not have to say anything, but it may harm your defence if you do not mention when questioned something which you later rely on in court. Anything you do say may be given in evidence.'

The shit had hit the fan.

# Chapter 44: You Did What?

Morton wished he could go home. Wednesday was fast turning into a nightmare.

'You look like you need a drink,' said a voice.

He looked up to see Kieran O'Connor standing in the doorway to his office, holding a bottle of Mortlach 1981.

'You could say that.'

Kieran sat down, produced a pair of nosing glasses from a travel case inside his big red QC's cotton damask bag, and poured two generous glasses.

'I hear you fucked up,' Kieran said.

Morton nodded. 'Possibly. One of my suspects backed me into a corner.'

'Do you think he did it?'

'No idea. I've got seven suspects, and any one of them could have done it. They're all smart enough, and they were all there. We're so far from cracking this case, and we now have...' Morton checked his watch. 'Less than 76 hours until the next murder, assuming our killer doesn't change course now they know we're on to them.'

'You know what you need to do. Follow Ayala's plan.'

'He told you about that?' Morton asked, surprised that Ayala and Kieran were in contact at all. They weren't exactly friends.

Kieran drained his glass. 'Who do you think suggested it?'

'Bloody hell. I thought it was a bit too sharp for Bertram to have come up with.'

'You know I've got your back. Let him take the fall. I can square it with the victims' families so he doesn't get lynched and we don't get sued.'

Morton sniffed his whisky cautiously. 'If I don't have anything by the end of tomorrow, you win. I'll arrest Ayala.'

'Sold. You going to drink that or just sniff it?'

Morton took a sip. 'Wow.'

'Wow, indeed.'

'How up-to-date are you with the investigation?'

'As up-to-date as you are. The Counter Terrorism Command co-opted me to sort the legal side of things for them. You must have a suspect.'

'I wish,' Morton said. He took another gulp of whisky. There was little burn, but he felt the warmth spread through him almost immediately. 'The best lead is the time. Ten o'clock. Why ten o'clock?'

'Could be anything. A significant event for the killer. Something that drives the compulsion. I've prosecuted a few cases that had similarly specific time elements. I think one of them was ten o'clock too. Saturday's a busy night.'

'Wednesday's the busy one for me,' Morton lamented.

'Then, I'd best cut you off,' Kieran said as he picked up the whisky and replaced the cork. 'And let you get back to work.'

'Cheers – for the Scotch and the company. Have a good one.'

Kieran headed out, and Morton was left alone with his thoughts.

Three days to stop a killer. Three days to save thousands. He half-wished that Kieran hadn't taken the bottle. With a yawn, he turned his attention back to the glare of his monitor. The answers had to be staring him in the face.

# Chapter 45: Two Days to Go

The clock was ticking down faster and faster. Ayala was off trying to find out where Babbage had been the previous Saturdays. Rafferty was looking into Maisie and Rudd. Counter Terrorism's Antonov had been assigned to investigate Eric, which left Morton with Danny Hulme-Whitmore.

He was, in Morton's considered opinion, nowhere near smart enough, but Morton still had to confirm that. A quick call to Vice's head honcho, Sylvester Fitzroy, ought to iron things out.

Sylvester was an old hand. He hated calls, especially unannounced calls, so Morton was forced to go through the man's secretary. He didn't have the number to hand, so Morton called the force switchboard.

'This is DCI Morton calling for Sylvester Fitzroy. Could you put me through, please?'

A nasal voice belonging to a man came back immediately. 'Hold, please.'

The line beeped as Morton was transferred.

'You've reached the office of Sylvester Fitzroy. This is Darleen speaking. How may I help you?'

'Hi, Darleen. This is David Morton. I need to speak to Sly urgently. Is he available?'

Sylvester had been trying to get a nickname to stick for years. He liked Sly or Fitz, though nobody really called him either. Morton knew that playing to his ego was his best bet of getting the man to take a call. It worked.

'David! Sly here.'

'Hi, Sly. I'm in a bit of a pickle. One of your boys, Danny Hulme-Whitmore, is a suspect in a murder investigation.'

'Murder? Danny boy? You're kidding.'

'I'm afraid not. What do you know about him?'

'He's brilliant,' Sly said. 'He was undercover for me for years.'

'Doing what?'

'Investigating the Bakowski Crime Syndicate, what else? They've moved more coke through central London in the last month than the Kray twins did in a decade. Even with Tiny on the run.'

A shiver ran down Morton's spine. One of the worst gangsters in London, Tiny Bakowski was the prime suspect in an old murder case. He'd evaded capture by fleeing overseas to God knew where. Morton had managed to get both of his brothers, but the main man was an enigma.

'He knows Tiny?'

'Danny was well on his way to becoming Tiny's right-hand man. By the time we pulled him out, Danny had worked his way right into the inner circle.'

The chill wouldn't leave Morton. Long after he'd finished his call with Sly, the name Tiny Bakowski continued to ring in his head. The murders were personal. It was between him and the killer.

Could Danny Hulme-Whitmore have crossed that line? Could he be hunting victims down to taunt Morton at the behest of Tiny Bakowski? If so, why now? Why these victims? None of this made sense.

***

Ayala had been tasked with finding Crispin Babbage. Thanks to the involvement of Counter Terrorism, Ayala didn't have to justify intrusions into the suspect's life as much as he normally would. As Kieran had explained, the case of *Leander v Sweden* gave states significant authority to breach human rights in the pursuit of counterterrorism. Ayala was concerned at how easy it was. Without much more than a name, he was able to have Crispin's phone traced.

He found Crispin in a gaming bar in Stoke Newington. It was, rather fittingly, called the Loading Bar. Crispin was oblivious to the world, his mind concentrated on his computer game. Ayala snuck up slowly behind him

'Babbage!' he shouted from behind. 'What're you doing?'

Crispin leapt out of his seat. As he jumped, he knocked his pint of beer to the floor. It landed with a smash so loud, half the bar turned around to mockingly applaud him.

When the attention had subsided, Crispin look at Ayala ruefully. 'That wasn't nice.'

'Neither is murder.'

'What on earth are you on about?'

Ayala decided to test him. 'I think you killed them.'

'Preposterous!' Crispin cried. 'Why on earth would you think that?'

'We know, Crispin. We know that fire turns you on.'

'Who told you that? It's a lie.' He had begun to turn a pale shade of beetroot.

Ayala slowly shook his head, hoping to come across as disapproving. 'Don't lie, Babbage. It won't do you any good. We have your computer records.'

Denial gave way to anger, then pleading, and finally, acceptance.

'Fuck you! How dare you?' Crispin balled his hands into fists as if he wanted to strike Ayala down. 'Please. Don't tell anyone. I didn't do it much. I can't... I can't help it.'

Ayala looked at the pathetic wretch before him and questioned how on earth they had rated him a ten. He didn't have the spine to kill in cold blood.

'Why do you do it?'

'I don't know. Don't you think I'd stop if I did? This isn't what I want. I'm ill, okay?'

Ayala's quick tongue got the better of him. 'How did you pass the psych test?'

'Please,' Crispin begged. 'I can't lose this job. All I've ever wanted to do is become a detective. Don't take that away from me. I'll do anything. I can help! I know who the killer is.'

'Isn't that something the killer would say?'

'I... I suppose.'

'Who do you think it is?'

'It's... it's Eric. His name isn't really Eric.'

'*What?*'

'I went to school with Eric O'Shaughnessy. He died ten years ago. Hearing his name annoyed me from the first lecture onwards. It could have been coincidence, but Eric doesn't even sound Irish. The man calling himself Eric isn't Eric. His real name is Taylor Bailey.'

*What the hell?* Ayala stared. How could Eric O'Shaughnessy be someone else entirely?

'Can you prove this?' he asked.

'I can.'

He did.

***

'Boss?' Ayala said. 'We have a problem. Eric O'Shaughnessy is not Eric O'Shaughnessy.'

'Excuse me?'

'The real Eric O'Shaughnessy is dead. Our man is an imposter. Crispin went to school with the real Eric. He's been digging into the imposter for weeks, and then got blackmailed into silence when he confronted him. Somehow, the imposter learned about Crispin's fetish. I don't know how. The imposter is Eric's cousin, Taylor Bailey. He's a former psychiatric in-patient at Maudsley.'

'How on earth did we miss that?' Morton's voice was shot through with anger.

'The real Eric died on holiday. He drowned when his boat capsized in Greece. It was never registered here.'

'Shit. Bring him in.'

# Chapter 46: The Trap

Morton had his own problems to deal with. If Ayala was right, Eric was a fraud, and not a very good one, at that. It didn't make him a killer, but Morton hoped he was. If Ayala had the killer in custody, then London was safe.

Until then, Morton had to proceed as if nothing had happened. His own remaining assignee was Danny. It was time to cajole an alibi from him by any means necessary. He didn't want another Sully moment; the timings were too tight. With two days left on the clock, he couldn't afford to make a mistake.

He called Villiers on his mobile.

'Kane, I need you to do something for me.'

***

Villiers agreed to the plan in no time, and Morton watched from a distance as Villiers met Danny Hulme-Whitmore outside the British Library. They sat on a bench facing the south entrance. Through the wire Villiers was wearing, Morton could hear everything.

'Forty quid an eighth? You been smoking your own product, Danny?'

Morton imagined Danny grinning, though from the distance, he couldn't make out much more than two blobs on a bench.

'I don't smoke this shit. Now, do you want it or not? You called me, remember?'

'It's good shit, right?'

'Only the best.'

'Fine.'

'Cheers. Pleasure doing business with you.'

That was it. Transaction complete. Morton briskly strode towards Danny as he walked away and tapped him on the shoulder. As Danny spun to face him, his face dropped. Morton could see him tense as if he wanted to run.

'Uh, hi, sir. Lovely night for a stroll.'

'Danny Hulme-Whitmore, you're under arrest for possession of marijuana with the intent to supply. You do not have to say anything, but it may harm your defence if you do not mention when questioned something which you later rely on in court. Anything you do say may be given in evidence.'

'What the hell? You set this up?' Danny eyed him angrily. 'It's just weed!'

'And murder is just murder.'

'Murder? I ain't no murderer.'

'Prove it. Where were you last Saturday?'

'Dealing! Look, I'll give you my clients if you want. I'll tell you where I was. I'll bet there's some CCTV nearby that'll show me walking past.'

'You're still under arrest.'

Two down, six to go.

***

Eric didn't lawyer up when Ayala arrested him. He seemed almost relieved to be dragged into New Scotland Yard on fraud charges.

Ayala half-wondered if he had an obligation to find him a lawyer anyway when he was clearly not completely compos mentis. While Taylor Bailey stewed in the interview room, Ayala looked into his background. To his surprise, he found his Facebook profile easily. It seemed that Eric really had been his own cousin.

'You aren't Eric O'Shaughnessy.'

'No.'

'Why did you pretend to be him?'

'Because you,' Taylor said, jabbing a finger at Ayala, 'wouldn't let me become a police officer.'

'You tried to join the force under your own name?'

'Uh-huh,' Taylor murmured.

'What happened?'

'I failed the psych exam. That was last year. This year I became Eric, and I had someone sit the test for me.'

*Jesus,* Ayala thought. How much worse could the background checking have been?

'Why do you want to be a detective?'

'I want to give back. I want to help the community. I want to be respected. Nobody ever treats me with respect. I'm *not* crazy!'

'Okay...' Ayala watched him and felt a sense of pity. This wretch could no more plot four murders than Ayala could learn to fly by flapping his arms as fast as he could.

Three down, five to go.

***

Rafferty felt like the odd one out. It seemed she was the only one not able to arrest the students she was assigned to investigate. Both Rudd and Maisie seemed positively tame by comparison. No drug dealing, no hidden identity, no refusal to offer up an alibi. They'd been rated low risk early on, and Rafferty stood by that assessment. Who had ever heard of a female serial killer? Other than the handful working with a male partner, like Myra Hindley, it was unheard of.

Rudd was interesting. They had been born biologically male. That much was in the personnel records. They'd passed the fitness test set for men, which had higher physical standards than the equivalent women's exam. It seemed weird to cast off that privilege and then bemoan the old boys' club.

Rafferty had to respect them for that. Doing it the hard way was much easier than simply accepting a place among the privileged few. They had a bit of a victim complex, and they certainly isolated themselves, but the interview they had done with Babbage had been lucid, eloquent, and principled. It was not, Rafferty thought, the tirade of a murderer.

Thursday was drawing to a close. Rafferty pinged Morton a quick text by way of status update, and then made the decision to call it a night. No doubt Friday would be even more stressful, and Rafferty knew she'd need a proper night's sleep to face what could lie ahead.

# Chapter 47: Desperate Times

He had made a promise, and he intended to keep his word. With great reluctance, Morton had to accept Kieran's proposal of using Ayala as bait.

It could backfire. If the killer didn't react as predicted, Morton could wind up with blood on his hands. But if he didn't act, he'd almost certainly have blood on his hands.

As Morton saw it, he had three tasks. First, he had to talk to the families in person and let them know about the gambit. He couldn't be responsible for hanging Ayala out to dry.

Second, he had to make sure the press were there when he arrested Ayala. A quick call to Martin Grant at *The Impartial* would sort that. The man was a gossip, and he'd tell every journalist he knew if he thought there was a free glass of wine in it for him.

Third, the easiest task. He had to delegate the interrogation of Sulaiman Haadi al-Djani. Antonov from the Counter Terrorism Command was still in the building, and he'd do perfectly. He had, so far, been oddly distant. He clearly didn't consider himself a part of Morton's team, not that he should. He had a standoffish personality which was at odds with the collaborative environment that Morton strived to foster.

With a yawn, Morton picked up the phone.

***

Antonov had initially objected to being 'assigned' to conduct an interrogation. He had acquiesced only when he learned of Sulaiman Haadi al-Djani's impressive curriculum vitae.

The man held a doctorate in psychology and had researched risk factors in serial killers. He was oddly overqualified to be studying to become a mere detective. He was the sort of man the Counter Terrorism Command would usually poach for the profiling team, and a worthy adversary to face.

The tape recorder had been set, the formalities sorted, and the interview under caution began.

'Hello, Sulaiman. My name is Antonov. You know why you're here.'

Sully ground his teeth. 'Because Morton's a racist prick? Oh, yeah, the Libyan guy did it. How original.'

'You think that's why he asked you?'

'He didn't ask anyone else.'

'Are you sure you simply weren't the first?' Antonov challenged him.

'It's not like I could know that. I've been under arrest, remember?'

'He's spoken to all of you.'

Sully's expression softened slightly. 'He still started with me.'

'Are you still refusing to provide an alibi?'

'I'm not saying anything,' Sully said stubbornly.

He looked less cocksure. For a moment, Antonov wondered if he was about to ask for a lawyer.

'Why is that?'

'I've told you.'

Antonov sighed. Round and round in circles.

'Sulaiman – can I call you Sulaiman?'

'Just call me Sully. I hate it when people butcher the pronunciation of my name, anyway.'

'Right,' Antonov said. 'Me too. You know we're looking for a serial killer. You know what the signs are. What have you seen?'

'Nothing.'

'Nothing?' Antonov echoed. 'But in your doctoral thesis, this thesis,' Antonov said, opening a folder containing a summary of Sully's research, 'you argued that epigenetic factors are the endogenous cause of violent psychopathy, did you not?'

'So?'

'So, how, in your opinion, do your classmates fit those risk factors?'

Sully frowned as if struggling to formulate his thoughts. 'Well, Kane, Crispin, and Eric seem like the biggest risks.'

'Because...?'

'They're men.'

'Right. But what epigenetic risk factors are present?'

Sully stared blankly. 'I'm sorry,' he said after a pause. 'Are you here to interview me or ask me to consult on your case?'

'A little from column A, a little from column B,' Antonov said. He spread the pages of Sully's research. 'You said that the rMNA transcription rate changes as a result of diet and social interactions. How would you apply that today?'

'I'd look for diet and social interactions.'

'Like what?' Antonov prompted again. He was growing impatient with Sully acting ignorant. 'You researched MAO and SNAP proteins and their effect on violent tendencies. Would you attribute this to any of your colleagues?'

Sully didn't answer.

He couldn't answer.

There was no way in hell he'd written his PhD.

***

The families of the victims were collected by uniformed officers and brought to a spare conference room. Mrs Teigan arrived first. She hugged Morton the moment she saw him, grateful that he had taken her plea to investigate Ed's death seriously. Brian King arrived second. He shook Morton's hand, looked him in the eye, and promised he'd do whatever he could to avenge Angie's death, whatever the press thought of their relationship.

Nobody came for Hudson Brown. Nobody loved him enough in death to turn up, even though Morton knew that his next of kin lived just down the road. Nor did anyone arrive on behalf of Donald Bickerstaff. When Morton was sure that Mrs Teigan and Brian were the only family members on the way, he began.

'Thank you for coming. As you know, I'm investigating the deaths of Angie and Ed. I believe that we're looking for a serial killer. After discussion with our in-house psychiatrist, we believe they're matching wits with the force in a twisted game. To put it bluntly, they think they're smarter than us. So far, they may be right.'

'So, what can we do about it?' King demanded.

'We need to lure them out. Again, to borrow an analogy from our chief psychiatrist, it's like a child playing Monopoly. The winning is only fun when your opponent is trying.'

Mrs Teigan leapt to her feet. 'You want to give up? After I trusted you!'

'No, Mrs Teigan,' Morton said calmly. 'I have no intention of giving up. I only want to make our killer think the game is over. To that end, I intend to stage a fake arrest to make our killer think we've found our man. If our hunch is right, this will provoke a reaction.'

'A reaction?' King asked. 'What kind of reaction?'

'Our psychiatrist believes the killer will reveal themselves in some way in order to show us how much smarter than us they are.'

'You keep saying "us",' King said. 'You mean you, don't you? What're you not telling us?'

Morton met his steely gaze with one of his own. 'I mean us. I have only just been formally assigned to these cases. This is a calculated risk, and I will only proceed with your blessing. It's our best hope at getting justice and preventing another murder. The clock is ticking, so what will it be?'

'Do it,' Mrs Teigan said. 'Whatever it takes.'

'I'll support it,' King said. 'On one condition.'

'Name it.'

'I want to be there when you take the bastard down.'

# Chapter 48: The Arrest

Ayala was arrested as he emerged from Westminster Station on Friday morning. Morton knew that an arrest at such a high-profile spot would get a great deal more publicity than arresting him at home.

Martin Grant had proved invaluable. The tip-off had ensured a healthy crowd of photojournalists were on the scene, and Morton's presence drew them like flies to honey.

As Morton approached Ayala, he felt a twinge of guilt. Ayala was in for a very rough couple of days, and, despite his obvious innocence, there would no doubt be some members of the public who would see the initial arrest in the news and nothing more thereafter, and those people would forever tarnish Bertram Ayala's stellar reputation.

Morton waited until the cameras were on him, nodded discreetly to Martin, and approached Ayala.

'Detective Inspector Bertram Ayala,' he said loudly, 'you're under arrest on suspicion of the murders of Angela King, Hudson Brown, Edward Teigan, and Donald Bickerstaff. You do not have to say anything, but it may harm your defence if you do not mention when questioned something which you later rely on in court. Anything you do say may be given in evidence.'

The cameras had begun to flash almost as soon as he started to speak. By the time he slapped a pair of handcuffs on a panicked Ayala, bystanders were filming with their mobile phones. He frogmarched Ayala to the car, pushed Ayala's head gently down to prevent him hitting it as he forced Ayala into the back seat, and fumbled with the engine long enough to let several journalists get their money shot of the perp being whisked away in a police car.

'Bloody hell, boss man, you didn't have to cuff me so tight. That hurt!'

'It's an arrest, Bertram, not a social call. Now, shut up until we get back to New Scotland Yard. You'll be processed with the rest of the criminals at intake, and then I'll have your laptop brought down to an interview suite so you don't get too bored.'

Ayala paled. 'Processed?'

'You didn't think we were just going to play-act the arrest, did you? You're getting strip searched like a common criminal.' Morton looked into the mirror again and saw Ayala looking distinctly unimpressed.

It was an exceptional sacrifice to make.

***

Kallum Fielder became the go-to guy for sensational news coverage once more that Friday lunchtime. After the news of Ayala's arrest broke at eight o'clock in the morning, his agent was offered a dozen talk shows. Kal picked the one with the highest ratings, rather than the most money, and was whisked into make-up by eleven.

Less than an hour later, he felt the glare of the studio lights as he appeared on *Unscrupulous Gentlemen*.

Host Frederick Vernon announced him to a round of applause from the live studio audience.

'Today, I'm with Kallum Fielder. He's come in to talk to us about Detective Inspector Bertram Ayala, the man arrested this morning in connection with no fewer than four seemingly unconnected murders. You've met the man himself, haven't you, Kal?'

The camera panned to a close-up of Kal. He could feel the heat of the studio lights above him and willed himself not to sweat.

'Yes, I've met Bertram Ayala. I always thought there was something sinister about him.'

'Why was that? What gave you the impression he was evil? He seems to have fooled everyone else around him, including the legendary DCI Morton.'

Kal wanted to laugh. He had that impression because they were paying him to. The truth was, he could barely remember Detective Inspector Ayala. They had barely exchanged a word.

'He just seemed so distant, so cold.'

'This was when your girlfriend – model Ellis DeLange – was murdered? Did he show any sympathy?'

'No,' Kal said, parroting the script he'd been asked to memorise an hour ago. 'It was weird, the way he looked at me. I thought at the time that he believed me to be a viable suspect. Reflecting back on it now, it's obvious what was going through his head.'

'What was that?'

'He wanted to know if I was a kindred spirit, a killer. When he realised I wasn't capable of that, that I couldn't have murdered Ellis, he looked at me with derision. He still had to investigate, of course, if only to satisfy the boss.'

Frederick Vernon leant farther and farther forward as Kal spoke, as if he was enthralled by the story that he had concocted off-screen. 'Do you think that's what made him a good detective, that ability to see himself in the killers he hunted?'

'Undoubtedly. Detective Bertram Ayala is evil, through and through. Like is attracted to like. It's only now that we're seeing the truth brought to light.'

# Chapter 49: Viva Voce

Mayberry needed to know how Sully had done it. He'd faked a doctorate without anyone becoming any the wiser. To get his PhD, he would not only have had to hand in a book-length tome, but he would have had to defend his research conclusion in a live viva voce exam.

It could be faked. Sufficient studying might let someone get through the interview element. But Sully seemed too dim to have managed that. Could he have bribed someone to do that as well?

The real question was: who had really written his thesis? Somebody had written eighty thousand words of articulate, nuanced, original research.

It was time for the old standby: ask Brodie for help. He had become something of a crutch for Mayberry. The big Scot didn't mind doing all the talking, and he seemed almost magic with a computer.

The big man was in his office that Friday lunchtime. He was facing away from the door, holding a half-eaten bacon sarnie on a paper plate.

'You seen this, laddie?' He gestured at the television in the corner of his office, which was showing *Unscrupulous Gentlemen* with the subtitles on. 'Bertram Ayala. I never thought he had it in him. How're you holding up?'

'He's n-not the k-killer,' Mayberry said.

'That's the spirit!' Brodie said. 'Of course he isn't.'

Mayberry wanted to punch him. 'It's a t-trick to l-lure the r-real killer.'

Brodie stared, unsure what to make of the information. 'What do you mean, it's a trick? Are you saying he got himself arrested, paraded on national TV, and humiliated online, all to bait the real killer?'

Mayberry nodded.

'Wow. I didn't think he had the cojones. Bertram Ayala, badass.'

The pronouncement that Ayala was a badass elicited a wan smile from Mayberry.

Brodie turned the television off, set his sandwich down, and turned his chair to face Mayberry. 'So, what can I do for you?'

Mayberry handed him a USB stick. He waited while Brodie loaded up a PDF of Sully's doctoral thesis. 'S-Sully d-didn't write th-this. He c-cheated–'

'And you want to work out who did write it? Okay. He could have paid someone, which would be hard to prove. He could simply have copied most of it from someone else's work. That's the most obvious solution. Let's run this through an anti-plagiarism checker and find out.'

Brodie uploaded the document, and then, while the search was in progress, noisily wolfed down the rest of his bacon sandwich. 'It's so good,' he said when he had finished. 'Irish bacon, Heinz ketchup, and some part-bakes thrown in the oven just before eating.'

That explained why Brodie had insisted on a mini oven in the IT department's staff room as well as a hot plate. Fresh bacon sandwiches were the order of the day.

'Don't tell the missus, laddie. I'm supposed to be on a diet. How anyone can expect a man to live without bacon, I'll never know. I love that woman to bits, but dear God, she eats like a rabbit.'

Mayberry smiled. She wasn't wrong. Brodie could stand to lose a few pounds.

'I know that look, laddie. You think she's right. Well, she is. But I'll take seventy years and bacon over four score and ten without, any day of the week.'

The search finished. Nothing.

'Hmm,' Brodie mused. 'What if he's a bit smarter than simply copy-pasting? This Sully, where's he from?'

'L-Libya.'

'Does he speak Modern Standard Arabic?'

Mayberry didn't know.

'Don't stress, laddie. I'll check the personnel files.'

It turned out that Sulaiman Haadi al-Djani did speak Arabic.

'W-what are you th-thinking?'

'When I did my degree, a couple of the foreign students there cheated too. They took essays written in their own language and translated them. It was in the wrong source language to get spotted, and even if there were suspicions, nobody called them on it because they were paying higher fees than everyone else, and then they all headed home after graduation. No harm, no foul, eh?'

'Y-you think S-Sully did that?'

'Let's find out. There can't be very many theses on the protein markers in serial killers written in Modern Standard Arabic, can there? Let me ping a translator and get us some proper search terms. Want a coffee while we wait?'

'H-hot ch-chocolate?'

Brodie grinned. 'I swear I've adopted a child sometimes. I assume you want my alcoholic marshmallows and a bit of whipped cream on top of that? If you're paying for it, I'll have my intern nip to Tesco for the cream now.'

Ten minutes later, Mayberry had his hot chocolate. He sipped it as Brodie typed away, furiously looking for Arabic language dissertations, and then sending the academic summary over to his contact. Mayberry had almost finished his drink when Brodie finally found a hit.

'Here we go. A nearly exact match. This,' Brodie said, gesturing at a PDF on-screen, 'is a thesis from eight years before Sully wrote his. It was written in an Algerian dialect of Modern Standard Arabic by a doctoral candidate at the Université Kasdi Merbah de Ouargla. That's where he got his research. Sully is a fraud.'

Sully couldn't have killed the four victims. He was too thick to even write his own doctoral thesis.

Strike another one.

# Chapter 50: The Taunt

By Friday evening, the suspect pool had begun to thin out. Ayala was, theoretically, in custody. In reality, he was downstairs working via a video link from the cells.

Morton watched bleary-eyed as Mayberry scribbled on the whiteboards. Every insane theory had been discussed. Planes, trains, buses, bombs, gas leaks, poisons, biological weapons... the possibilities seemed endless.

*Babbage – 10*
~~*Sully – 9*~~
*Villiers – 6.5*
~~*Hulme-Whitmore – 6*~~
*Maisie – 5*
*(not) O'Shaughnessy – 4.5*
*Rudd – 3*
~~*El-Mirza – 2*~~

Sully, Danny, and Almira had been discounted. Babbage and Villiers seemed unlikely, but couldn't be definitively ruled out. Eric – or Taylor, as Morton now knew him – was patently insane but didn't strike him as a killer. Rafferty didn't like the look of Rudd or Pincent, either.

That left them at a dead end. There was no more information to go on, no more leads left to pursue.

'Five suspects,' Morton lamented. 'Four victims.'

'Could we be looking for multiple killers?' Ayala asked by video link. 'We've not alibied everyone for every Saturday.'

'The "everybody did it" theory?' Morton said, dubious of such a ridiculous proposal. 'I can't prove it isn't.'

Rafferty knocked at the door. In her arms were several bags of takeaway food. 'Who's hungry?'

Morton's stomach groaned. It was getting on for seven o'clock, and he hadn't eaten since breakfast. The food was welcome relief from the stress.

They ate in near-silence. Paper plates were scattered all over.

Halfway through their impromptu dinner, Mayberry stammered his thanks to Rafferty. 'T-t-thanks, Ashley. D-do you want some m-money towards this?'

She looked bewildered. 'I didn't order it. I just happened to be walking through the hallway when the delivery guy arrived and said he had a delivery for DCI Morton. He specifically said your name.'

'Then, who the hell did?' Morton looked around the room. 'Nobody?'

Panic flooded the room. If they hadn't ordered the meal, who had?

'Shit.'

Morton lunged for the bin. He snatched it up, retched, and vomited. He heard the others run from the room, likely to do the same. Could the killer have sent the Thai meal to poison them?

A final retch convinced Morton that he had purged as much as he could without an emetic. He didn't feel unwell beyond the usual nausea from throwing up. Could the killer be messing with them? Could it be wheels-within-wheels logic? Could the killer have sent an unpoisoned meal so Morton and the team would waste hours at the hospital?

Morton's head hurt. This investigation was driving him insane. He was second-guessing everything: the evidence, his team, his gut. The killer seemed to be spreading misdirection everywhere. Could even the time be a red herring meant to send him careening down the wrong rabbit hole?

Rafferty and Mayberry reappeared after a few minutes, looking the worse for wear.

'Who exactly brought in the food?' Morton asked her.

'One of those motorbike delivery drivers. I don't know. He asked for you, and I assumed you'd ordered it.'

Fuck. It was targeted to him. Everything was personal.

'Was there an invoice or a receipt?'

'Hang on,' Rafferty said. She began to dig through the remains of the meal and found a slip of paper in the bottom. It listed all of the items, their prices, and the contact details for Panang Cuisine just north of Camden.

'Panang?' Morton echoed. It was one of his favourites. Kieran had introduced him to their food a few months back. Whoever had sent the meal knew Morton's preferred choice of takeaway.

A shiver ran down his spine. He was being watched by a serial killer.

'Yeah, and there's a name. Kieran O'Connor.'

Damn. Had the food been a gift after all? Morton was about to dial Kieran's phone when Rafferty spoke again.

'Uh, boss. You need to see this.' She handed him the note. On the back, in all caps, someone had written the following message:

*Well done. You added two and two and got four, but can you make it five? You trained me. Now, I'll train you.*

***

A quick call to Kieran confirmed he had had nothing to do with the order, though he knew Panang Cuisine well because it was his local. Mayberry was dispatched to talk to the restaurant owners. The drive took Mayberry almost half an hour in traffic for a three-mile journey, and it took almost as long to find somewhere to park. As was usual for Camden on a Friday night, the place was rammed. There were hipsters and students drinking up and down the canals, past the railway track, and along the entire stretch between Mornington Crescent and Camden Town tube stations.

Panang was right by the railway line. Trains whizzed overhead as Mayberry walked in. He made a beeline for the counter, shoved past the queue, and accosted the woman serving. He flashed his ID at her.

'Hi, I'm D-d-detective Sergeant Mayberry. You d-delivered an order to N-new Scotland Yard.'

'No refunds!' the woman said, pointing a large red sign behind the counter.

'I'm not here for a refund. I need to know who placed the order.'

The woman shrugged. 'We busy.'

Maybery eyed the woman carefully. She seemed to be putting the accent on a bit thick, as if it were a deliberate tactic to get rid of him.

'Do you have C-C-C-CTV?' he arched his neck to look around.

'No.'

'Can you r-remember anything about this order? It was a v-very l-large order. It was in the name of K-K-Kieran O'Connor.'

'No. We busy. I don't see who order. I just serve next customer.'

Mayberry grew exasperated. 'D-does anyone else work here?'

'Chef. He in back. He no see customers. You buy food?'

'N-no, I'm not buying food.'

'Then move out way. We got customers.'

# Chapter 51: Counter Terrorism

Morton didn't go home that Friday night. Instead, he pulled out an old fold-up bed and a rather worn blanket and kipped in his office. The others did the same, taking shifts to stay awake in case any new information came in. Morton slept fitfully, knowing he was being taunted.

They rose at five for breakfast. This time, Morton personally went to the twenty-four-hour bakery around the corner.

They had seventeen hours left on the clock.

The Counter Terrorism Command had already made sounds that they were unhappy. Their contingency plans were ready to roll: over fifty thousand extra officers deployed to strategic sites around London.

'We have to,' Antonov said simply. 'It's protocol.'

'It won't do any good,' Morton said. 'This killer is too smart to hit the obvious targets. They'll hit somewhere soft.'

'Where?'

'I don't know,' Morton said simply. 'If they follow the pattern, it'll be an evolution on the murder suggested in class. That's the game they're playing. We know from last night's taunt that they still want us to play.'

'What was the exact murder they planned?'

'Using a drone to deliver an explosive payload,' Morton said.

Antonov slammed a chubby fist down on the conference table, causing the pastries to leap into the air. 'Then, we need a no-fly zone in place. We need sniffer dogs. We need bomb disposal on standby.'

'They won't use a bomb or a drone. You've been investigating my students. Do any of them strike you as having the connections necessary for a bomb?'

'No,' said Antonov. 'But I've got to do it. The home secretary must be briefed immediately. We need to raise the threat level to critical, keep people inside, and stop whatever is being planned by any means necessary.'

'You do what you have to do,' Morton said. 'But if I shout, you'd better come running. It's going to be our knowledge of the students that breaks this, not a blanket safety net. The killer will be trying to hit a soft target outside your perimeter. You can't have people everywhere.'

'What kind of attack do you think it'll be?'

Morton hesitated. He had an idea, but it could be misdirection. He showed Antonov the note again.

*Well done. You added two and two and got four, but can you make it five? You trained me. Now, I'll train you.*

'And?'

'Look at the language,' Morton said as he pointed at the note. 'You trained me. Now, I'll train you. Is that just a reference to a student-teacher relationship, or have they used the word "train" twice on purpose?'

'You think it'll be a bomb on a train?'

'It could be. It'd be a softer target. You can put men all over the major stations, but can you prevent someone leaving a bag behind on a busy train as it pulls into central London?'

Antonov paled. Transport for London handled over a billion passengers a year, covering hundreds of miles of track, and that didn't include any of the regional train operators or the Docklands Light Railway.

'See what I mean?' Morton said. 'They could strike anywhere. It doesn't have to be a bomb, either. It could be gas or a chemical agent or something else entirely.'

'Then,' Antonov said, his resolve clearly stiffening, 'we must have sniffer dogs on the trains.'

'That might not be a bad idea,' Morton said.

As he spoke, he wondered if the killer was one step ahead of them. If they were arrogant enough to taunt him, to provoke the Counter Terrorism Command into raising the threat level to critical, to challenge legions of police, then surely, they ought to have considered sniffer dogs, bomb removal robots, and the like?

What else was there? Morton strained to think. If it wasn't a bomb, poison, or gas, what could the killer do? Was he reading too much into the word "train"? Was the killer luring them to the wrong conclusion? He would have to release Ayala soon, but not too soon that the killer might notice. He needed all the man power he could get.

***

By six o'clock, the Home Office had been briefed. The prime minister appeared bleary-eyed on BBC News to announce that the terror threat level had been raised to critical.

Within a matter of minutes, every news channel was carrying the video statement as breaking news. Speculation ran rampant: was it international terrorism that had prompted the change? So-called experts began to brief the public on avoiding flights, staying home, and reporting anything suspicious.

It was a mass hysteria the likes of which had not been seen in decades. Airports ran empty with flights across London being cancelled for security reasons, and supermarket shelves were emptied of everything from bread and milk to cans and bottled water.

It was as if the apocalypse had been announced.

***

It was exactly as I expected. The police were clueless.

Even the lame-duck prime minister had become a puppet in my game. They had brought in tens of thousands of new officers, moved sniffer dogs and bomb disposal units. They would no doubt lock down the capital's railway stations tighter than a nun's arsehole.

None of that mattered. They had no way of knowing where I would strike, only when. The clock was ticking down. The final countdown had begun.

I was winning. And in less than sixteen hours, it would be game, set, and match.

# Chapter 52: Puzzling

The Counter Terrorism Command abandoned Morton's Incident Room shortly after breakfast. They had a divergence in approach, and each team had their own way to proceed. The moment they were gone, Morton sprung Ayala from his cell. He'd have to keep a low profile until the evening, but they needed him in the room.

The taunt had to be the key. 'I'll train you.'

The killer was playing with him.

The thing about games was that there had to be a chance either side could win. The killer didn't want to play fair, but they seemed to need a victory. To beat Morton without giving him a shot would be a pyrrhic victory.

Wherever they were targeting had to be connected to the railways.

'Mayberry, get me a map of London. I want overlays showing every train, every tube, and even the DLR.'

The projector flashed to life as the bulb warmed up. Mayberry, silent as usual, did as directed.

Lines snaked across the London map.

'Now, mark in red anywhere that the Counter Terrorism Command are going to put extra staff.'

'H-have y-you got a l-list?'

He had a point. Antonov hadn't given them explicit details. 'Let's assume they're going to cover every major hub station, all zone one stations, and any station where tube lines interact.'

That would be where Morton would put the extra staff if he believed in the same logic as Antonov.

At Mayberry's command, a large knot of the rail network in the centre of the map turned red.

'Now, put anywhere with a high population density in green.'

The areas that lit up were close by the commuter lines going in and out. They were busy enough to carry thousands of passengers, but not important enough to guard.

'If you wanted to kill a lot of people, where would you hit? Rafferty? Ayala? Any ideas?' Morton turned to look at his two senior detectives.

Both were asleep.

Morton paced the Incident Room, then tapped each on the shoulder. Neither woke.

'Sod it,' he said.

He raised a hand into a giant fist and slammed it down on the conference table between them. They jumped up immediately. Their eyes went wide as if they were afraid they were under attack.

'Good morning, you two,' Morton said. 'How nice of you to join us. We're trying to work out where the killer will strike. Any thoughts?'

'It has to be somewhere just outside the safe zone,' Rafferty said. 'The biggest threat is coming into central London. You can't hit Waterloo or Paddington because it'll be so busy with police. This is a killer who wants to be smart, not just violent. If they wanted to kill people, they'd have done it without taunting you and without sticking to an arbitrary schedule.'

'About the taunt,' Ayala said. 'What if the choice of takeaway delivery is important? They chose a place in Camden. What's around there?'

'Camden Market?' Rafferty volunteered.

'That's not a train,' Morton said. 'It has to be railway-related.'

'Does it?' Rafferty said. 'What if it's just a coincidence? What if they meant it like the verb, to educate, not the noun train? They could hit a bus, or a convention, or a church. Every time we push the security perimeter back, we move the people to a new, weaker spot just outside it.'

Just outside. 'Hmm,' Morton mused. 'Which stations are immediately outside the big interchanges?'

'C-Clapham J-Junction?' Mayberry volunteered.

It was possible. It was one of the busiest interchanges. There would no doubt be some presence there, though, and it was a high-CCTV area.

Morton shook his head. 'No. We're not thinking outside the box enough. Our killer isn't going to just throw a backpack on the floor and walk out. They're not suicidal. They'll know we've got dogs, marksmen, and metal detectors. Everyone is on high alert. They're going to strike in a way that's smarter than a bomb.'

'What if they kidnap a train driver?' Ayala said. 'They could force him to ram a platform or run a red and collide with another train.'

The image of two trains crashing at high speed appeared in Morton's mind. There would be carnage.

'They'd have to be willing to die with the train driver when the train crashed,' Morton said. 'They'd also have to convince a train driver to commit suicide during a terror alert. It's not impossible, but it's desperate rather than smart. We know they'll strike at ten o'clock. What trains are running then? Mayberry?'

Mayberry tapped away for a moment. 'H-hang on.'

From the other end of the table, Morton saw him open Skype and call Brodie.

The Scot's rough brogue echoed through the conference room. 'Need a hand, laddie?'

'Brodie,' Morton called out. 'We need live train times for tonight. What trains are there that'll be within three miles of central London at ten o'clock tonight?'

'How precise a time, boss?'

'Plus or minus fifteen minutes. But sort the results by closest time and proximity to major population centres.'

'On it.'

They sat in silence for a while. Eventually, Brodie knocked on the conference room door in person. That was a surprise; it was rare to see him emerge from his cave.

'I've got it all here, boss,' he said as he held a USB stick aloft. 'May I?'

Morton waved a hand. 'By all means.'

Brodie took over Mayberry's laptop, and a series of red dots appeared on top of the railway lines.

'Each red dot is a train. This is at 21:45. If I move the time forward, the map changes like this.'

As Brodie slid the timer to the right, the red dots moved. Hundreds of trains coming in at varying speeds.

'Speed,' Morton said suddenly. 'If this isn't a bomb, and it's actually about a crash, you need speed to do damage.'

'Okay,' Ayala said. 'Force equals mass times acceleration. I'm with you there, boss. But you just said they couldn't crash a train.'

Bile rose up Morton's throat. 'You don't need to kidnap a driver. You don't even need to be on board.'

'A hack?' Brodie said. 'I don't think the trains are networked. They're still largely manual.'

'Not a hack. Something simpler.'

'Something on the track?' Ayala suggested.

'That could do it.'

'How many lines go through an area with a population density of over, say, 5000 people per square mile?'

Brodie pulled up the census data and layered it over the map. There was scant overlap between soft targets and a population density that high.

'Okay,' Morton said. 'What one target could you hit with a train and do the most damage?'

'Somewhere with a utility plant?' Ayala suggested.

'What about waste treatment facilities?' Rafferty chimed in.

'A bridge?' Brodie suggested. 'A fast train could do a lot of structural damage.'

That was it. If a train could be derailed to hit another target, the killer could take down large numbers of people.

Morton glanced at his watch. It was fast ticking toward six.

'We need to get teams out to every location that derailment could cause mass casualties. Look for buildings near train lines: hospitals, universities, high-rise tower blocks. Anything outside the usual security perimeter. Exclude anywhere like Clapham Junction. We want trains travelling at speed. Come back here in an hour with your best guesses.'

That would leave them three hours to cover the highest-risk spots. They were cutting it fine, and they still didn't have a concrete idea. Fingers crossed that someone would come up with a target that made sense.

# Chapter 53: On Location

The list had been divvied up, and Morton had sent his team out separately. Each had backup from the Counter Terrorism Command. True to his word, Morton had also called in Brian King, who turned up with his partner in tow, armed to the teeth.

Morton himself had taken the most obvious target: the approach to Euston. It seemed like the takeaway had to be a clue. Why had the killer chosen to use a Thai place in the middle of north London? It could just be that it was the least suspicious action choosing somewhere Morton ate, but if the intention was merely to provoke him, it had been a lot of work finding that out.

Clues were still ringing in Morton's mind. Ten o'clock. Panang Cuisine. It was nearly half-past nine. There were thirty-six trains coming in to Euston in the thirty-minute window running from quarter to until quarter past ten. Of those thirty-six, twenty-eight would be going fast enough to do serious damage.

'Brodie.' Morton spoke into the microphone attached to his ear. 'Can you hear me?'

'Loud and clear,' Brodie said back after a second's delay.

'Are you in contact with the others?'

'Yes.'

'Can you patch in Brian King and his partner?'

There was a brief crackle before Brodie replied, 'No problem.'

Morton sent Brian half a mile up the line. If there was to be an incident between them, they'd be spaced out far enough to deal with it.

Something was bothering Morton. The taunt echoed in his mind, over and over.

*Well done. You added two and two and got four, but can you make it five? You trained me. Now, I'll train you.*

What was he missing? Two and two was four. Why did that seem so cryptic? Conversely, "train" seemed too obvious.

*Can you make it five?*

Why five murders? Why ten o'clock?

As the time ticked down, the others checked in from outside Marylebone, Paddington, Victoria, King's Cross, and Liverpool Street. In total, there were almost two hundred trains that could be targeted.

It had to be North London. Panang meant something.

Quarter to ten. The window was open. If the killer was going to strike, it would have to be now. Who could it be? It wasn't Sully, Danny, or Almira. They'd been ruled out. Danny was still in custody, and Almira was streaming to her clientele; Brodie had checked, and seemed exceedingly cheerful about that assignment. Taylor, not Eric, was too unstable to let walk, so Jensen had had him committed for further evaluation.

Babbage, Villiers, Pincent, and Rudd were still in contention.

None of them lived in North London. None ate at Panang. None seemed to have a connection to ten o'clock.

Who would they want to kill? Babbage's anger would surely be directed at anyone he felt was responsible for his parents' deaths. Villiers was an unknown, as were Pincent and Rudd.

Ten to ten o'clock.

Who had a connection to Panang? The only answer was Morton… and Kieran.

'Brodie, where does Kieran live?'

'Mornington Terrace.'

Minutes from Penang. A few metres from the railway lines out of Euston.

*You added two and two and got four, but can you make it five?*

Five. Not thousands. Five. There was one target. One single victim hiding among the many.

Kieran.

The lawyer's voice echoed in Morton's mind, only slightly muddied by the whisky they'd enjoyed that night.

*I've prosecuted a few cases that had similarly specific time elements. I think one of them was ten o'clock too. Saturday's a busy night.*

'Brodie, can you search Kieran's old cases for a reference to ten o'clock?'

'Sure. Any reason why?'

'Just do it. Fast.'

Morton paced the track as he spoke. If one of the students was going to derail a train, it would be nearby. He headed north towards Kieran's.

'Brian!' Morton yelled into the radio. 'How close are you to Mornington Terrace?'

'Ten minutes out. Should we head over?'

'One of you go,' Morton said. 'One of you hold position.'

Morton broke into a run. Six minutes to ten. Somewhere along the lines between Morton and Kieran, one of the students was going to derail a train.

'Boss,' Brodie's voice echoed. 'Kieran prosecuted an unlawful death case against the police a few years back. He lost.'

'Who?'

'Dean Walker.'

Morton remembered the name. 'What did he do?'

'He shot some teenager on the railway line. He thought they were putting something dangerous on the track, but they were just larking about.'

Something on the track. Just as Morton had expected. There was one thing that could be put on the track that fitted perfectly: a train derailer.

'All units, we're looking for a derailer. It'll be somewhere on the track. It's a safety device intended to stop a train going down the wrong route. They're usually a bright orange, but the killer might have painted it. Repeat, we're looking for a derailer.'

'Boss?'

'Yes, Brodie.' Morton was sprinting along the track, scanning for a derailer.

'Dean Walker killed himself after he was acquitted.'

It all clicked in Morton's mind. That was why Angela King had been the first victim. Her husband was a surrogate.

# Chapter 54: Unexpected

Kieran was watching the news eagerly. He had no part to play in tonight's manhunt, but he was invested nonetheless. It was his friends who were risking life and limb to hunt down a serial killer.

He had a tumbler full of whisky on the coffee table and a pizza in a box by his side.

As the clock ticked towards five to ten, he heard a knock at the door. Had the pizza guy forgotten something?

He unlatched the door.

'Don't move,' said a woman's voice. A gun poked through the gap in the door. 'Take three steps back and keep your hands where I can see them.'

Kieran complied. 'You don't want to do this.'

'Oh, don't I? Why's that?' The woman shut the door behind her. She kept her voice low and even.

'Because this isn't smart,' Kieran said simply. 'I assume you're the one who killed Angela King, Hudson Brown, the old man, and Ed Teigan.'

'I did.'

'Why?'

'You know why,' she said. 'Don't you remember me?'

'Should I?' Kieran asked.

'Ruth Middleton. Surely, you remember her?'

Kieran shut his eyes. He did. She was the teenage girl who had been playing on the railway tracks. She'd been shot by Dean Walker, a man he'd been tasked to prosecute.

'You knew her.'

'Knew her?' the woman said. 'I loved her.'

'Killing me won't bring her back.'

'No, but it might make me feel better.'

Kieran held his hands up.

'Don't move.'

'Okay. It's... Maisie, isn't it?'

'Oh, so you do know me now.'

Kieran looked her directly in the eye. 'I'm sorry I lost the case against Dean Walker. Juries don't always do what I tell them. For what it's worth, he killed himself afterwards.'

'Coward!' Maisie spat. 'He killed the first girl I ever loved.'

'I'm sorry,' Kieran said simply. 'That doesn't excuse killing four innocent people.'

'Innocent? Pah,' Maisie said. 'Brian King killed someone, you know. I saw it in the paper. You haven't even brought charges against him.'

'That was an accident.'

'You'd better hope my finger doesn't accidently slip.'

Kieran eyed the clock on the mantelpiece. Three minutes to ten.

'Why did you kill Angela? Shouldn't you have killed Brian?' Kieran said.

'Dying isn't a punishment. It's nothingness. Living without the love of your life, that's hell on earth. I wanted him to feel what I felt. I shot Angie so he'd have go through life without her, just as I have to live without Ruth.'

Kieran needed to keep her talking. Morton would work it out in time, wouldn't he? 'Okay, but what about Hudson Brown?'

'He hated everyone who isn't a straight white male. I couldn't let that bigot live.'

Kieran couldn't disagree. He wouldn't have killed the man, but neither would he have pissed on him if he were on fire.

'The old man, then. What did he do?'

'Nothing. I didn't even know his name. Wrong place, wrong time. He wasn't long for the world, anyway.'

'So, why did you kill him?'

'That hospital is where they took Ruth. They didn't save her from the gunshot. I wanted them to feel that pain, that helplessness. They tried to help this time, and the old man died.'

Kieran exhaled deeply. The pain in Maisie's voice ran deep.

'And Ed Teigan?'

'I needed someone to jump, and he jumped.'

'He killed himself?' Kieran parroted.

'Just like Dean Walker. He looked a bit like him. That's why I followed him. When I saw him smoking on the roof, it was too perfect. I took this gun up with me.'

'And said what?'

'I said he had two choices,' Maisie said. 'I could shoot him, and he'd definitely die. Or he could jump, and he might live. He chose to jump.'

It was the perfect murder. Make a man kill himself, and the police would never have anything to go on.

'And now me.'

'Yes. Then my Ruthie can rest easy.'

'Before you do, can I ask how you killed Angie King?'

'Oh, that was easy. I know a lesbian when I see one. She saw me as hot young meat. She was no innocent in all this.'

'I didn't ask you why. I asked how.'

'I know. It'll be even more fun to send you to your grave without an explanation. Enjoy eternity in hell.'

Kieran looked at the clock. Nine fifty-nine. He shut his eyes and waited for oblivion.

# Chapter 55: Out of Reach

*Five to ten.*

Morton sprinted as if his life depended on it. He ran along the track, minutes out from Kieran's flat. There was no way he could get there in time. He knew Brian was closer, but ten o'clock was fast approaching, and Kieran's life hung in the balance.

Trains whizzed by as he ran. If the killer wanted to kill Kieran, they had to be in the area. His track was the one with the derailer. The light was dim, and it was hard to see. Morton held his phone in front of him as he ran, illuminating ten feet of track at a time.

'All units, the target,' Morton panted, 'is Kieran O'Connor. Repeat: the target is Kieran O'Connor. The derailer is nearby. All units, converge.'

Where was the Counter Terrorism Command? They had tens of thousands of men, but none had been assigned to the railway running through Camden.

Just as he was about to give up hope, Morton tripped.

'Fuck!'

'Morton!' Rafferty's voice crackled over the radio. 'Morton! Are you okay?'

'I just tripped.'

He looked down at his ankle. It was already beginning to swell, and he could run no further. That was when he saw what he'd tripped over. It had been painted black, and looked not much larger than a crowbar. It was the derailer. The flag had been removed, and the high visibility orange was gone, but this was it.

'Brodie!' Morton yelled. 'I've got it. How do I take it off without electrocuting myself?'

'Quickly!' Brodie yelled. 'You've got a train coming in less than a minute.'

*Don't touch the rail,* Morton thought. He pulled at the top of the derailer. It didn't budge.

The sound of a train horn made him look up. He had only seconds left to move it.

There was a twist lock on the inside edge. Morton pulled it, but it was too stiff. He heaved, his finger straining against the metal.

A shadow seemed to loom over him as the train pulled closer and closer. Morton placed his whole weight against the derailer, his hands clawing at the lock mechanism. It gave way, and Morton tumbled backwards, still clutching the derailer.

The train whistled past, seconds from crushing Morton to death.

He exhaled deeply. He'd done it. London was safe.

Except for one man: Kieran.

# Chapter 56: Instinct

Brian King left his partner, Abby Fields, trawling the track. He had discarded his body armour for speed, and ran carrying his Glock 26 in the direction of Kieran O'Connor's building in Mornington Crescent. He found the building quickly enough, but from the track side.

He tossed his gun over the fence, careful to leave the safety on, and clambered up. Razor wire on the top tore into his flesh. By the time he landed heavily on the other side of the fence, he was dripping blood.

He picked up his gun, switched the safety back to off, and ran. The apartment block was enormous, and after what seemed like an eternity, he found the front door – but it was locked. He hit every doorbell.

The buzzer went off, and in he ran.

'Brodie!' he yelled. 'What flat number?'

'Ninety-five.'

King cursed. It was on the ninth floor, and the sole lift was marked out of order. Three minutes to ten. He swore and ascended the stairs three at a time. His lungs burned. His muscles screamed.

The door to 95 was visible from the stairwell. He ran forward. One minute to ten.

He heard voices inside.

'Before you kill me, can I ask how you killed Angie King?'

'Oh, that was easy. I know a lesbian when I see one. She saw me as hot young meat. She was no innocent in all this.'

Anger rose up inside him. Something snapped. He kicked the door without a second thought, held his Glock in front of him, and fired.

***

Kieran heard the gunshots rather than felt them. If this was what dying felt like, it wasn't so bad after all.

'Open your eyes,' a voice commanded him. It was almost comforting.

'Do I have to?' he murmured.

'You're not dead, idiot.'

His eyes snapped open. Brian King was standing before him.

At his feet lay Maisie Pincent's body, riddled with bullets.

He didn't know why, but he stepped toward Brian King and hugged him.

'Get off me, you daft eejit.'

# Chapter 57: Evaluation

Silverman was waiting when Morton arrived back at New Scotland Yard at nearly midnight.

They had sent officers to Maisie's home to look for evidence, and the result was on Silverman's desk. The tech team had found a 3D printer. By reprinting the last file from its memory, Brodie had cracked Angie King's murder: Maisie had 3D-printed a gun, hidden it inside a long-range camera lens, and used it with the frangible copper bullet that Morton had discovered with Chiswick. It was an ingenious solution that left no gun, no striae, no bullets, and no paper trail.

'You got lucky,' Silverman said accusingly.

'*We* got lucky. This was your cock-up as much as anyone else's,' Morton said, smiling sweetly. 'You should never have assigned those two murders to Rafferty, and you should never have relegated me to teaching duty. Without both of those mistakes, fewer victims would be dead.'

'How dare you!' Silverman screamed. 'You arrogant, self-centred, narcissistic son of a bitch. This is the second case you've screwed up under my watch.'

'Difficult circumstances demand difficult decisions. May I remind you that we stopped a train from being derailed today, we prevented the murder of a prosecutor, and we stopped a serial killer.'

'You mean you had a rogue officer shoot a serial killer.'

'No,' Morton said slowly. 'I'm sure I remember you specifically authorising Brian King to work with the task force.'

Silverman looked at him dumbfounded, and Morton had to resist the urge to smile. 'Oh, yes, and when exactly did I do that?'

'Right after you illegally redacted the pathology report on Hudson Brown, and right before you reinstated me.'

If looks could kill, Morton would have died on the spot. He could see the cogs turning in Silverman's brain.

'Fine,' Silverman said through gritted teeth.

'I'm glad we had such a productive meeting.' He spun on his right foot and hightailed it from her office.

He was back.